MOONSHINE & MAGIC

A Southern Charms Cozy Mystery

BELLA FALLS

Evermore Press

ISBN-13: 978-1984313102

ISBN-10: 198431310X

Cover by Victoria Cooper

For my Family and the Magic of their love.

Also by Bella Falls

A Southern Charms Cozy Mystery Series

Moonshine & Magic: Book 1

Fried Chicken & Fangs: Book 2

Lemonade & Love Potions (a short in the Hexes & Ohs Anthology)

For a FREE exclusive copy of the prequel Chess Pie & Choices, sign up for my newsletter!

CONTENTS

Chapter One

My motorcycle sputtered and shook under me as I slowed down on the almost abandoned two-lane road to address the young man and woman standing next to a motionless car with its hood popped open. The guy waved his arms in the air like a maniac while his companion scowled at her cell phone.

Raising the visor on my helmet, I reveled in the fresh air that smelled heavy of humidity and heat. Memories flooded my senses, squeezing my heart.

"Excuse me, can you help us?" The guy pulled my attention back to his current predicament. If he remained polite, maybe I could overlook his surprise that underneath the helmet existed a girl.

His wife or girlfriend chimed in before I could respond. "Our cell phones don't seem to work." Her lower lip extended her pout another millimeter. As the guy opened his mouth to explain, she continued, still staring at her uncooperative phone. "It's the craziest thing. We were driving down this road I guess because the GPS wasn't working right or something. And it ends with a small barricade and a sign. No warnings before that."

The guy nodded. "So we turned around, but as we were driving back, our car just gave out."

"Who doesn't post up warnings that it's a dead-end road? I thought that was the law or something. Maybe it would be if we weren't out here in the sticks." She shook her phone in frustration.

It took her a few more seconds before Miss Pouty finally looked up and noticed me. My lips grinned with false friendliness. She scowled back at me.

Best to kill her with kindness instead of hex her with hate. Smiling harder, I thickened my accent. "Bless your hearts, I guess you haven't had much of a Southern welcome. I do apologize for that."

The man gave a sheepish grin and raised his hand. "It's my fault. I'm the one that wanted to drive down the smaller roads and see where they took us."

"*You* got us lost. And our car sits here broken down miles away from any kind of civilization." The girl narrowed her eyes and examined me up and down. "I don't suppose there's anything *you* can do about it." The tiny sniff at the end of her sentence punctuated her point.

Oh, the list of possibilities of what I *could* do was long. Make her face break out into the worst case of pimples? Not nice, but not the worst idea I'd ever had. Cast a love spell and steal her boyfriend? Okay, I wasn't *that* evil. Plus, not sure he'd be worth the effort.

Show them that she was messing with the wrong girl by teleporting her into the nearby swamp area? Okay, that tempting option passed through my mind...more than once. But no need to blow through the last of my magical reserves by being spiteful. As Nana always said: an ounce of spite is worth a pound of unicorn manure.

Also, I didn't need the hassle of being arrested by the magical wardens of the area. Again. My return already came with significant obstacles to overcome. No need to add another brick in that wall.

Turning off the bike and parking it in the middle of the road, I dismounted, took my helmet all the way off, and locked it down on the cracked leather seat. "Sure." I plastered a wide smile on my face. "I'd be happy to help y'all. Let me see what I can do."

Moving around to the front of the car where the opened hood blocked their view of me, I made thoughtful noises as if actually inspecting their engine.

"I should help her," the guy offered, and my heart raced. He needed to stay put if I had a chance to work my magic. To help out the situation, I wiggled my butt a little in their direction, keeping the rest of me out of sight under the hood.

"Derek, don't you dare. You will stay right here next to me," the girl demanded with a clipped tone. A little natural jealousy beat out a spell any day.

Focusing my energies on the engine, I waved my hands over the hunk of metal. *"Pay attention to the magic I yield. Over this car, create a shield. Get these people on the road, and help me not turn her into a toad."*

Magic poured out of my fingers and palms, forming a liquid blanket that wrapped itself around the engine block and all the metal, rubber, and wires. As the shimmering layer grew in size and strength, my already-low energies depleted even more. Once all of the parts under the hood were covered, I willed the end of the spell and took a brief second to gather my wits so I wouldn't pass out as soon as I stood up.

"Try it now," I yelled out from under the hood. The car dipped as Derek got in. It took a couple of tries and some minor magic sparks, but eventually, the engine roared to life.

Closing the hood, I wiped my hands on my jeans as if getting rid of the stain of non-existent oil. The girl raced around the trunk and hopped in the passenger seat without so much as a murmur of thanks or a murderous glance.

I took cautious steps to the driver's side and bent down to talk through the window. "That should do it. Y'all be careful from now on. Sometimes getting a little lost can get you into trouble."

"Let's get out of here." The girl tossed her phone on the dashboard and crossed her arms. "Now."

Poor Derek. He flashed me an apologetic look and mouthed his thanks as he rolled up his window. I stood in the middle of the road until the red of the tail lights disappeared.

Well, looky there. My spell worked perfectly. I didn't turn her into a toad after all.

With a chuckle, I returned to the motorcycle. My smile faded when it refused to start. "Come on, Old Joe. You gotta work." Three more tries. Still nothing. Karma. Ain't she a witch. "I swear, I wasn't really going to turn her into a toad. I just needed something to rhyme with *road*," I shouted into the air. Only the buzz and clicks of cicadas in the trees answered me back.

With my last attempt, I closed my eyes and wished very hard, holding back the curses on the tip of my tongue. The bike rattled and vibrated under me before it gave out. "Yes. Come on, Old Joe. You can do it. We're so close to home. *Your* home. Don't you wanna get there?"

As if the object perked up at the promise, it sprung to noisy life with a little more oomph. Taking it off the kickstand, I eased it down the road toward the proverbial dead end. The large sign hammered onto a dilapidated wooden barrier loomed ahead. With slow deliberation, I inched Old Joe closer to it.

Light tingles worked their way down from the tip of my head to the bottom of my boots. Revving the engine a couple of times, I drove the bike forward and straight into the barrier.

Like a puff of smoke, the glamour disappeared around me, and the two-lane road extended ahead as I drove through. Live oaks rose from the ground on either side and spread their branches like a canopy over the old pavement. Spanish moss hung down in grey-green strands, blowing in the breeze. The last of the day's sun dappled between the waving leaves, the effects of light and shadow lulling me into a drowsy state.

Pixie poop, I'd forgotten to ward myself from the final protection barrier. Any non-magical being who somehow stumbled in and made it that far would fall into a deep slumber and wake up sometime much later, somehow transported to a different destination far from this area.

Without needing words, I willed a simple spell to block the effects. A feeling of emptiness in the pit of my stomach warned me that I couldn't keep that up for much longer, so I leaned over the handlebars and cranked the gas to move as fast as the motorcycle would allow. Which, turned out, wasn't very fast as the rumbles and trembles underneath me grew increasingly sporadic.

Old Joe huffed and puffed and wheezed its way to the border security gate. As it rolled next to the gatehouse, it spluttered one last time before dying with an undignified shudder.

"License, please," a squeaky male voice requested from the small open window. "Well, bless my beard and boots. If it ain't Miss Charlotte Goodwin come back. This really is turning out to be one big ol' homecoming week here in Honeysuckle."

"Evenin', Mr. Flint." After digging in my pocket, I held out my license. "Isn't it First Night festivities? Guess you drew the short straw."

Taking a wand from his breast pocket, he waved it over the small rectangle of plastic. "Somebody has to stand guard. I don't mind. My girl's bringing me goodies." Sparkling runes and geometric signs floated above the surface of my license, but he barely glanced at them and winked. "It's just a formality. Everyone knows you belong here."

A scoff escaped me before I could stop it. "We'll see about that. I didn't leave on exactly the best terms."

He stroked his beard. "Well, come to think of it...no, you didn't. But there're more than a few who understood and a sight more who will welcome you back with open arms."

"And a few who might curse me where I stand the first glance they catch." My head spun as I stated the truth that had my gut churning the whole day of travel.

An unnaturally high-pitched woman's voice broke into our conversation. "Why Flintmore Hollyspring, can't you see this dear girl here is running on vapors? For such a nice gnome, you really are a genuine numskull. Not sure you deserve this bevy of good fixings that I brought you." Pink fairy dust peppered down from Gossamer's agitated wings as she bobbed in the air, handing off a large cup to him and balancing a plate loaded with all kinds of food that had my stomach growling.

"Flinty, pass her the sweet tea." She waved her free hand at me, more fairy dust flying and a chicken leg threatening to fall. "Hey, Charli. Long time since your path brought you home. You staying for good this time?"

Lifting the cup to my lips with a shaky hand, I took a long, hard gulp. The sweet nectar of the South ran over my tongue and down the back of my throat. My heart beat heavy inside my chest. *Home.* "Don't know yet. But I didn't want to miss out on this year's Founders' Day celebrations."

After another couple of icy gulps, my energy meter ticked up a few notches. "Although I might not be moving anywhere fast. Think I've been gone too long for the old protection spells to still be working on my bike. Actually, Dad's bike. Was his bike." Patting the faithful piece of machinery, I blinked away the mist of tears on my eyelashes. "Seems that the barrier protections might have gotten to Old Joe here."

"Let me take a look." Flint jumped down from his seat, and his whole body disappeared. Only his pointy hat rose above the window. Pushing the door open, he sidled up beside me, inspecting the bike.

"Well, you missed a huge event while you were gone," Gossamer insisted, flying over and handing me a large square of cornbread.

"Indeed, you did." Flint leaned down and inspected every inch of the motorcycle, his brow furrowed.

"What'd I miss?" I held back an obscene groan from a bite of the yellow crumbly goodness.

Gossamer's wings flapped so hard that her pink dust got in my nose and made me sneeze. "We got married!" she tittered. "I'm now Mrs. Gossamer Hollyspring. Could you just die?"

Genuine happiness fueled my wide smile. How long had it been since that had happened? "I am so pleased for the two of you. Congratulations."

Gossamer nearly bowled her husband over hugging me around the neck. "Thanks. I'm sorry you missed the festivities. But hey, I'm glad you're back. So much has changed."

"And I'm sure a lot has stayed exactly the same." In fact, I was counting on that. "We'll see how everything goes. So Mr. Flint, what's the verdict?"

He wiped the sweat from his brow and shook his head. "It ain't your magic bindings. They're weak but still there. Strong enough to get you through. Nope. Looks like you've simply run out of gas."

My hand smacked my forehead with enough force that it stung. In all my excitement to get back, I'd forgotten the one crucial thing left that I needed from the human world.

"You just leave your bike thingy parked here by the gatehouse. No one will mess with it, and you can come back for it later. For now, finish your tea and get on into town. You'll catch the tail end of tonight's potluck in the park. Lots of tasty food made by fine folk waiting for you," Gossamer suggested.

I stared down the long and darkening roadway towards town. "Any chance you can put me on the fairy path?" Any shortcut would be appreciated so that I didn't arrive a hot, sweaty mess from all the walking.

Gossamer kissed Flint on the cheek as he meandered back to his seat and dug into the plate of food. "Sure thing, honey. On one condition."

"What's that?"

She scrunched her nose. "You let me spruce you up a bit. You look...a little road weary."

My hands went straight to my hair. If it looked as bad as it felt, it might take some serious magic to help. Wearing a helmet did as much damage to its condition as the heavy humidity. "Is it that bad?"

Gossamer nodded. "And maybe a little change to your clothes. Just a temporary one. Long enough for you to—"

"Go to the ball?" I finished, clapping my hands in mock excitement. "Oh thank you, Fairy Godmother, thank you. Does it change back at the stroke of midnight?"

Flint choked on a piece of chicken as he tried not to laugh. Gossamer placed her hands on her hips, her wings quivering in agitation. "No, Miss Sass. At best maybe an hour or two." With a flourish of her hand, a pink wand appeared, and more pink dust whirled in the night breeze. She lifted an eyebrow in my direction as if waiting for permission.

After a sigh, I acquiesced. "Go ahead. Bibbity Bobbity get 'er done."

A current of wind swirled around me, and my body tingled from the potent magic of the tiny fairy. It tickled like mini feathers poking me all over. When the sensation ceased, I looked down at her results. Instead of a sweat-stained T-shirt, a pink and white checkered peasant blouse flattered my curves. A clean pair of jeans that fit like a glove replaced my older ones. I wiggled my toes free from the boots now clad in some sandals. My pink toenails practically sparkled all on their own. Patting my head, I no longer felt an untamed mess.

"Thanks for not putting me in heels." I winked at Gossamer. "Love the color."

"It's my signature hue. Now come on. Park your bike, and I'll open the path for you."

I wheeled Old Joe to a safe place behind the gatehouse. Taking out the keys and shoving them in my pocket, I opened one of the saddlebags and tugged out a smaller leather backpack, slinging it over my shoulder.

"That's all you're taking with you?" Gossamer asked.

I shrugged. "I left with very little, and I'm returning with pretty much what I've got on me." I looked down at the glamour of new clothes. "Well, sort of."

Waving her wand again, a pink vertical line formed in the air and straight down to the ground. With her hand, she dug her fingers into the line until it ripped open. The sound of laughter, talking, and music floated through. The familiar sight of the end of Main Street right before the park shimmered on the other side.

In a soft voice, Gossamer urged me. "Come on, Charli. You don't want to miss your homecoming."

Doubt crept into my gut, and I questioned my choice. Once through, there would be no turning back. Literally. Unless I wanted to walk the few miles all the way back to the border. As the night grew dark. Alone. Well, me, a few hundred cicadas, and whatever else lurked in the woods.

A cool breeze blew across my face, the moss in the trees bending to its will. Balling my fists, I did my best to summon my courage. Was I a Goodwin or was I a mouse? I ignored that tiny voice in the back of my head telling me that I was indeed small and squeaky with big ears and a long tail. Faking every ounce of bravery, I plastered a smile on my face, told that voice to shush, and walked toward the fairy's shortcut.

Right behind the rip in the air stood a large wooden sign in peeling white paint. Its old-fashioned black lettering needed a touch-up. But it loomed there like a grand announcement...or a big warning.

Welcome Home to Honeysuckle Hollow

Stepping onto the path, I hesitated as something on the sign caught my eye, goosebumps breaking out all over.

Did the population number on the sign just tick up by one?

Chapter Two

Chills followed the goosebumps as the distance I traveled from one place to another folded into the difference of one step, my internal balance faltering for a second. Choosing the fairy path always gave me the heebie-jeebies, which is why I hardly ever used it despite having friends who offered.

With footing on solid ground, I turned in place, taking in the familiar scenery. Stores lined the sides of Main Street, their darkened windows hiding what was waiting inside for the daylight. Fairy lights hung in strands across the street, giving off an otherworldly glow. Someone had added strings of mason jars with different hues of glows inside each of them. Everything underneath reflected their colors like they were lit up by psychedelic fireflies.

"Charli, wait up." Gossamer flitted to my side. "I gotta get some more sweet tea to bring back to my Flinty."

I pointed at the lights. "Did you help with the decorations?"

"Just the pink ones," she nodded.

"They're nice." My thoughts buried themselves in the past.

We walked down to the far end of Main Street, a heavy silence growing between us. The noise of the town's population grew with every stride, and my pace slowed.

With a tiny huff, Gossamer flew ahead of me and turned around, her body bobbing up and down in the air in front of me. "Listen, sugar pie. You gotta face the music at some point. Might as well be tonight when everyone's full of food and fun. Plus, you got a limited time to show off my masterpiece." She flourished her hand at my ensemble.

I wiped the beads of sweat off the top of my lip with the back of my hand. "I know." The unspoken *but* hung in the air between us.

My fairy friend shrugged. "Well, I wanna get back to my husband sooner rather than later." She flew over and hugged me around the neck. "Let me be the first to officially welcome you back. Good luck with whatever you choose to do." She disappeared into the distant crowd, a cloud of pink sparkles left in her wake.

Be brave, be brave, set the cadence for my feet to move forward, one in front of the other. At the last second, I turned left down an alley instead of heading to the opening of the park. The music grew louder as I worked my way toward the light at the end. I'd still make it to the park, but perhaps to a less conspicuous side of it.

When brick gave way to grass, I pushed through a few bushes and onto a cement walkway, wending my way around the curves and past abandoned benches. My eyes sought out the activities of the big party.

Every year, our little town took its Founders' Day celebrations so seriously that the events stretched it out to an entire week of things to do and participate in. Everyone looked forward to the First Night because it allowed us all to mill around, eat food we all prepared, and in general remember that we're a community that supports each other first and foremost. My choosing to return on this particular night had less to do with fate or coincidence than I wanted to admit.

The squawk of a crow startled me out of my sentimental reveries, and a figure moved in my direction. Adrenaline rushed through me. "Who goes there?"

All fear blasted away at the sound of a friendly guffaw. An even more familiar voice cheered me. "My dear, I think it would be more appropriate for me to ask *you* that question. Seems like you're practically a stranger, skulking over here in the dark rather than addressing your kinfolk and friends. Come on over here and give your old Uncle Tipper a squeeze."

An older man dressed in a seersucker suit and bowtie with a stomach as big as Santa's and a countenance like Colonel Sanders stepped into the light of an overhead lamp and opened up his arms, the crow on his shoulder flapping its wings to keep balance.

With relieved enthusiasm, I wrapped up the kindly man in my arms and gave in to the warmth of his tight embrace. "Hey, Uncle Tip. How ya been?"

He rocked me back and forth. "Been missing you, Charli Bird. You flew so far, far, far away. It's good to hold you again."

That nickname shot an arrow straight through my heart. Only a select approved few ever dared to use it. Anybody else who tried got smacked with a light hex or hand at the least.

"I think I missed this place in a small corner of my soul," I muffled into his shoulder. "I definitely missed you, too, Uncle Tipper." After a few more seconds, he released me when his crow chirped an annoyed caw. "And I missed you, too, you old bird."

"Biddy here's been my one companion who tolerates my shenanigans since you left. No one wants me to have any fun anymore. No getting away with anything. Someone's always watching. They're all gunning for me, I just know it. And they forget...I know things. Things that are worth knowing." He shook his finger in the air, his eyes darting back and forth. When they landed on me again, he paused his ramblings and swallowed.

With a clearing of his throat, his entire face dropped its wild concern, a mask of carefree indifference returning. "Now give me your hand, darlin'." Holding onto it, he held me captive under his intense scrutiny. "I've been missing my red bowtie. You know, the one with the tiny white polka dots. As a walking, talking divining rod, I'm hoping you can make my day and at least give me some general whereabouts to check."

If it had been anyone else in town to come right out and ask me to use my magic for a dog and pony show, I'd tell them they could search where the sun didn't shine. But because Uncle Tipper would always be one of my favorite people, I risked the little energy store I had.

With a sigh, I gave in. "You know the drill. Concentrate on that particular object. Help me find what you most want." Closing my eyes, I waited.

Sparks exploded in the dark, and the color red came into foggy view. Like turning a dial to find the right radio station frequency, I tilted my head and concentrated, drawing on Tipper's desire to pull the picture of the object into clearer focus.

"It's laying somewhere. On the floor. A wooden floor. In the shadows. Underneath...a bed." Concentrating, I willed the brightened vision to sharpen and zoom out. "Next to something. A shoe...no...heels. Red stilettos. Blood red. And next to that, something delicate and lacy with a tiny satin red bow—" I gasped and opened my eyes.

Tipper practically vibrated with glee. "No need to fill in the rest. I know *exactly* where it is." He kissed my cheek. "Thank you, my dear. Seems like your time away has been put to good use. Don't remember your gift being as sharp before. And now for your reward." He positioned my hand in front me with purpose.

With a wave of his fingers, a cool glass of liquid appeared with a small pop. The ice tinkled as I attempted not to drop it.

He smiled in satisfaction. "There. Now that's true hospitality. I hate to see anyone without a drink in their hand." With a snap, a glass materialized in his own grip.

I raised my cup to him. "As long as the drinks were unclaimed, I appreciate it."

His left eyebrow rose, and his lip curled up at the side.

"Tipper, you didn't steal these from someone did you?" My gut already knew the answer.

"My ungrateful niece, your Aunt Nora, and her even ungrateful-er daughter, darling Clementine, can fetch new ones." He looked wistful as he looked me in the eyes. "Your mom really was the best of the Walker bunch since...well, me." He tousled my hair. "And my present company ain't so bad either." Biddy squawked and nodded her head.

As much as I appreciated the drink and needed the sugar after the little use of *my gift*, if Uncle Tipper was bouncing from ideas to crazy accusations to stealing things with magic, perhaps others weren't entirely in the wrong to watch his so-called shenanigans. No telling what else he'd been up to.

Reaching inside his jacket, Tipper fumbled around until he pulled out his desired object, a silver flask. "Aha. Now it's a party." Unscrewing the cap, he poured some of its contents into his cup. He shook the container in front of me. "Care to partake?"

To ward him off, I brought the drink to my lips. Sweet tea with a floral bouquet. Nowhere else on earth used honeysuckle flowers to sweeten its tea as they did here.

Another marker of home. "No thank you. I'm good with it as it is."

He tilted his head. "You sure?" His chin gestured toward the crowds, a loud voice echoing off the nearby buildings to gather everyone for an announcement.

Kissing him on the cheek, I smiled at his signature scent of bay rum aftershave. "I am. Any consequences of my choices are mine to bear. Better to face them dead on and get them over with."

Uncle Tipper cupped my chin with his free hand. "My dear girl, you couldn't remind me more of your mother Rayline, our beloved sunshine, any more if you tried."

A single tear ran down my cheek, and he brushed it away with his thumb. "That's the best thing anybody has ever said to me," my voice broke in a cracked whisper.

He patted my cheek and took a sip of his spiked drink, the ice tinkling in the cup. When he glanced back at me, tears rimmed his own eyes. "What am I going to do when I'm gone? Who's going to take my place?"

No good could come from dredging up old complications and inherited problems.

I reached out to take away his drink. "You've got lots of kinfolk left. And not all of them are as much trouble as me."

He maneuvered out of reach, protecting his libation and sniffing. "You're right, of course." Taking a long swig, he smacked his lips. "Besides. I don't plan on going anywhere anytime soon. I'm the oldest representative of the Walker side of the founding families. If they want to stop me, they'll have to do it over my dead body." He shook a fist at the moon with enough force that his crow flew off her perch on his shoulder and lighted on top of the lamppost. With a mania I'd yet to experience with him, his eyes widened.

Concern coursed through me. "Of course they will, Tipper. Now, are you gonna escort me to the party?"

With his fingers, he smoothed over his mustache. "If you will pardon me, I think I shall go hunting for some pretty prey tonight. I hear the Widow Macintosh is like a sweet apple, ripe and ready for the picking these days."

"Ever the heartbreaker. You be careful out there." I crashed into him for one last hug, a little of his spiked concoction splashing on my arm. Out of all people in the town to run into first, I'd definitely won the lottery so far. Maybe my luck would continue.

He patted my back and released me. With a chivalrous bow and a tiny salute, he bid me adieu. "Come on, you old Biddy. We've got things to do." His crow flew down and landed on his shoulder.

I watched him walk away, my spirits lifted with his jubilance. He'd always been a little *touched,* as we liked to call it, but I'd never seen him so agitated before. Another mystery I'd have to solve once I got settled.

The commotion from the announcer beckoned me from the shadows. Downing the rest of the tea and pulling my shoulders back, I started the march to join the rest of the crowd.

A hand on my shoulder stopped my progression, the grip tightening until I winced. The deep voice from behind startled me, and I dropped my glass.

"I should arrest you right where you stand, Charlotte Vivian Goodwin."

Chapter Three

"You'd have to catch me first." No way would I let this guy get the upper hand.

"Already have," he insisted.

A stomp on the foot and an elbow into the gut got me released. I ran across the grass, but my pursuer caught me too soon. He picked me up, crushing me with his arms until my feet flailed in the air. "Give up?"

I nodded, and he put me down on the ground. As my foot lifted to stomp again, his fingers dug into my sides with furious purpose. Uncontrolled giggles stole my breath. "Cut. It. Out."

"Not until you give in," he said. "Do you?"

My sides hurt from the pressure of the tickling. "No."

"Give in."

"No."

"You're so stubborn, Charli Bird." His fingers increased their intensity until it was too much to take.

"Okay, okay. I give. I surrender." Holding my hands in the air, I gasped for breath.

The strong arms released me and spun me around to face him. "You are such a brat and pain in a unicorn's backside. Some things never change, do they, sis?" My older brother wrapped me up in a fierce hug.

"Hey, Matty D." My eyes fluttered shut, the comfort of his embrace washing away months of self-enforced loneliness and pining for family.

It took him long minutes before he let me go. With a sigh and a deep inhale, he pushed me back to look at me. "You should have let us know you were coming."

"Didn't know myself," I lied. "You look so official in your warden's uniform. You're on duty tonight?"

He straightened with pride. "I volunteered so I could have the night off for the barn dance. Plus, nothing really out of the ordinary to catch my eye. If you don't count Uncle Tipper."

"Yeah, he's out there stumbling around in the night, looking for some woman to woo. But there's something up with him. You're gonna have to fill me in."

My brother looped his thumbs in his belt buckles. "There's also the surprise return of a runaway."

My stomach dropped. "Can't be a runaway at my age. I just...left. You know why." A pebble on the ground looked so interesting that it needed my full attention.

"Hey, I missed Dad. Mom as well. Don't you think there were more of us hurting than only you?" Pain and resentment rolled off him like a heavy wave. He pursed his lips and shook his head. Blowing out a hard breath, he relaxed. "But that doesn't matter right now. I'm glad to see you, Birdy. You look surprisingly good."

"Don't call me that." I smacked his arm. "Not my doing. Ran into Gossamer at the border. What's really under here is a sight to behold. So how about you escort me to the party while I look more like a supermodel than like road kill. With you in uniform, maybe people won't stare at me too much."

Matt scrunched his nose like he used to when we were kids. "Oh, they'll stare, all right, uniform or not." He opened his mouth to add something, then closed it. Opened and closed. Opened and closed.

"Spit it out, Matt."

"Maybe you should head on back to the house. Nana's there. She'll be over the moon to see you."

Surprise bowled me over until panic filled me. "What? Nana's not here? Why? Is she okay? Is she sick?"

Matt waved his hands in front of me. "No, no, no. She's fine. She just didn't want to be here tonight."

My panic subsided, but curiosity perched on my chest instead. "Why? What's going on?"

"Charli..."

"Don't treat me like a kid." I tapped my foot in annoyance. "You know what, forget it. If you won't usher me over there, I can go by myself." I stomped off, ignoring the pleas in his voice as he called out my name in a loud whisper.

The lights from Main Street had nothing on the colorful twinklings that floated above the townspeople. Everyone milled about in groups, talking and eating. Music played while a few danced in front of the gazebo stage. All sizes of containers and dishes lined the long tables under tents where people showcased their best recipes. My mouth watered at the endless possibilities.

Next to the table with cakes and pies stood Blythe and Alison Kate, two of my best friends. With nervous anticipation, I pushed my way toward them when the music died, and Hollis Hawthorne stood at the microphone in the center of the stage.

"Welcome, everyone, to First Night. It is my absolute pleasure and duty as the sole founding member representative here to declare tonight a triumph." His smile echoed his polite words, but his stiff demeanor represented the same old Hollis—all business and no play. To think that he could have ended up my father-in-law.

Someone pulled on the straps to my bag. "Charli," hissed my brother. "Let's go."

I swatted him away. "Why? You're acting weird. More than usual." With a wave of my hand, I tried to dismiss him.

Hollis continued. "Tonight, there's more to celebrate than just the beginnings of our Founders' Day celebrations. It's a proud day for my family, and we wanted you to share in our joy."

Clapping my hands with slow deliberation, I leaned into Matt. "Yeah, right. He wanted to show something off."

My brother kept trying to pull me away, but I planted my feet. I was in the thick of things and had no intentions to run again.

"As I was saying, tonight is a proud night for the Hawthorne family. I'd like to ask my son, Hollis Tucker Hawthorne IV, to come up."

A spotlight shone right on the young man who climbed the stairs and made his way to stand by his father with the whitest of smiles and the straightest of teeth. The rest of the world dropped away as I beheld the one person who'd changed my life. The reason I'd left. And the one whom I'd jilted.

Tucker shook his dad's hand. "Thanks, Father. As many of you know, this has been a transformative year for me. My investment business is booming, thanks to all of you and my partner, Ashton Sharpe."

"You mean best friend, right?" Ashton called out.

Best friend? Since when did Tucker have a best friend? And who was this Ashton Sharpe?

Tucker pulled attention back to himself with a chuckle. "Well, yes, you have been loyal and stood by me through the good and the dark times."

"He better not be talking about me," I muttered.

Matt gripped my arm. "Birdy, you might not want to be here right now. Trust me."

"I. Said. Stop. It," I gritted through my teeth.

A few people around us turned and stared. They leaned in and whispered to each other, their eyes darting to me. Those few tapped the shoulders of some others, and in what seemed like a blink of an eye, a lot more heads turned my way than looked at the stage.

"If y'all don't mind, I'd like to ask someone here on the stage. She's the person who's affected me the most. Without her, I'd be a different man."

Butterflies fluttered in my stomach, and I rung my hands. How had Tucker heard about my return? In the letter I'd left behind, I explained that we'd talk about things when I came back. However, that conversation wasn't meant to be had in front of the whole town. There was no way my behind was going up on that stage. If I had to, I'd use all of my magic to teleport me away, even if it killed me.

Tucker beckoned with a wave. "Come on up here, Clementine."

Mouth open in disbelief, a skeptical screech escaped me. "Clementine?"

If there were any eyes not turned in my direction, my outburst cured that. All heads whipped to stare at me, including those of my Aunt Nora, Tucker's mom and dad, and the man himself. The smile leached away from his face as abject dread replaced triumph.

My cousin Clementine took nervous steps onto the stage, her lips forming a shaky smile. When she reached Tucker, she touched his arm and leaned on him for support. He continued staring at me until she pinched him.

"What? Oh...right. Um...Clementine. My *darling* Clementine." He patted her hand, and I rolled my eyes. Didn't he remember we called her that as a joke, not a term of endearment?

Getting down on one knee, he held out his hand. A velvet box materialized in it, and the women in the crowd gasped. Everyone loved a proposal. Except me.

"Miss Clementine Leonora Walker Irwin, would you make me the happiest of witches and agree to marry me?"

I seemed to recall him reciting the same thing to me not that long ago in the woods under a waning moon and stars.

"Yes," she squeaked, her right hand flying to cover her mouth and her left hand extended. "Yes, I will gladly and with honor become Mrs. Hollis Tucker Hawthorne IV."

"Those two are gonna drown underneath their mighty names," I sneered.

Pixies wearing laurel leaves like crowns and togas appeared out of nowhere, carrying trays of full champagne flutes to pass around. A banner fell from the rim of the Gazebo that read, *Congratulations, Tucker & Clementine* in cursive script.

Instead of applause, silence filled the air. The heat of hundreds of staring eyes bore into me. Maybe they wanted a spectacle of tears, a tantrum of anger, or a crazy outburst from me.

Snatching a glass from a nearby flying pixie, I held it up high. "To the betrothed couple. May you both have all the happiness in the world." The words tasted like ash.

Like deflating a balloon, the tension diffused, and

everyone followed suit. Soon, the merriment returned, and life moved on around where I stood glued to the same spot. My eyes tracked Tucker's movements as he waved at people while escorting my cousin off the stage.

Matt patted my back, pulled my bag from my shoulder, and excused himself as a rush of screaming girls surrounded me and shut out the rest. They talked all at once, throwing arms around my neck and bestowing kisses on my cheek. I did my best to hide the emotional storm brewing inside me.

"Well, Charli knows how to take a heck of an exit. I guess we should have guessed she'd make a whirlwind of a return." Blythe Atherton, the tallest of all of us, winked at me.

"I think she acted fabulously considering how surprised she must have been. You were surprised, weren't you?" Alison Kate Johnston licked frosting off her fingertips after handing me a red velvet cupcake. "Taste this and tell me if you can tell what the secret ingredient is."

Lily Blackwood put a protective arm around my shoulder. "Leave her alone, Ali. Can't you tell that she's—"

"—a ticking time bomb," her cousin Lavender finished. "Her aura is all wobbly." Born in the same month under the Gemini sign, those two acted more like twins than cousins although they looked nothing alike.

"I'm just trying to cheer her up," pouted Alison Kate.

Pulling up my theoretical big girl britches, I obliged with a bite of the cupcake. "You are, Ali Kat. It's gonna take more than a minute for me to get comfortable in my own shoes again." The cupcake tasted like sand, but I managed to chew and swallow. "Is it flavored with some honeysuckle syrup?"

Alison's face dropped. "How did you know?"

"Because everything has honeysuckle in it. Frosted fairy wings, you can be dense sometimes." Blythe argued back and forth with Alison.

Lily and Lavender discussed the morphing colors of my aura, Lavender attempting to manipulate it by pinching her fingers around me. And I grew more and more comfortable in the chaos of my friends. My tribe. Suddenly, the world righted itself again.

Until the sound of a throat clearing interrupted. "Girls. Thank you for celebrating with us this evening. Have you seen my Clementine's ring? It will truly take your breath away."

Aunt Nora dragged my cousin in front of everyone, her eyes never leaving mine. She nudged her daughter, and Clementine held out her hand.

"That's a real beauty," I admitted. The rest of my friends made agreeable noises but shared knowing looks between them.

That particular ring had been just as shiny and beautiful on my hand, too. But it also had looked sad and dejected when I left it on top of my farewell letter. Who was to say it wasn't exactly where it should be now?

"Congratulations, Clem." I gave her a hug, which she stiffly returned. "I truly do wish you all the happiness."

My cousin narrowed her eyes at me as she curled her lips in a cold smirk. "Thank you, Cousin Charlotte. Although we didn't expect your presence here tonight of all nights. But I appreciate your sentiments. I really should be getting back to *my* Tucker."

Clementine left in a snit, but her mother remained. She grasped my hand in her icy grip. After an awkward pause, Aunt Nora leaned in and planted a cold kiss on my cheek. "May you have a happy homecoming," she proffered through clenched teeth. "Girls." She nodded at my friends and took her leave.

We watched her glad-hand her way through the different groupings of people, no doubt bragging about her perfect daughter marrying into the most prominent founding family.

Alison Kate shook her head. "That cousin of yours is..."

"A real witch?" I finished. "Yeah, we've never been close." I did my best not to notice Lavender touch Lily's hand for a second. At one point in my childhood, I would have given anything for my cousin to be that close with me. No chance of that. Especially now.

Lavender sighed. "You'd think your aunt's aura would be all shiny with love and hope for her daughter's future. She's all cloudy."

Blythe crossed her arms. "I can't believe those two are related to you."

"Hmph. As Nora would gladly tell y'all and remind me, not by blood. I'm not a real Goodwin or Walker since I'm adopted, remember?" My aunt never lost an opportunity to tell that to people. No doubt she reveled in the triumph that a real descendant of the Walker's was engaged to a Hawthorne.

How my mother ever put up with her sister, I'd never know or understand.

More Honeysuckle Hollow residents came over and hugged me hello, welcoming me and avoiding all semblance of curiosity about how I felt. In the long run, I realized that maybe I'd dodged a bullet. Without the awkward engagement, everyone would be focused on my departure. But now, most of them feigned concern for me. Better to play the victim than the villain.

"Charli, what is happening to your hair?" Alison Kate pointed at my head.

"Oh no. Gossamer's glamour must be wearing off, with my emotions in such a tangle." I'd burned right through her magic much quicker than if I'd had my wits about me. "I'd better call this a night and head home before I make an even bigger scene when everyone sees what I'm really wearing."

It took another long round of hugs and promises to get together again in the coming days before I could leave. Matt excused himself from a nearby conversation and put his arm around me as we walked.

"You going to Nana's?" he asked.

"Yep."

"You gonna say more than *yep*?"

"Nope."

"Brat."

"Yep."

Matt captured my head in the crook of his arm and gave me a noogie as I fake fought him off.

"Leave me alone. You know I don't need anybody. The streets are lit, and most everybody is here. I'll be fine."

He raised his head and looked down his nose at me in full inspection. "You gonna stay put? If I come over tomorrow, will you be there?"

My insides turned mushy, and I threw my arms around him. "Of course," I mumbled into his chest. "I'm not going anywhere anytime soon."

He rested his head on top of mine. "Good. Missed you."

"You, too." Tears soaked into his uniform shirt, so I pushed back. "Wouldn't want to ruin your reputation as a tough warden."

He ruffled my hair and handed me back my bag. "Night, Birdy."

"Don't call me that, Matty D."

My brother walked away, turning around to taunt me. "If not me, who else?" He waved. "See you tomorrow."

Same older brother. Same feelings of absolute love and childish annoyance. Someday, we'd be old and decrepit and still be having the same conversation.

I walked out of the main entrance to the park and onto the middle of Main Street. Humming under my breath, I danced under the lights and illuminations. I'd survived the night. From here on out, life would be much easier.

A shadow darkened the light of the moon, and a loud squawking interrupted my relief. The large bird circled overhead, its constant noise garnering my attention. When it didn't stop in its repetition, I guessed its identity.

"Hey, Miss Biddy. You gonna accompany me home?"

The crow cawed at me twice and flew away. Not sure what to do, I turned in the direction to walk home. Biddy dive-bombed me, the whoosh of her feathers fluttering right above my head.

"What are you doing, crazy bird?" My hands waved her away.

The black figure circled above me a few times and flew in the opposite direction. Since I had no desire for the next thing she attempted to get my attention, I sighed and followed her insistent cries.

We made it around a couple of buildings and down an alley until we hit the edge of the park, close to where I'd been before.

"Hey, bird. Does Uncle Tipper want to talk to me? Did he send you?"

Persistent squawks answered my futile questions, and I did my best to follow her screeching with spoken reassurances. She finally landed on a park bench, flapping her wings and hopping next to a ponderous figure.

"Oh, hey, Uncle Tipper. You done bird doggin' the ladies tonight?"

No chuckle. No smart remark. Only a very uncomfortable hush.

Biddy hopped onto the seat of the bench and then back up to the top of it. Her noises were quieter, sounding different. Like whining. Or pleading.

My great-uncle was probably passed out. He hadn't earned

the nickname Tipsy for nothing. Still, I approached him with caution and dread.

"Come on, Uncle Tipper. Time to walk me home." The tremors in my hand unnerved me as I reached out to touch his shoulder.

As soon as my fingers landed on his body, a cold zing zapped up my right arm, and I knew. I just...knew. Still, I shook him to be sure. First a gentle push. Then a second one with a little more force.

"Uncle Tipper?" my voice wavered.

His head slumped forward. My bag fell to the ground. And my scream filled the night air.

Chapter Four

My nose twitched with the temptation of delectable smells. Bacon. Coffee. A warm cinnamon-y concoction probably dripping with sugary frosting. A crash of something hitting the floor and muted fussing pulled me out of the deepest slumber of my life, like being yanked out of quiet deep waters and forced into the air and light.

Sitting up, I rubbed my throbbing head, and I tried to piece together where I was. Someone had been chasing me in the dark, right? Or no, that had been a nightmare. And yet, deep down in the pit of my stomach, my gut screamed at me that all was not well. My right arm tingled with a strange ache, and I massaged it, taking in my surroundings.

A pattern of tiny baskets of delicate flowers repeated over faded pale yellow wallpaper. Wooden furniture from different eras filled the enclosed space. Everything reflected a refined and austere taste save a chest of drawers that matched nothing else. Various bright colors decorated each drawer with every knob painted in contrast. It sat against the wall in utter rebellion against the other objects, a symbol of a young girl marking her territory. Above it, a framed cross-stitched sampler offered the sage advice to never accept an invitation to a dragon's barbecue.

Nana's house. My room, my brain registered. Sunlight spilled through the lace curtains. My hand ran over the quilt covering me, relishing every handmade stitch. Filled with joyful glee, I snuggled down into the bed and pulled the covers over me, wrapping myself up and giggling. No better protection existed than being under this quilt, in this room, in this house.

A light knock on the door interrupted my revelry. "Charli Bird," Nana's voice sang. "Get up, sweetness. Morning's here to greet you with her shining light."

My grandmother's standard wake-up call cheered me even more. Playing an old game, I barked out, "Nobody here but us chickens."

She pounded on the door a little harder. "Well, them chickens better roost their sorry behinds out of bed, or a certain bird will miss out on some fine breakfast. Now shake your tail feathers and get yourself up and presentable."

"I'm up, I'm up," I yawned, planting my feet on the creaky wooden floor. "Hey, Nana?"

"Yes, Charli Bird?"

"What am I wearing?" My fingers plucked at the delicate

ruffles on a nightgown from a bygone era that covered my entire body.

"What I put on you after bathing and tucking you in. Now, you gonna use your mouth for complainin' or eatin'?"

My stomach punctuated her well-made point with a growl. I grabbed my bag first but found it empty of clothes. A stack of them clean and folded lay on top of a nearby wicker-seat chair, my panties neatly creased into a tidy square. After a quick trip to the bathroom in the hall to brush my teeth and pull my hair back into a messy bun, I ventured toward the sounds and tempting aromas. Nana's cat Loki blocked my way, rolling his gray striped back on the hallway runner, his generous pale tummy mocking me.

"Move it, cat."

With feline indifference, he licked his paw and stretched longer. Stepping over him, I made my way to the staircase. On the way down, the little stinker bit my ankle and zoomed underneath me, almost causing me to fall to my death.

"You better run before I hex your tail off, stupid cat," I yelled after his tubby behind.

"Don't disparage my sweet boy," Nana chastised as she met me at the bottom.

"*He* bit *me*." I stood in front of her, hands on my hips.

"It's his nature. You can't fault someone for being who they are." She cocked an eyebrow at me.

"Yeah, but you didn't have to name him after the God of Mischief as a kitten. No doubt that contributed to his natural state of being a little devil."

She mimicked my stance. "I don't know. Seems to me you fit your name quite well. You sprouted wings and flew away, didn't you?"

"Nana," I protested, not prepared to defend myself without some food in my belly.

Her expression softened, and she opened her arms. "Thank goodness you found your way back, though. Now quit your sassin' and give your old grandmother a squeeze."

She rocked me back and forth, and I clung to her with a wretched thirstiness, drinking in all the things that made her *her*. After Mom's death, Nana took us in to help Dad and the two of us kids stay afloat from our sadness. Echoes of the life that we'd lived all those years here crashed against me. I didn't notice the copious sobs racking my body until Nana forced a handkerchief into my hand. Its flimsiness made me laugh through my tears.

"I don't think this will get the job done," I sniffed, lifting it to my face and taking in the scent of my grandmother's perfume. "It's too pretty to snot on."

Nana wiped the wetness from my cheeks with her fingers. "But that's what it's made for. So snot away." Her knuckles dashed under her own eyes before she grabbed me by both shoulders.

Her eyes examined me while her fingers squeezed my arms. She moved her hands up my neck and cupped my cheeks, tilting my head back, mumbling under her breath something unintelligible. When she cranked my head forward and got close enough that her nose almost touched mine while she stared into my eyes, the level of my discomfort broke my stunned paralysis.

"Nana, whatcha doin'?" I asked through squished cheeks between her fingers.

"Hmm, what?" She narrowed her eyes one last time before shaking her head and returning to her normal expression. "Oh, forgive me. Just checking to make sure you're really here well and whole standing in front of me."

"O-o-kay." Not for a second did I believe her lie, but hunger outweighed my curiosity. "Can we go eat?"

Releasing me, she gave me another hard squeeze before patting my rump. "You go on into the dining room. I'm gonna open the front door."

"Why?"

"It'll make things easier. Now get." She shooed me away with her hand.

With tentative steps, I entered the formal dining room, the source of all the mouthwatering scents. The long oak table was covered with steaming dishes, a plate stacked with pancakes, pans of various ooey gooey baked goods, a mound of bacon and sausage piled high, a pot of coffee, a pitcher of orange juice, and another of Bloody Mary's.

"Pick your poison and dig in." Nana gestured at the stack of plates at one end of the table. Her eyebrow raised as she watched me rubbing my sore arm again, so I stopped. With her lips pursed, she disappeared into the kitchen.

I scooped some of everything onto a plate until some of it

threatened to fall off. A piece of bacon hung out of my mouth as I poured my first cup of coffee.

Nana clicked her tongue at me as she came back with a plate of hot corn fritters. "Oh, Charli. Don't tell me you've lost your manners while you were away."

"There's enough food here for all of Honeysuckle. I can't eat all of this." By my calculations, if I ate the rest of the pancake, there'd be room on my plate for a fritter plus a scoop of grits and sausage casserole. And a sticky cinnamon bun.

"You let me worry about the food. You worry about fueling up. When your brother brought you to me two nights ago, you were dangerously close to needing Doc Andrews."

My mouth stopped in the middle of a syrupy bite. "Two nights ago?"

Nana's face softened. "Eat first. Talk later, darlin'."

Flashes of the night I returned to Honeysuckle Hollow popped into my head and disappeared. I tried to remember the specifics, but the images shimmered in and out of focus. Weird.

A loud knock on the front doorway interrupted my confusion. "You want me to get that?"

"No," Nana said. "The door's open. Whoever it is will figure out what to do. Now, make me some room. I've got more food to bring in."

Stuffing the cinnamon bun in my mouth and standing, I maneuvered a few dishes to make a hole right in front of me.

Working on my mouthful, I took stock of the bounty on

the table. "Nana, there's enough here to feed an army of rabbit shifters." The pounding grew in intensity.

Nana's head appeared again from the door to the kitchen. "Girl, watch what you say." She disappeared again.

The pounding had stopped and a deep voice echoed from the foyer. "Ms. Goodwin. You home?"

My grandmother walked into the dining room carrying a stacked plate of biscuits and a china gravy boat, a smug smile perched on her lips. "In here," she beckoned in a sing-song tone.

The voice didn't ring any bells. The generous bite of cinnamon bun currently residing in my mouth needed to disappear as fast as possible. Before I could swallow it all down, a tall, broad man filled the entire doorway to the room. His amber eyes ambled over the food all the way down the long table until they lit on me.

Heat flooded my cheeks and flowed all the way down to my toes under his scrutiny. For a long second, he held his intense stare until he blew out a breath and shook his head.

With a scowl on his face, he addressed my grandmother. "Wanted to let you know I'm here to continue working on your porch, ma'am." His Southern drawl reverberated through me.

"For the last time, you call me Ms. Vivi, please. Where are my manners? Let me introduce you to my granddaughter, Charlotte. Charli, this is Dashiel Channing. He's new to Honeysuckle."

No kidding, Nana. "Pleased to meet you." I stood up with

typical grace, knocking my fork off my plate, and extended my hand.

He shook it, but when he pulled away, he frowned while wiping what must have been sticky frosting from the bun on his jeans. "Pleasure."

"Dash, why don't you make yourself a plate. There's plenty, and the two of you can get acquainted while I bring out some more." Nana's tone dripped with honey as did her entire face until she looked at me. Her finger tapped her lips as she silently mouthed, "*Wipe*."

After the seconds it took to comprehend what she meant, I dabbed my napkin across my lips, looking in horror at the glob of white frosting left behind. Pixie poop. The fire in my cheeks could light the entire table on fire. I couldn't even venture to peek at Dash to figure out what he must think of me.

"No, thank you, Ms. Goodwin. I wanna get going on my work. Thanks for the offer." His deep, growling voice both terrified and intrigued me at the same time. He nodded his head in my direction when I dared to peer back at him and disappeared.

"Nana," I hissed and threw my napkin at her. "You could have warned me."

She rearranged dishes to make more room. "Could've. But didn't. Oh, sweet honeysuckle iced tea. Gird yourself." She pointed at the foyer.

A storm of commotion brewed in the other room as female voices roared with deafening magnitude. Nana's friends and their granddaughters, my own gaggle of girlfriends, streamed into the dining room, holding dishes and supplies, finishing conversations as they set their offerings down on the table.

"How are you feeling, honey?" asked Ada Atherton. "My sweet-tempered grandbaby told me all about the engagement."

"Granny," Blythe slammed her dish down on the table. "I thought I told you not to say anything."

"Well, it's the talk of the whole dang town. It might as well be the topic of conversation at the table. Here. These are for you." Mimosa Blackwood handed me a large bouquet of colorful blooms wrapped in tissue and cellophane from her store.

"Those gerbera daisies are for *cheerfulness*," Lavender explained. "No need to see your aura to know you could use some of that this morning."

Lily pouted. "I wanted yellow chrysanthemums to commemorate your sorry ex-fiancé. *Slighted Love* indeed. But Grandma and Lav insisted on daisies."

"Thanks, Ms. Mimsy. And both of you, too." The flower wrappings with *Mimsy's Whimsies* printed on them crinkled in my hands.

"Here, let me put those in some water." Nana grabbed them from me.

Lily's younger sister popped a piece of biscuit in her mouth and sat down without ceremony next to me. "So is it true that you found Tipper's dead body?"

The news of my great-uncle's death bothered me. My brain searched for the answer but couldn't find one, even though I knew in my bones I should be able to. Panic filled me to the brim.

"Linsey," her sister and cousin warned.

The color in Linsey's cheeks deepened. "What? It's the biggest story going. If I could get the first scoop, maybe DK will let me do something more than just the Dear Delilah advice column for The Honeysuckle Holler. I'm sick of making up responses to stupid questions like what's the best way to wash out hex marks. *Dear Dingbat - The best way is not to get yourself hexed in the first place.*"

Blythe scowled at Lily's younger sister. "That's good advice. Shame you don't take it yourself." She wagged a finger at the offender in warning.

My head tried to figure out what Linsey meant but nobody would look at me. "What's she talking about? What happened to Uncle Tipper?" The pain in my right arm ached a little more.

"Guess your spellcasting worked a little *too* well, Vivi?" asked Ida Mae Johnston as she placed a platter of scones on the table. "Getting a recipe down pat takes time for experimentation."

"And you would know all about getting the recipe just right, Meemaw. Here, Charli, why don't you try one of her lavender and honeysuckle scones." Alison Kate handed me one with an apologetic look. "I helped her bake them this morning."

Blythe rolled her eyes. "I don't think that's gonna solve anything right now."

I shut my eyes to the din of everyone talking and arguing back and forth around me but not *to* me. What had happened to Tipper? And why was I involved? A dull ache throbbed in my head as murky images attempted to break through the fog.

The screen door slammed and my brother called out from the foyer. "Nana? Where are you?"

My grandmother pinched the bridge of her nose. "In here, sugar pie."

Matt walked in and paused. "Didn't know this was a party." He looked at the table of food with longing but walked over to me. "Charli, I'm sorry, but I need you to come to the warden station with me."

"For what?" I stood up, my chair scraping on the floor.

"I'll explain on the way, so please just come and don't ask questions right now." He touched my shoulder.

Nana fixed him in her gaze. "Young man, you will not come into this house and treat your sister like a common criminal. Please explain yourself."

"My fault entirely," a strange man's voice said. He stepped into the room. "I apologize for interrupting your meal, but we've given you more than enough time, and now your granddaughter needs to answer some questions. Deputy Warden Goodwin here is following my orders."

"And I told you two nights ago that as I fill the High Seat of the town council that she would answer your questions when she's ready." Nana stood tall, walking over to face the stranger head-on, more of a formidable force than an old lady. "I thought I'd made myself clear, Detective Clairmont. We don't work this way here in Honeysuckle Hollow. A little politeness and consideration go a long way in a small town like ours."

All the girls pushed Matt out of the way and shielded me like a protective ring hiding me from sight, crossing their arms, while their grandmothers stood in solidarity behind mine.

My brother pleaded with me. "Charli, please. The sooner you get this over with, the sooner you can come right back. I promise."

"Get through *what*? I have no idea what any of you are talking about." The panic growing in my gut stirred up my confusion, and I rubbed my temples. Something locked away in my head needed to come out, but I couldn't find the key to let it. The pang in my arm throbbed again. "I have to go."

Elbowing my friends out of the way, I bolted through the back doorway that led to the living room and ran through to the parlor into the foyer and toward the stairs.

"Stop right there, Miss Goodwin," demanded Detective Clairmont. "Under warden command."

My body halted at the foot of the stairs, unable to move. Indignant voices erupted as everyone questioned the man's authority. Nana screamed that he had no right throwing a spell around in her house. Matt attempted to reason with his superior. The rest of the women henpecked him while I tried my best to budge.

The screen door banged shut with enough force to stop everyone. "May I be of service, Ms. Goodwin." Dash blocked the outside daylight with his hulking frame, his amber eyes flashing.

"You will stay right where you are, werewolf," Detective Clairmont ordered, contempt dripping off his words.

"I'm a wolf shifter. There's a difference." The muscles in Dash's jaw twitched, and his hands curled into fists. "Now let her go."

"You have nothing to do with any of this. If you want to keep it that way, you'll get back to work."

"And if I don't?" The shifter's lip curled up in a snarl.

"Then I'll take you *and* Miss Goodwin down to the station and question both of you. Come to think of it, where exactly were you two nights ago? Can someone vouch for your whereabouts?"

Nana walked forward and stood in between the two men. "Now that's enough. Dash, I appreciate your presence, but maybe it would be best if you went back outside." She placed a gentle hand on his chest.

"No," he refused. "Not until he lets Miss Charlotte go."

Matt stood next to Detective Clairmont. "Come on, Mason. This is going overboard. It sounds like she's not going to be much help anyway until my Nana's spellcraft wears off."

The detective sighed. With a snap, he broke the bond and

my body slumped with the release of the invisible force. "And exactly when will that be?"

Nana came over to hold me up. "When it does. Detective, do you have family? Any children of your own?"

A shadow passed over his face like clouds in front of the sun. He caught himself and cleared his throat. "No. I don't see what that has to do with anything."

With a hug around my shoulders, my grandmother stood next to me. "If and when you do, you'll understand the lengths you will go to take care of and protect your own. For now, you can get off my property. And I don't want to have to report your actions here today, which could be seen as prejudicial rather than judicial." She nodded her chin in Dash's direction.

Sheepish shame flashed on Detective Clairmont's face for a brief second. "My apologies, Mr. Channing." The frown in his lips spoke more than his words.

Dash grunted in reluctant acceptance. His glowing eyes found mine, and a chill ran down my body. Except...was he checking on me or thinking he'd like to devour me with his great big teeth he must possess when he shifts? He released me from his gaze and walked outside after a polite bow of his head to my grandmother.

The tension grew as thick as molasses, and all I wanted was to pull the quilt back over my head. "Detective Clairmont?" My quiet voice garnered the attention of everyone left standing.

"Yes?"

Rubbing my sore arm, I gave it my best shot. "I don't

remember what happened, but it sounds like you need me to. I promise, as soon as I do, I will come down to the station on my own. Will that suffice?"

His attention dropped to my limb. "Has that been hurting you for long?"

"Mason, is her promise enough?" asked Matt, standing up for me as much as he could.

We all held our collective breath until he nodded. "Yes. As soon as your memory returns, make sure you fulfill your word."

Holding up three fingers, I put a bigger stamp on my promise. "Witch's honor."

My friends gasped. "You don't owe *him* that," Blythe barked.

"I'll only get potentially hexed if I break my promise," I reassured her. Looking straight at Mason Clairmont, I raised my eyebrow. "And I stand by my word."

Without saying anything or even uttering a polite apology or farewell, the detective turned on his heel and left. A heated exchange of words from outside drifted in through the screen door. The tension around us popped like a thin soap bubble, and I blew out all the air in my lungs, bending over and grabbing my knees.

"Well done, Charli Bird." My grandmother patted my back.

Matt came over and ruffled my hair. "Nana, he means business. There's more going on, and we need Charli to talk to us."

"Surely, that can wait," she insisted.

"Not for long," he replied.

"Oh for unicorn's sake, don't start that again." Standing up straight, I crossed my arms. "Now, two things are gonna happen. Y'all are all going back in that dining room and stuff yourselves until we have to roll you out the door. And while you're doing that, you're gonna tell me what it is I'm supposed to be remembering."

⚜

AFTER MY STOMACH stuck out and my brain was crammed with so much info that both might burst, I fixed a plate of food, grabbed a glass of iced tea, and excused myself from the hubbub.

With my hip, I bumped open the screen door. Dash stood with his back to me, bent over the railing, his sweat-soaked shirt clinging to his body.

"Uh...I brought you some food," my voice squeaked.

Dash stopped working but didn't turn to me. "No, thanks."

"How about some iced tea?" I shook the glass at him. "It's so...*hot*."

The shifter had faced me, sweat dripping down his forehead. "That I'll take."

My feet remained planted, forcing him to come to me. When he reached for the drink, I handed him the plate. When he reached for the plate, I remembered he wanted the drink and pulled it away, thrusting the tea at him. He clasped my wrist in his big hand, holding it in place, and pulled the glass from my grip. It took him a second to let me go with a scowl and another murmured thanks.

"Sorry about the way he treated you. That's not usually how things are here."

After a few large gulps, he caught his breath. "I'm used to it."

"You shouldn't be."

His lip curled up. "What world did you grow up in?"

I pointed down. "Right here in Honeysuckle. And I hope that I can prove that it's not like that here. We're not like that."

He scoffed. "Thanks for the tea." Without hesitation, he walked away.

"Thanks for sticking up for me."

His broad shoulders shrugged, every cut muscle moving like a well-oiled machine. "I try to do the right thing. When I can." He went back to work, making as loud a racket as possible.

"So do I," I muttered as I headed back inside.

Chapter Five

"You sure this is a good idea?" From behind a tree across the street, I watched the final trickle of people caught up in intense conversations file into the town hall. It didn't take a genius to figure out the topic of gossip on everyone's lips.

My brother shushed me from the front of the tree. "The whole point of being stealthy is to, you know, not give yourself away by talking. Nana insisted I make sure you attended tonight's meeting. It might help you fill in some blanks and get you caught up on current events."

The prospect of being seen and caught at the center of the drama filled me with dread. I should have followed my instincts and stayed home. Under my quilt.

"The sooner the details are clear for you, the sooner you can come in and talk to Detective Clairmont. Then Mason can get off my back. Look, here comes TJ." Matt's voice brightened at the sight of his wife. "She's gonna sneak you in." They embraced as soon as she met them.

"Eww, keep it clean, you two." I scrunched my nose and stuck my head out from behind the trunk. "Well, what do you know, Traci Jo?" Due to a couple of animal emergencies, she hadn't been able to make it to Nana's house that morning.

My sister-in-law yanked on my hand to pull me into a hug. "I know that we've all missed you lots while you've been gone. Also that telling people not to feed their pets or familiars the same food that they eat goes in one ear and out the other. You do *not* want to know what I've helped clean up today."

A flying shadow passed over us, and with a couple of caws, the familiar large crow landed in the branches above. The three of us watched it tilt its head as it inspected our motley crew.

"That's Biddy, right? Tipper's crow?" asked TJ.

"Pretty sure." I reached out my hand towards the bird. She hopped down a couple of branches closer but stopped just shy. Her presence dredged up details from my murky memory and solidified them. Talking to Tipper. Finding him on the bench. And everything else in between. Rubbing my right arm, I shivered.

Matt watched me with brotherly protectiveness, no doubt debating whether or not to risk Nana's wrath to send me back home. With reluctant resignation, he pointed at the building. "Let's get you inside. TJ, you go in and open the side door. We'll meet you there."

Once his wife crossed the street, my brother turned to

me, his stern look suggesting serious business. "I was against this, but there's no talking Nana out of anything. All the women in our family have a stubborn streak a mile wide."

I smacked his arm. "Hey, I resemble that remark."

He swatted me back. "Pay attention. You go hide up in the projection room. I don't want anybody talking to you before you're ready."

"Sure. And you also would like not to get into trouble with your boss if I talk to anyone but him first, right?"

The wrinkle between Matt's eyebrows deepened. "He's not my boss. When he transferred from his big job up North, he came with his rank. Big Willie wasn't too pleased, but there wasn't much he could do."

I'd bet the last of the money in my savings that Sheriff "Big Willie" West didn't enjoy having a city boy trying to run things in his small town. I'd also bet Detective Mason Clairmont had a talent for ruffling feathers wherever he went. He must be over the moon to have a big case to work.

Mocking my brother, I tiptoed behind him across the street like an idiot. One person leaving early or arriving late, and the jig was up. But we made it to the side door with no problem. A quick knock and it opened with a tiny squeak of its hinges.

"Want me to come with you?" offered TJ.

I shook my head. "Naw. I know my way around."

The stalwart building was old stomping grounds for my friends and me. Unbeknownst to the town officials, including my grandmother, we'd sneak in to share a snatched mason jar of moonshine and snacks. The place served multiple purposes, including town meetings, use of the stage for things like the community theater group, and especially as our only movie theater. All of us kids at some point worked the projector when a new movie came to town. Well, new to us meant practically classic to the rest of the world.

I jiggled the old knob on the door to the projector room, and it gave way like it used to. Walking up the stairs covered in frayed thin carpet, I crept toward the projector window and slid it open, cringing when it gave way with an audible scrape. I poked my head up, relief replacing fear as everybody focused on Nana, who sat on the stage in the larger of the three chairs, the one to her right empty and the one to her left occupied with a frowning Hollis Hawthorne.

"As I said, due to the town's loss of Tipper Walker, we will be suspending any town business until we officially fill his seat." Nana's voice rang clear and true throughout the entire building.

A tall man stood up as my grandmother recognized him to give him the floor. He spoke in a clear, snooty British accent. "You'll forgive me, but I was led to believe that holding the meetings and then forcing the vote was crucial at this time due to so many town citizens returning for the yearly festivities. It is our best chance to have any prospect of an opportunity to present the issues and have a fair and balanced decision." A smattering of applause followed his frustrated words.

Hollis smacked the table in front of him. "I must agree

with Ralph, the venerable gentleman vampire. There are serious issues that need decisions now. Begging your pardon, Vivian."

"It's Raif, sir," corrected the tall man.

"What?" Hollis blustered.

"My name. It's Raif, not Ralph. A common mistake." He sat down without pushing his point further.

A woman next to him whispered something in his ear sharp enough for him to wince away. In a huff, she stood up and maneuvered her way to the end of the aisle. Her full name escaped me, but I knew her as Eveline. Technically, *Lady* Eveline, if memory served me. Some old aristocratic title she carried over from her days prior to being turned. Dashing away what looked like pink tears from her eyes, she rushed out.

Before Nana could utter a reply or grasp control again, someone raised their hand and cleared their throat. With confidence that radiated off of him like sunbeams, the guy that claimed to be Tucker's best friend stood up. What was his name? Ashton Something?

He addressed the two members on stage. "This has more than just a seat on the council at stake, if you'll pardon my use of that word, Raif." He nodded his head at the former speaker. "There are matters that need attention that affect the business and economy of the town. Both Tucker and I have worked hard on preparing our proposal." He gestured next to him, where Tucker sat, nodding his head.

My grandmother held up her hand. "Which will not go

ignored. However, I believe that observing a brief suspension of town business is more than called for in this instance. Considering the considerable amount of change that will be happening," she gestured at the empty chair next to her, "I ask for the town's patience so that our transition forward, whatever that looks like, will be a smooth one that is in all of our best interest."

Hollis shot a sideways glance at my grandmother and a stern glare at his son's friend, who sat down. Nobody dared to add anything else, and the silence gave space for Nana to conclude business.

She shook her head. "We were all sad to hear of our dear friend Tipper Walker's passing two nights ago. Arrangements are being made for his parting ceremony by his surviving niece, Leonora Walker."

My stomach dropped. If Aunt Nora were in charge of Tipper's estate, that would mean she'd be the one to inherit the third seat on the council as the next in the Walker line. With that sour-faced woman in a position of power and Hollis Hawthorne as a potential ally, who knows how things might go sideways in our little town? But Nana was right. Now was not the time to think about those kinds of changes.

"In honor of Tipper, I'd like to ask everyone to please stand." Nana scooted her chair away from the table and waited. In unison, everyone stood up. "Let us honor his memory with a moment of silence."

The sounds of a few sniffs peppered the air. My own eyes watered. That silly old man had been a horrible and entertaining influence on me all my life. He'd embraced mischief like an old friend and danced with abandon on the edge of sanity. But his heart had beaten strong and true. At least up until the end when somehow it had stopped. Why had I been the one to find him? Nothing clouded my memory anymore, and I hugged my arms around my body, giving into muffled sobs.

"And now, since last night's festivities in the park were canceled due to the unfortunate incident, I can think of nothing more appropriate than letting the Honeysuckle Hams perform their little play written by Tipper himself, all about our town's humble beginnings. Hollis, would you please dispose of our table and chairs." Nana walked off stage left, leaving an extremely displeased Hawthorne family member to use his magic to move the furniture.

Several people in mix-matched antique garb filled the back of the stage. One of them, Beauregard Pepperpot, stepped to the front, the bright makeup on his face giving him the appearance of a cross between a ghost and a clown.

Taking off his hat, he addressed the restless audience. "Before we start, I just wanted to say that Tipper Walker wasn't simply *my* best friend. He was loyal to our town and a friend to pretty much everyone here. In his honor, we perform his words as he wrote them."

Oh boy. No telling what version of history we were about to watch.

One of the troupe pulled out a fiddle and played a somber melody almost in tune. Three others stepped forward and stopped in the middle of the stage, holding wands in their hands and bringing the tips of the wooden props together.

Wands? Since when did we need those to practice magic? Perhaps Uncle Tipper had somehow gotten his hand on some popular books about witches, wizards, and magic from the outside world. This did not bode well.

"Woe to our nation and its peoples," proclaimed the one on the right with dramatic intensity. "Where can we go where we will not be persecuted and can live in perfect harmony?"

The woman in a vintage dress with too tight of a bodice and a swinging hoop skirt that kept knocking into the two next to her brandished her wand in wide arcs. "Why, Prentice Goodwin. You do bring up a valid point. I, Norberta Walker, propose that we shall found our own town. One in which more than just us witches can live in freedom. To do as we please without judgment or censure from anybody else. Especially those who would seek to topple us."

Beauregard stumbled from a wayward nudge of the hoop skirt and looked directly out at the audience, his ears redder than a ladybug. "I, Hollis Prissypants Hawthorne, shall offer up my land for this good work for witches."

My shoulders shook from containing giggles. No way did the esteemed Mr. Hawthorne appreciate what must be coming up based on that little jab.

The man playing the Goodwin ancestor paced away from the other two, holding a hand over his heart while the one holding the wand gesticulated wildly. "Alas, if we do not offer the freedoms to all who possess magic, then I cannot agree and must away to find another haven."

The woman sashayed her way next to Prentice, her skirt swinging like a bell. "Fear not, for I am in complete agreement with you. Freedom for all or sanctuary for none." She paused and waited. When nothing but silence followed, she cleared her throat and spoke in a booming voice. "I say again...Freedom for all or sanctuary for none!"

Playing along, the audience clapped, although probably not as loud as Tipper had anticipated or wanted.

Norberta turned her head to the third actor. "What say you, Mr. Hawthorne? Do you yield or do you stand in opposition?"

Beauregard, playing his role as the Hawthorne descendent, rubbed his chin in staged thought. "While I do not agree with everything you say, I shall not stand against you for now. I admire you, Ms. Walker, and declare that you and your family to come must be the smartest and handsomest that 'ere our town shall know."

Laughter rippled through the audience, and I stifled more snickers behind my hand. The whole production had Uncle Tipper's stamp all over it.

Beauregard continued. "And as I admire you with such great adulation, I shall offer you the most attractive tract of land to establish your long line while I take the least tempting for myself."

Sweet honeysuckle iced tea, Tipper outdid himself. Everyone who had ears had heard him tell tale of how his great-great-great whatever so many times removed had won the land his large estate sat on in an ill-advised run of cards and gambling. The animosity between the two families had fueled town gossip for generations.

Tucker stood up and made his way out the aisle, followed by Ashton and his mother. No doubt his father had already taken his leave. Maybe my aunt and cousin were joining them somewhere in the back where I couldn't see from the tiny window.

The three founding surrogates took out objects and held them up. They pantomimed digging a hole on the stage and then burying the objects.

The woman playing Norberta Walker swayed back and forth, her skirt knocking into the other two players. She waved her hands and the wand in the air as she declared, "We sacrifice our personal treasures and bury them in good faith that our town shall be protected forever more."

The squeak of a pulley pierced the air, and a drop cloth painted like a tree rose from the stage, growing from the spot where they'd buried their treasures. I stifled a giggle at their childish re-enactment of the founding events, imagining how much Tipper would have enjoyed it.

The three on stage traipsed in front of the tree. With the tips of their wands touching, they recited some nonsensical poem, and the ends shot off tiny fireworks. The fiddler stomped his feet and changed the song to a quick, merry tune. The rest of the troupe's costumes made more sense as they represented the different supernatural beings that came to live in Honeysuckle Hollow. They danced around the tree with joyful abandonment while the audience clapped along.

From the side of the stage, a figure walked to the front, waving his hands and getting in the way of the ridiculous spectacle of merriment.

Detective Mason Clairmont held up some sort of badge in his hand and attempted to yell over the commotion. It took a few comical moments for the whole troupe to comprehend what was going on until a single elderly female dressed as a fairy waving a sparkly wand with a star on the end ran into him mid-skip.

"My apologies for the interruption, but as everyone is gathered here in one place, it makes it easier to address the ones I need to talk to." He stared out into the audience as he reached into his pocket and pulled out a folded piece of paper.

Nana reappeared on the stage and rushed to Mason's side. He bent his head to listen to her. By the looks of the theater group members, what she said couldn't have been too pleasant. Having been on the receiving end of her displeasure, I took perhaps too much glee in Mason's apparent discomfort.

A dull buzz in the air rose to indignant murmuring. It died down when my grandmother held up her hands and addressed everyone. "Ladies and gentlemen. While I agree that perhaps the methods of Detective Clairmont are...lacking in propriety, I suggest that we allow him some latitude as I am sure that what will follow will be in all of our best interest."

"Is it about Tipper?" someone yelled out.

Mason frowned. "We are not prepared to make any formal announcements at this time. However, with your cooperation, if we can get on with it, then things will be over more quickly." He rustled the paper.

That arrogant man must be as dumb as a post, using his city ways on small-town folks like these. All he'd managed to do was stir up a hornets' nest of drama and gossip.

"Would the following people please remain here while the rest of you exit as quickly and quietly as possible." Without hesitation, Mason read off a short list of names.

With wide eyes and concerned whispers, the rest of the crowd filed out, their heads turning around to try and figure out what to do. Nana remained on the stage despite the detective's evident agitation at her presence.

By my count, nine people remained. And every single one of them had one thing in common.

"This is outrageous," Raif declared. "Madame Goodwin, surely you cannot condone this kind of blatant profiling of your small vampire population."

Beauregard sat down on the edge of the stage, his makeup running from sweat. Or maybe tears. "Tipper would have hated this." He sniffed and pulled a hanky out of his pocket to wipe his nose.

I hated to disagree with him, but I was pretty sure that wherever Uncle Tipper was, he was *loving* the mayhem.

"Would you please explain yourself and what you want from us? I would prefer to leave this *witch hunt* as soon as possible," Raif demanded. The rest who rallied around him, staring up at Mason on the stage.

The detective counted the crowd. "This isn't everybody."

Nana spoke up. "A town hall meeting is an invitation for everyone to attend and participate. It is not mandatory."

Mason frowned. "Then I'll collect what I can and pursue the rest later. I need each of you to tell me your whereabouts during the First Night festivities."

Raif stepped forward. "Why us, sir? Why make our lives harder by holding us as responsible for Tipper's murder?"

"I did not say that he was murdered."

"You all but did!" shouted Raif. "To the entire town!" The other vampires joined their tall companion in expressing their outrage.

Mason maintained a stoic stance on the stage, sweat glistening on his brow. "I'm trying to rule you out, not arrest anybody. For reasons I cannot, nor will, not divulge at this time, questioning all of you is necessary."

His eyes swept the room, and I swore he glanced in my direction. Ducking down, I held my breath. Voices echoed from below, but from my crouched position, only some of what was said remained clear.

Mason may not have said the word *murder*, but his zeal to question me and now this particular group told me enough. What happened to Tipper that night hadn't been natural. And his ramblings that I thought showed how touched in the head my distant family member had turned might have had some truth to them.

My mind raced to organize the details of talking to Tipper. People wanted to end his fun. He knew things. And he'd said that if someone had wanted to stop him, they had to do it *over his dead body*.

What else had we talked about? He'd wanted me to help him find his bowtie. The whole thing was probably to test out my abilities to locate things so that I could help him in some upcoming adventure. Except...

With a gasp, I scrambled to my feet and hurried down the stairs. Turning the old knob and opening the door a crack, I checked for anyone around. The coast being clear, I snuck to the side door and did the same, pushing it open into the night air and running around to the back of the building out of sight, trying to piece together a plan.

My locating abilities required touching something or somebody to pick up on whatever I searched for. A thought or memory of someone I'd never truly been in contact with wouldn't work.

The flap of wings and the familiar screech near my head alarmed me until an idea struck me. Taking a chance and trusting my gut, I spoke directly to the bird. "Biddy, I need to find someone. Now. Can you help me? For Tipper?" I held out my arm in hope.

Without hesitation, she flitted down and landed on me, her head cocking side to side so her dark eyes could regard me. Recalling a picture of the person I sought in my head, I contemplated how to make a connection through Tipper's bird to find them. Before I found my solution, the crow nodded her head.

Spreading her wings, she took off into the darkened sky, the moon lighting up her silhouette. Disappointment filled me until she called out a stray cry, circling overhead.

"You know exactly where I want to go, don't you, you old Biddy," I muttered. Knowing I must be a little crazy but trusting my instincts, I readied myself. "Lead the way."

Mason was right. Not everybody on his list was still there in that room. Someone had left early. Someone who'd walked up the aisle and out of the town hall. Someone who'd been wearing blood red heels.

Chapter Six

Following a bird flying in the night sky while avoiding being seen proved to be a challenge. Biddy's flight path didn't take into consideration trees, hedges, bushes with thorny bits, or the occasional vole hole to step in. She squawked in impatience, circling above me when my efforts moved too slowly for her liking.

The large crow glided down to perch on top of a mailbox, flapping her wings and cawing. A dim light glowed inside behind drawn curtains. My heart rose in my throat while blood pumped fast in my veins. The plan in my head had gotten me as far as finding where the intended target lived. What came next?

Biddy took off and landed on the porch, hopping around and squawking. Afraid that her boisterous insistence might draw attention to us, I rushed to her, making more noise trying to pacify her.

The unlatching of a lock startled both of us quiet. The front door opened, and a well-dressed woman stepped out. "Biddy, is that you?"

Without hesitation, the crow hopped up and landed on the offered arm. The lady scratched the bird's head, mumbling sweet things to her.

"Good evening, Ms. Eveline." No doubt her vampire abilities had already alerted her to my presence. "I mean, Lady Eveline."

She smiled at me, the tips of her fangs peeking out of her lips. "No one calls me that here. Least of all you. Tipper spoke of you often and with much love, Charli, if I may call you that. Won't you please come in?" Opening the door wide, she beckoned me to come inside.

Following a vampire into their house might be considered ill-advised anywhere else except in Honeysuckle. That reassurance didn't stop my heart from racing as I stepped in front of her and made my way inside.

Large antique pieces and ornate decorations in her foyer met my expectations of what would adorn a vampire's house. But when I followed her through her formal parlor into an inner living room, the old-world elegance gave way to furniture that could be found in pretty much any Honeysuckle household.

Without a sound, Biddy lifted off of the vampire's shoulder and rested on the mantle, making herself at home. Eveline glided to me after I sat down on a fluffy couch. "May I offer you something to drink? Tipper enjoyed his libations whenever he joined me here."

No doubt she meant something with a little kick. But I needed my wits about me. "Some sweet tea?"

With another polite grin that showed off the sharpness of her teeth, she made her way towards her kitchen. "Ice or no ice?" she called out as her blood-red heels clicked on the hardwood floors.

"Ice, please."

The time it took for her to bring the drink didn't give me much opportunity to gather my thoughts. When she came back, she took a seat across from me, crossing her long legs and folding her hands in her lap. In a panic, I realized she was giving me the control of the conversation.

"So, uh, I guess you and Uncle Tipper were a...I mean, you two sometimes got together...no, I don't mean to imply..." I fumbled and sipped on the tea to calm my nerves.

"You mean to say that Tipper and I were something of an item. The answer to that is, yes. Let us speak plain with each other, much like Tipper and I did. It makes things much easier." Her foot in her pointed shoe bounced. "To that end, I must say that when I expected company tonight, it never crossed my mind that it might be you."

"Who were you expecting?"

She sighed. "I thought perhaps Raif might stop by."

"You mean after you addressed him at the town hall meeting?"

Her eyebrows raised. "You saw that?"

I nodded and pressed harder. "It looked like you were unhappy with what he said."

Eveline stood up with such speed that her movement blurred in front of me. She stood next to the mantle, staring at Biddy. "You've been absent for a while, right? So you're not caught up on current events here in town." Biddy leaned her head forward to let Eveline scratch it. "Raif has been at the forefront of a campaign to get a non-witch onto the town council. You can imagine what a proposal like that might do to a town like this or how it might go over with some."

My mouth fell open. During my lifetime in my hometown, I could only remember one incident of someone pushing for a major change like that. I must have been six. No, seven. Old enough to recognize how controversial it had been but not mature enough to understand the outcome. From what I remember, whoever it had been that suggested the change eventually left Honeysuckle, and it had stirred up some unrest amongst the non-witch magical community for a long time.

"And Raif wouldn't let the issue drop, no matter how much I tried to convince him that now was not the time. Especially tonight of all nights," she continued. "But he *is* right. There should be more representation of non-witches at a higher level of the town leadership. However, discussing that with Tipper showed me how volatile it might get if any of us pushed."

For all of his good parts, Tipper possessed a deep-rooted stubborn streak and could be very difficult to deal with.

"Guessing he focused on how bad change would be, and clung to tradition above all else."

Eveline smiled. "You knew your family member well. Tipper was no fan of Raif's zeal. There were a few nights where it drove a wedge between us." Her grin faded. "I suppose those were silly fights, considering I will no longer be able to verbally spar with him anymore. How I will miss that exasperating old man."

She slipped a dark lace handkerchief from inside her sleeve and dabbed at the pink tears pooling in her eyes. "You must excuse me. His passing has weakened me in a way I did not expect."

Rubbing my sore arm, I watched her emotions take over as she gave in to quiet sobs. No one who witnessed the display could dispute that her feelings for Tipper were genuine. I replayed her explanation in my head to try and figure out heads or tails of Mason's motives.

"Maybe you can shed some light as to why the wardens would detain Raif, Beauregard, and other vampires at the end of the meeting? Do you think the campaign for a council seat is the reason?"

Eveline dropped her handkerchief. "Please, tell me that you are in jest. They held back all the vampires in Honeysuckle?"

Did her fangs just grow longer and her eyes flash red? Attempting a brave face to cover my growing unease, I affirmed the information. "It's true. Detective Clairmont read off a list of names, which included yours. And Raif protested."

She narrowed her eyes. "I would think so. It will fuel his enthusiasm for making changes twofold, that you can count on. And it will have won no friends for that detective."

"Pfft. Detective Clairmont succeeds at that all on his own," I uttered without thinking.

"It must mean that they suspect one of us for Tipper's demise." She tapped her finger in thought against her lips. "No, your visit shall not be the only one of the night, if I were a betting person like our Tipper. And that man almost always won whatever he gambled."

A stinging tingle shot down my arm and I couldn't hold back the shiver. The more we talked about my great-uncle, the more the ache increased.

"So you think Uncle Tipper's death wasn't natural?" I gritted my teeth against the growing pain.

Eveline shook her head. "I don't know what to think. He would occasionally rant and rave about things in a manner that, well, I'm not sure how to say this without insulting his memory."

"He sounded a little touched in the head? I talked to him briefly the first night I returned to town. I think I understand what you mean."

Sitting back down, she leaned forward. "He was sure that someone was after him. Sometimes I'd have to calm him down, he'd agitate himself into such a tizzy. And then like that, he'd snap out of it. But never in my wildest...my dear, are you quite all right?"

The pain in my arm throbbed with such intensity that the

discomfort blocked my ability to pay attention. Unable to hide it, I clutched my limb and cursed. With concern, she rushed to my side.

I waved her off. "I'm fine. But may I use your powder room?"

She pointed at a nearby door. "I have a half-bath there if that will do."

Sweat breaking on my brow, I made it to the small bathroom with a little dignity intact. Splashing water on my face, I stared at my reflection in the mirror. A stray thought caught me off guard and made me smile through my pain. Did vampires actually need mirrors?

A loud knocking on the front door interrupted my silly musings. Biddy cawed in agitation. The rapping persisted until the front door creaked open. Eveline spoke to whoever joined her, but the voice that answered caught me off guard.

"I'll ask again, where were you tonight?" Mason's tone left no room for polite chit-chat. Holding my breath, I listened in.

"I attended the first part of the meeting but chose to leave before its conclusion. Why?" Eveline asked. I noticed that she didn't offer him any refreshments that might encourage him to stay longer than his welcome.

He kept things vague after a pause. "I am interviewing all persons of interest at this time."

"Including me. Do not dance around the reason why, Detective. It will only prolong your time here," added Eveline.

Biddy squawked with thunderous indifference.

"Is that your bird?" Mason asked.

"You know full well it is not and whose it is. Was. That is Tipper's crow Biddy, and she is welcome here anytime she wishes to visit."

"So she's familiar with your residence?"

"Let us not play games, Detective Clairmont. Tipper and I did have a relationship of sorts."

"Will you elaborate on that for me?"

Eveline sighed loud enough for me to hear through the door. "I mean that from time to time, we would come together."

"You were a couple?"

"We were together when we wanted to be. Is that clear enough for you?"

He coughed twice. "And what do you mean by being together?"

"May I presume by your line of questioning that you found something of interest in your examination of the body that leads you to suspect those of my kind?"

Mason's tone darkened. "What do you believe was discovered, Lady Eveline?"

"By my guess, you found a bite mark. Not fresh, mind you. But still present." A chair creaked, and I guessed that Eveline sat across from the detective much as she had me, probably unnerving him a bit.

"Despite it being against the law, you would bite him?" An edge to Mason's voice suggested a level of discomfort.

"From time to time, it would happen in a moment of uncontrollable, raw passion."

Eww. No part of my mind wanted to think about Tipper being passionate. Joking that he could be a Southern Casanova was one thing. Having it confirmed with possible mental images took it to a whole other level.

After a pause, Eveline's voice rolled out like a cat's purr. "Why, Detective, I believe you are blushing. Is it possible that you understand the effects of losing control of one's self and giving in to the raging fire that sometimes burns within us?"

The thought of her approaching Mason, maybe flirting with him, or even perhaps touching him did something inexplicable to me. Before I could explore the random reaction, the cold ache throbbed to life again. My hands gripped the sink to steady myself.

Mason cleared his throat. "So, uh, the biting was consensual?"

Her voice came out smooth as silk. "Of course, detective."

"One more question. Where did you stand on the issue of changing the town council?"

Good. He managed to ask a question that nagged me as well.

"Like all relationships and politics, we attempted to avoid confrontations when together to keep the peace." Eveline's response offered some insight but held back a lot more.

"I see," said Mason, not as confident as before.

Eveline's tone returned to one of annoyance. "And now that you have your answers, will you stop bothering the vampires of Honeysuckle?"

Carefully, I leaned against the door and listened. "I have

responses to some of my questions. Not all. But I suppose that is enough for tonight."

"Yes," agreed Eveline. "Considering that you are here unofficially and I am not under arrest."

"Yet," underlined Mason. "Ms. Winthorpe, I will advise you the same way I told everyone else I interviewed tonight. Do not leave town anytime soon."

"Detective Clairmont, Honeysuckle is my chosen home. Out of all places in the world, I choose to live here. Not because it is the richest place or most fascinating, but because it is the safest place I have found. At least until now." A cry from Biddy punctuated her statement.

"Crazy bird," Mason muttered under his breath. "Ma'am, I assure you, my job is to keep this town safe, no matter what people think about me while I do what needs to be done to make it so. I'll see myself out."

Through the fog of pain, I worked out the facts so far. Tipper's body must have shown bite marks. Although, if Eveline was to be believed, they were not fresh. Reason number one, Mason targeted vampires. He also knew about Raif's campaign, reason number two. But that issue didn't point to only one set of Honeysuckle citizens.

My gut instinct told me that no vampire had anything directly to do with Tipper's demise. But then why single them out?

A light tap on the door interrupted me. "Are you okay in there, Charli?"

Was I? A quick inventory of how I felt gave me an answer

I didn't like. Coming out of the small bathroom, I lied with a tiny crack of a smile. "I'll live. And you? Are you okay?"

She clicked her tongue. "That man has no idea how to comport himself. If he is not careful, he will find himself on the wrong end." Intense emotion flashed in the lady vampire's eyes, and I held back the desire to ask her—*the wrong end of what?*

"I should get going myself." With careful steps, I entered the living room again.

She walked me to the front of her house in uncomfortable silence. When she opened the door, Biddy flew past me into the night without so much as a caw of goodbye.

Eveline touched my shoulder, and a chill rocked my entire body. She ran her fingertip down to my hand. "It hurts, right?"

In disbelief and discomfort, I affirmed her assumption. "Like nothing I've felt before."

"Is it hot like coals burning inside of you or cold like ice freezing in your veins?"

"Cold. Ice cold. Like no amount of fire could burn it away."

Her eyes dropped and she shook her head slowly. "Oh, Charli. I'm so sorry."

"I don't understand."

The house seemed to shake when she smacked the door frame. "That man," she huffed. "That silly, stupid, delusional, irresistible man."

Confusion battled the ache in my arm. "Are you talking

about Tipper? Is there something he did to me? I don't understand. "

Without more of an explanation, she pushed me out the door.

"It means you need to get out of here. Now." She shoved hard enough to make me stumble onto her porch. "Forgive my rudeness. And above all, try to forgive him." Eveline began shutting her door.

"Forgive Tipper for what?" I squeezed my arm. "This doesn't make any sense."

She held the door open for another second, the light from inside streaming into the night and framing her silhouette. "Go straight home, Charli. Tell your grandmother everything. If this is what I think it is, only she might know how to stop it." Eveline offered me a final glance of sympathy before shutting the door and leaving me in the darkness.

Chapter Seven

The amount of effort to take one step at a time on the way home exhausted me. Instead of going for stealth, I walked on the edge of the road, hoping that someone would pass by and maybe offer me a ride. At the slow pace I could manage, it might be dawn before I made it on my own. But in a small town with not much to do, the chances of fortune being on my side were slim. Where was a fairy to give me a shortcut when I needed one?

Stumbling more than once, a light from behind illuminated the road in front of me. It grew brighter as the sound of a car rumbled and slowed beside me. The smile of relief on my face for catching a break faded when the window rolled down.

"Miss Goodwin. Fancy finding you out here in this neighborhood. Need a ride?" Mason's voice dripped with smugness.

Taking my hand away from gripping my arm, I waved at him. "I'm fine on my own, thank you, Detective Clairmont. I promise to come see you tomorrow."

His car matched my slow pace, the tires rolling over the pavement and crunching over gravel. "Don't be silly. You look like you could use a little help."

"Not from you," I muttered under my breath. But another shooting pang in my arm threatened to trip me. I stopped in my tracks, my current choices frustrating me.

Mason threw his car into park. "You gonna stand there all night talking to yourself, or are you gonna get in the car, Charli?"

His use of my nickname caught me off guard, as did his softened tone. "Fine."

Mason reached across the front seats and popped the passenger's door open. With grumbling resentment, I settled in and buckled the seatbelt. Maybe I had to give in, but I didn't have to be happy about it.

He pulled the car back on the road, his eyes focusing in front of him. Mine were trained directly on his face, trying to figure him out.

"How is it that you just happened to be driving by?" I asked.

"I watched Eveline Winthorpe shove you out of her house and followed you." He didn't flinch once while revealing that little nugget.

Pixie poop. He'd been watching me? "How'd you know I was there?"

"I knew somebody was in her house. A half-drunk glass of what I guessed was sweet tea dripped condensation onto the table where someone had left it before I arrived. I didn't know who that *someone* was until I saw you. Care to tell me what you were doing there? Or what you overheard?"

"We were discussing Tipper. Sharing our condolences with each other."

"You two are great friends, are you?" His eyes glanced my direction.

I shivered, half under his scrutiny and half from the pain racking my arm. He reached out and wiped the beads of sweat from my forehead. "You don't look good."

"Just what a girl wants to hear from a guy," I managed, leaning my head against the cool glass of the window and away from his touch.

He drove his car to the far end of town and down the length of the dirt driveway to Nana's house, guided by the lights burning on the front porch. The car pulled in at an angle to get me as close to the house as possible. With more energy than I possessed, he shot out and rushed around the front of the car until he opened my door. With a gentleness he hadn't shown me in our first encounter, he helped me out.

The screen door slammed, and Nana met us on the porch. "I felt something was up. I hate it when my old bones are right. Help her inside, please, Detective."

Without warning, he scooped me up in his arms like a baby. My ability to rebel weakened to a brief shake of my head. "Don't think because you're acting like a big hero that I like you."

The effort to carry me didn't even make him huff with exertion. "So noted." His eyes flashed to mine for a brief moment.

"Set her down on the couch, please," directed Nana. She carried a glass of something dark brown with an unpleasant stench.

As if I weighed nothing, Mason set me down without jostling me. "Don't think because you're a damsel in distress that I'm your Prince Charming, either." He winked, his face relaxing into something resembling a normal person rather than a soulless machine.

Nana sat on the coffee table in front of me, her fingers pulling open my eyes and examining me. She thrust the smelly liquid in my face. "Here. Drink this down."

My stomach turned. "I don't think I can."

"Don't make me make the detective put you in handcuffs and force it down your throat. And don't argue with me Charlotte Vivian Goodwin."

I tried to point my finger at her. "Don't middle name me." *In front of him*, I held back.

"If you don't drink this, I can come up with a concoction that's five times worse." Her eyes pleaded with me.

"Drink it, Charli," added Mason, the concern in his eyes genuine.

"Fine," I resigned. Holding my nose, I downed a few gulps before spluttering.

"All of it," insisted Nana. She whipped a kitchen towel out of nowhere and wiped off my lips and chin.

Left with nothing else to do but obey, I swallowed the rest as fast as possible, praying that I wouldn't spew it out and embarrass myself.

A warm buzz like a bee inside my veins tickled its way down my arm. The pain dulled to a bearable ache. My eyelids grew heavy, and Nana and Mason fluttered in and out of sight. Their voices floated on a sea of dreams as I sunk into oblivion.

"I've seen this before," Mason stated.

"That crazy old goat. If I could, I'd bring him back alive just to hex his behind dead again." Nana sounded angry and worried. That meant I should be, too. But no amount of effort could throw off the blanket of sleep that claimed me.

As I drifted into unconsciousness, I tried my best to cling to the final thread of Nana's voice. "If we don't do something, there might be two deaths in Honeysuckle Hollow."

❧

ANOTHER MORNING of waking up in confusion and another attempt at gaining my bearings again. My memory remained intact, and to my relief, the pain in my arm didn't overwhelm me. When I made it downstairs to the table, I stopped in the doorway.

Mason sat bold as brass, drinking a cup of steaming coffee

and looking like he'd been waiting for me. The watchful eyes of Doc Mason observed my every move.

"What are you doing here?"

Nana walked in with a cup for me and a refill for the two men. "Don't you remember? Detective Clairmont brought you home to me last night."

I recalled the actions of an actual man emerging from underneath his shield of professionalism that gave me pause. "But what is he doing here now?"

"We need to talk," he insisted.

Nana flashed him a look. "Not until Doc has checked her out."

"Yeah, can't it at least wait until I have food in me and can come down to the station?" No way would I sit down to the plate of eggs scrambled the way I liked them with bits of ham and onion mixed in and toast with strawberry jelly on it. Not while Mason sat there.

I narrowed my eyes at my grandmother when she set a plate of eggs over easy with bacon and toast in front of Doc. And another in front of Mason. Traitor. "Since when did *he* become welcome in your home?"

Nana pointed. "Sit down, Charli. There are things that need explainin'." Her glare squashed any more questions, and like a sulky kid, I trudged over and plopped into the seat.

"Go ahead. I'm all ears." Without looking at any of them, I started in on the eggs.

Nana started. "The night you came home, what happened when you found Tipper?"

So, there'd be no preamble or build up. Right to the heart of things. "I followed Biddy, and she led me to the far side of the park. Tipper sat on a bench, and I thought maybe he was just drunk and passed out."

Mason leaned forward. "You touched him to check, right?"

"Yes. So what?" The piece of toast I'd picked up hung in the air. Nana and Mason shared a look, and my patience gave out. "Would you guys stop dodging me and get to the point."

"Fine," my grandmother relinquished. "You touched Tipper with your right hand, and you felt something zap your arm."

"Like cold lightning," added Mason.

It was my turn for my eyes to bounce back and forth between the two of them. "How did you know?"

"I've seen it before." Mason frowned.

Doc stopped chewing his bite to glance at Nana. "It's been ages since something like this. Are you sure?" When she nodded at him, he went back to watching my every move with tight scrutiny.

My brain did its best to keep up. "Eveline told me I needed to forgive Uncle Tipper for something. Nana, what did he do?"

Crossing her arms, Nana glared at the table. "That old fool spellcast something on himself. Alone. I'm sure he meant it to hurt whomever he thought was after him."

Dropping the toast, I waved my hands in front of me. "Whoa. I did *not* kill Tipper. Doc, tell 'em. Tell them that

Tipper died of natural causes." My arm ached the truth, but I wanted the lie.

"I can't. Tipper's death makes no sense." The town doctor and healer leaned forward in his chair and rested his elbows on the table. "The man drank like a fish, but otherwise, he was in perfect shape, at least for a man of his age. I'd just examined him, too. No issues and healthy as a horse. Heck, we should all be lucky to live as long and as hard as he has. Had. And then for him to up and die of a heart attack. Something doesn't add up."

When I'd talked with my uncle, there'd been no signs that he didn't feel well. In fact, other than his paranoia, he'd remained his crazy, off-beat self. The man that I'd loved and respected as much as my mom did.

Taking a sip from my cup, I grimaced at the foul taste. Instead of coffee, Nana had mixed up some version of the same concoction from the night before. I knew better than to refuse it, but that didn't stop me from shooting some serious side eye in her direction. "So then why are we treating it like he was murdered?"

Mason scooted his chair closer to me. "That's where you come in. I want to hear everything that happened between you two. What did you see? What did you hear? It might help us figure out who the killer is."

As all of the attention of the room pointed at me like sharp daggers, comprehension dawned on me. "Surely, you don't believe that *I* killed him?" When my eyes lit on Mason, fear gripped my insides.

"I'll admit," he started. "When I saw you clutch your arm yesterday, I guessed what might be the cause. And yes, your innocence was in question. As it should have been. But after discussing things with your grandmother last night, now I'm not so sure."

Nana nodded. "You see, a spell like this can be tricky. It's meant to punish the one who commits the murder, but sometimes it can have unintended effects if not executed with perfection, which is why it's outlawed and forbidden." She sounded more like the head of the town council than my grandmother.

My mind connected the dots, and realization dawned on me with devastating surety. "Uncle Tipper wasn't all there anymore, was he? So in his paranoid state, and with a fractured mind, he didn't spellcast correctly."

"That's what we conclude." Mason ventured a look my way. "If the death curse were performed right and you were the murderer, your time would be coming to a painful end."

"But I'm not the murderer. Surely that should break the... did you call it a death curse?" The goosebumps on my arms gave birth to more chills.

"You found the body. And best I can tell, the only way to break the wretched thing is to find the one responsible." Nana's lower lip quivered. "And, yes. It is called a death curse."

A new possibility sunk in. "Wait. What happens if we don't find the killer? Can't Doc here cure it or something?"

Everyone avoided my gaze. Nana pounded her hands on the table and stood up, her chair crashing to the floor. "That old fool." She clutched her hand to her heart, giving into despair. Her lack of holding it together frightened me down to my bones.

"Listen, it does us no good to think about that outcome. Your grandmother and Doc here will do what they can to slow the effects," instructed Mason.

"I do not want to have to drink that unnatural-looking, gray slime all the time and sleep my way to my end. I refuse to be Sleeping Beauty, waiting for the hero to wake me up." My cheeks reddened at the reminder of last night's brief exchange with the detective. Definitely no need to think about exactly how the princess got woken up.

"Your grandmother is the strongest in magic here in Honeysuckle, although I'm sure she would protest that sentiment. Combining our knowledge, we've already adjusted your medicine." Doc nodded at the cup in front of me.

"It still tastes awful." And looked like sludge from the bottom of a lake.

Nana cocked her head and raised her eyebrow in that *because-I-said-so* way. "Well, what did you expect, cotton candy? It's medicine. Stop your whining and get to finishin' it."

All three watched me as I raised the drink to my lips. Holding my nose, I downed a couple of gulps but couldn't keep back the shivers of disgust. "There. So, how can I help solve the murder, Detective?"

"You are going to tell me every little detail from your encounter with Tipper. And then you will leave the rest of it to us wardens." He stood up.

I joined him. "No deal. If this curse is on me, then I'm going to do all I can to get it off me. That means you've earned yourself a new partner."

"I work alone, Miss Charlotte."

Oh, so I was no longer Charli? "Not anymore. You need me."

Doc crossed his arms. "I agree with the detective. I don't think it's a good idea that you be stressing yourself out, Miss Charli. It would be better if you rested."

"If this curse thing is as bad as all that, then I refuse to go out with a whimper. I won't die curled up in a ball, waiting for death." My lower lip trembled.

Nana righted her chair. "As much as I'd like for my granddaughter to remain safe at home with me, I've learned not to argue too much with her when she gets like this. We Goodwin women tend to get our way. And she's right. It is her curse. She should be allowed to do what she can to break it."

Mason shook his head. "She may be putting herself in harm's way."

I threw up my arms. "According to all of you, I'm already harmed. Besides, you need me."

He walked over and stared me down. "And what do you bring to the table?"

I gulped. What did I bring? No college education. No job. Not a whole lot of power behind my magic. My shoulders slumped.

Nana jumped to my defense. "My Charli has amazing

locating gifts. If there's something you need finding, she's the one for the job."

Doc's face relaxed for the first time. "That's right. Our girl here is the best there is at finding things. Remember that one time when we couldn't find a key to our filing cabinet? Me and Queenie turned the office inside out and upside down until Vivian sent us Charli. Took her no time at all to help us find the small thing."

Nana beamed with pride. "And she was all of seven-years-old at that point."

Mason furrowed his brow. "Locating? You mean, tracking? You're a tracker." For the first time, admiration shone in his eyes. The way he said *tracker* made my pride sit up and take notice.

Heat rose in my cheeks again. "I don't know what you'd call it. I've spent the last year trying to find others with similar abilities to learn from since there's no one around these parts who can train me."

He looked at Nana. "I thought powers like that were inherited."

"I'm adopted, Detective Clairmont," I admitted in a quieter voice.

"Charli's the daughter of our hearts," explained my grandmother. "Blood doesn't make a family. Love does."

Unable to stand the awkward silence that followed whenever we told someone I was adopted, I strode around Mason and snatched a piece of bacon from his plate. "Like I said. You need me. And I need to be a part of the investigation. So let's go through that night, and then I'm going to give you the biggest gift of them all."

He snapped off the end of my stolen bacon and shoved it in his mouth. "And what's that?"

Sitting back down at the table, I picked up my cup of not-coffee. "I'm gonna teach you how to be a local."

Chapter Eight

"You need some serious work on your people skills," I accused, waving at Leland Chalmers, Sr., the father of my childhood friend Lee, dropping off something in the mailbox.

Mason frowned as he walked next to me down Main Street. "I'm not here to be everybody's friend. It would cloud my objectivity."

Stopping at a large store window, I glanced inside Life's A Stitch. A few women sat around, knitting and talking in one corner. The store worker had her back turned to us, helping someone pick out needlepoint or cross stitch floss. But the quilt on display hanging on the back wall squeezed my heart, knowing who'd made the pattern and stitched it. After ringing up the customer, the woman who worked there glanced up at Mason and me watching from the sidewalk. She gestured for us to come in.

My feet stayed rooted where I stood. A part of me longed to go into the store that had so much of my own life sewn up into it. But a bigger piece of my heart wasn't ready.

"I'll wait for you here if you want to go in," Mason offered.

I shook my head at both him and Ms. Patty Lou, the current owner. She waved back at me with a sad smile and joined the knitting group.

"No, that's okay. I'm not ready yet."

"What does a person have to do to get ready for a store like that?" Mason joked.

My eyes darted to the ground, and I willed the pool of tears forming in my eyes not to spill. "It was my mom's store. Well, hers and Patty Lou's together. I practically grew up in there."

Mason emitted a small sound of sympathy but coughed to cover it up. "So, you can sew?" He took a few steps away from the store, allowing me to follow in my own time.

"Nope. I'm horrible at it."

"Knit?"

"I tried once. What came out of my efforts might have been a scarf. If it had ended up about three times as wide as I made it." I smiled despite the sadness still sitting in my chest. "And I don't quilt or do needlework patterns. But I loved watching my mom do stuff. She was amazing."

No chance of catching the tear that escaped. I wiped my cheek and sniffed. "What about your mom? Did she do any handiwork like that?"

His confident gait faltered. "No. Not that I know of." His face darkened.

"Sorry. Didn't mean to get too personal with you." Stupid me, ruining my plans with him before I got started.

"You didn't say anything to apologize for. I just don't tell people." He picked at a scab on his arm and blew out his breath. "I don't know if my mother sewed or anything. I didn't grow up with her."

"Oh." The air around us thickened with nerves.

"I didn't grow up with a father, either. So when my powers showed up in a regular foster home, you can imagine what it did to my childhood."

My fingers itched to hug him and reassure the hurting child inside him. I figured the biggest surprise of the day would be that I had a Death Curse working through me. Who knew that Mason Clairmont sharing a piece of himself would be the bigger bomb.

"How'd you manage?" I asked. "Gah, sorry. Don't mind my nosy self. I'll just take it with me inside."

He reached out and took my hand. "No. It's fine. A social worker who was also a witch showed up. I guess there are those out there that look for specific problems like I was. She got me placed in a home with other witches, and I got the care that I needed."

But what about love? I wondered to myself. Giving him the space to continue or end, I remained quiet. When a couple of people passed us with polite recognition but curious eyes watching our hands, he released me and cleared his throat.

We moseyed forward again, but the moment of sharing passed.

I pointed at my friend heading to the Harvest Moon Cafe. "That there's Flint. He works the front gate to the town and helps his brother with his gardening service. Come on." Unsure if Mason would follow, I headed for the only restaurant in town.

"But we already ate a big breakfast." He crossed the street behind me.

Before we entered, I addressed him. "Now, the best advice I can give you is to keep your mouth shut, your ears open, and whatever you do, eat every last bite of whatever they put in front of you."

The jangle of the bells on the door marked our entrance. Since it was mid-morning, not too many people populated the cafe. But enough of the usual suspects were there that it might turn into an effective lesson. I steered him to the stools at the counter.

"Why, Charli Goodwin. Welcome home, girl. You're lookin'...well, it's so good to see you," gushed Sassy. Her wings fluttered, and she bounced up and down in the air, her green hair pulled back into a ponytail swinging in enthusiasm.

Under my breath, I leaned into Mason. "You weren't kidding when you told me I didn't look good, were you?"

"You look just fine now," he whispered back, his lips forming a rare grin. The man had the straightest teeth I'd ever seen. The smile did something to his face that struck me in the strangest of ways.

"Blythe isn't working until tonight, if you're looking for her. But first, introduce me to your boyfriend." She hovered close to him.

"Sassafras, this is Mason Clairmont. Detective Mason Clairmont. Not my boyfriend. I'm sure you've seen him around before. Mason, this is Sassy." The small fairy needed to back off a few clicks.

She batted her eyes. "Oh, I didn't recognize you. You've got a real nice smile, Mason." Placing a menu in front of him, she continued ignoring me. "Order anything you want from here and it's yours."

My eyes rolled so hard to the back of my head that they threatened to get stuck there. "I'll take a piece of pie and a cup of coffee, please, Sass."

She waved her hand at me as if to dismiss my request and leaned her elbows on the counter in front of Mason. "And for you?"

"The same." Relief washed over me, hearing the return of his cold demeanor.

"What kind of pie you got?" I asked, almost waving a hand in front of her face.

"The usual. Pecan, chocolate chess, banana cream. Nobody makes a better pie than me. My crusts are the absolute best, and the fillings will make you want to marry me." She dared to wink at the detective.

The statement about her baking skills might be close to the truth, but her delivery stomped on my goodwill. "Sassy here is the Queen of Flaky for sure. Get us two slices of pecan, please."

Sassy shot me a look to kill and hovered closer, touching Mason on the hand. "You sure you want the same, honey? I'm waiting on a delivery of strawberries from Boyd if you care to stick around."

He slipped away from her touch. "Yep. Pecan pie. Please and thank you."

Mr. Steve, the owner and cook, poked his head through the window to the kitchen. "Sassy, finish taking their orders and get back here."

With a pout, she promised to be back in a flash. For all I cared, she could take a quick walk off the end of a pier. Or fly herself there. Whatever, she needed to keep her wings and her winks to herself. Bless her heart and hex her tiny hiney.

"Well, my first lesson to you was to be friendly to everyone. Maybe more to some than others." I regretted my words the second they left my mouth, hating that I sounded like a jealous girlfriend.

Flint caught my eye and waved me over to join him. I hopped down from the stool. "Here's lesson two. Keep your ears open."

I greeted the gnome and the group of retirees that sat at a table in front of the window, holding court. They all welcomed me back with smiles and handshakes.

Flint patted my arm. "Did Matt tell you that he came to get Old Joe?"

The motorcycle. I'd completely forgotten about it. "No. I didn't see it parked at the house."

"That's the thing. It won't start again. Nothing we did could make it work. My guess is he took it down to Leland's for him to work on it."

"So what you're saying is that I drove that bike into the ground?" Matt might hate me for that considering I'd claimed our father's treasure for myself in my grand escape.

"Hey, it brought you back in one piece. And Leland and his son are miracle workers when it comes to figuring out the combo of spellwork and mechanics." Flint picked up his coffee mug. "So, is it true that you're the last person to see Tipper?"

The rest of the retirees stopped their conversation and tuned into my reply. Heck, all movement in the entire place ceased in order to eavesdrop. I gave them a few details but withheld a lot more.

"I heard that Tipper'd won a big card game, and that's what got him dead," one of the gentlemen offered.

The guy next to him shook his head. "No, he was against making changes to the town council. You know that man wouldn't switch out his underwear if he could get away with it in polite company."

"Shush, Henry," the man next to him chastised. "My apologies, Miss Charli, for his crudeness. But they're all wrong. I heard tell that someone was challenging his right to his land."

Henry shook his head. "Nah. It actually has somethin' to do about changes to his will and who inherits."

The accusations stirred up the talk until they all argued with arms gesticulating and voices getting louder. With a wave, I extricated myself from the heated discussion and returned to my seat at the counter where the pie, coffee, and Mason waited for me.

He made notes in a small notepad. "I see what you mean."

Taking a forkful of pecan pie, I smiled. "You get more flies with honey. And you get more gossip by knowing people and letting them chew your ears off." The pie couldn't hold a candle to Nana's. The mouthful of sweetness tasted like victory in more ways than one.

"Chances are they're wrong." Mason put his pad away and took a bite of pie under Sassy's watchful eye. He nodded at her in approval, and her wings quivered in absolute jubilation.

Ignoring her, I tried not to talk with my mouth full. "But they might not be, and now you've got some possibilities that maybe you didn't have beforehand."

He chewed on his second bite. "Maybe one."

Flint slapped the table, interrupting everyone. "I'm telling you, it's the drink that took him. That man drank like the rest of us breathe air."

Henry waved a finger at his friend. "Well, duh. But that doesn't mean it killed him. His drinking more likely preserved him than killed him."

As the volume of the debate lowered, the last accusation bounced around in my head. No one paid attention when

Tipper got tipsy. We all expected that of him, so giving that detail any importance never occurred to me. Until now.

"We gotta go," I whispered to Mason, trying not to look conspicuous.

The bells on the door chimed, and everyone stopped to greet the gargantuan being that walked in. Big Willie West, the town sheriff, strutted to the counter and sat down next to Mason, his massive amounts of hair sticking out of every crack and crevice of his uniform.

"Well, well. It's good to see you takin' an interest in our community, Detective. And Sassy here makes the absolute best pies, ain't that right, Miss Sass?" His boisterous voice boomed throughout the entire place.

"Yes, sir." Mason returned to his professional manners, ignoring my light tapping on his leg underneath the counter.

"I've just come in to get the lay of the land. See what's what with Tipper. But looks like maybe you beat me to it since you seem to be getting quite cozy with Miss Goodwin there." He leaned back in his stool to look around Mason at me. "Been quite a welcome home, wouldn't you say, Charli?"

"That it has been, Sheriff," I agreed.

"Hey, now that you're back, I've got a list of things the missus swears I've misplaced somewhere. Any chance you'd be able to help me out? If you can get me even a foot outta the doghouse, I'd be mighty obliged." Big Willie looked down greedily at the three pieces of pie that Sassy placed in front of him.

Sliding off the stool, I nodded. "Not a problem, Sheriff. I

can make arrangements to help you later. But right now, we've got to be going." We needed less talk and more walk.

Sassy pouted again. "So soon? But we just got the strawberries in for me to get started on tonight's pies for the contest. Why don't you stay to have a taste?" I was pretty sure her offer didn't extend to me.

Big Willie slammed his enormous fist on the counter, making everything and everybody jump. "That's right. I forgot we were switching the fair to tonight." He slapped Mason on the back hard enough to make the detective cough. "You know, son, you should represent the wardens this year."

"Represent? For what?" The priceless look of surprise on Mason's face made me sad I didn't have a camera on me.

"In the pie eating contest. Not only will you get to consume as much of Sassy's fine strawberry cream pies as you can eat but you'll also be doing the department a favor by ingratiating yourself with the locals. That's a win-win in my book." Big Willie paused long enough to pick up a slice of pie and take a generous bite. "Sassy girl, you've outdone yourself."

I tugged on Mason's sleeve as he attempted to protest. *No* didn't exist for the sheriff. Also, we had things to do if my new revelations were true. My efforts to save the detective went to waste, and Mason worked his way into the direct line of fire.

Big Willie narrowed his eyes. "Boy, you may have been a big shot from wherever you came from. And you may think you've got more experience than an old Southerner like me. But around these parts, you're a guppy amongst the big bass. Got me?"

Mason's shoulders slumped a tiny bit, but he straightened his back. "Yes, sir."

Bits of crust and pie filling dotted Big Willie's smile, and crumbs stuck in his shaggy beard. "Good. Then I'm sure I'll be seeing you in attendance at tonight's big shindig."

The bells on the door tinkled when we left. Outside, the humidity clung to our skin, and the sun beat down hot on the pavement.

"I think I'll head back to the station." Mason's whole mood dropped.

"Don't," I implored, wanting to give him a good reason to stay. "We haven't gotten nearly any good information yet. And there's something I need to tell you."

He put his hands in his pocket. "You can gather what you can on your own. I'll go back and organize all my notes."

"You can't let him get to you. He's a decent guy."

"Big Foot, you mean."

My eyes widened. "Don't let him catch you calling him that. He's a sasquatch. And on that note, do yourself a favor and stop treating everyone like they have to live up to whatever they are."

He shot me a quizzical look. "What are you talking about?"

Holding up my hand, I counted off his offenses. "When you talked to Dash at my house, you treated him like he should already be behind bars for being a werewolf."

Mason stuck his chin up. "I have my reasons."

I narrowed my eyes. "He's not even a werewolf. He's a shifter. And he's right, there's a difference."

He smirked. "Since you seem like an expert on Dash and his being a wolf something, I won't say anything."

Heat rose in my cheeks. "Don't. Because then you called out all the vampires in town. I don't care what your reasons were. You could have done it in a more subtle way rather than treating them like suspects in a lineup. At this rate, you're going to alienate every single citizen here." I took a breath to list another thing he'd done wrong.

"You're right," he interrupted, holding up his hands in surrender. "You're right, Charli."

My mouth hung open, but the words died on my tongue. Having that man admit that I was right made me forget for a second that my arm had started to throb a little harder again.

About the time I gathered enough brain matter to continue, I spotted Linsey zooming in on the two of us. "Oh, pixie poop."

"Hey," Mason pointed at me. "That sounds a little prejudiced, too. And dirty."

Speaking to him out of the side of my mouth, I pulled him in the opposite direction of Lily's pesky younger sister. "It can't be dirty. I've heard it's full of glitter."

"Charli," Linsey called out. "Just the person I wanted to see. Hello to you, too, Detective. Fancy runnin' into the two of you. Together." Her eyes sparkled with mirth.

"What can I do you for, Lins? We're kind of busy." Whatever she wanted, she'd better not ask me—

"Is it true that you found Tipper's dead body? And that you might somehow be involved in his death?" The reporter wannabe batted her eyes at me with faked innocence.

Mason placed a protective hand on my shoulder. "Miss Goodwin is not at liberty to say anything at this moment as she is a part of an active investigation. If you want answers, come to the station. And there, you'll get the same response. We are not officially commenting on the nature of Mr. Walker's passing at this time."

Linsey didn't take the response as final. "When you say that she's a part of the investigation, does it mean that Charli is a suspect or that she's helping you solve it?"

"Isn't there a pile of letters waiting for your extensive and knowledgeable advice at the newspaper?" I asked through gritted teeth.

Linsey looked between the two of us and finally gave up. "Well, if you won't give me a quote, maybe DK will print the article I've written up about your infamous return to Honeysuckle, Charli. Got a quote for that?"

One step closed the gap between us girls. "Sure."

"Charli," Mason warned.

I held a finger up at him. "Print this. I'm officially happy to be back in Honeysuckle Hollow, my true home." Whipping around, I took a few steps away.

"You plannin' on sticking around this time?" she shouted after me.

The true answer to that question weighed on me. It no

longer mattered if I wanted to live in Honeysuckle. It mattered whether or not I got the chance to.

"As long as I'm alive," I managed. Mason brushed the back of my arm with his hand.

"Thanks for your time," Linsey uttered.

Making sure Mason didn't notice as we walked away, I glanced behind us and found her watching us with interest. With my middle finger, I flipped her off and left her in the dust.

When we got some distance between us and the pest, Mason ventured to speak again. "Are you going to tell me what we're so busy doing?"

Some people nodded at us as they passed. Unwilling to share with the whole town, I grabbed the detective and dragged him across the street and down an alley. Before telling him anything, I checked around us for company.

With the coast clear, my theory could be presented in a low voice. "You know, Flint was right. Tipper drinking was his default status."

Mason stepped in closer. "So you think he drank himself to death? Plausible, but wouldn't Doc have determined that?"

I shook my head. "Not if it wasn't the alcohol that killed him, but—"

"—something *in* the alcohol," Mason finished.

Adrenaline raced through me. "Exactly. So if you test Tipper's flask, maybe there might be something in it to tell you whether or not I'm right. That Tipper was—"

"—poisoned," we both finished at the same time, breathing hard and staring wide-eyed at each other.

It took me too long to realize that our fingers were entangled as we clasped hands in shared shock. Withdrawing mine, I backed away from him.

Mason frowned. "You know, if you're right, we've got a problem."

"What's that?"

"I've gone through everything we collected that night. Twice. More than that. And I'm pretty sure we never logged in a flask."

Excitement shifted into smugness. I cracked my knuckles in self-satisfaction. "Well, Detective. Looks like we've got something to go find."

Chapter Nine

The slight pressure of the protective ward around the area where I'd found Tipper's body pressed into me. Sadness and anger threatened to crash against the wall I needed in order to work my magic. Still, the tears pooling in my eyes threatened to fall at any second.

Mason closed the space between us, his presence a surprising comfort. "The tracker I worked with before used objects from the people he was hired to find. Is that the same way your talent works?"

His words stirred me from my reverie of sorrow. "For the most part. I'm better at finding objects than people. And then my magic is strongest if I can touch the person who wants me to find whatever it is. When I was growing up, it was more trial and error, or rather more error than success sometimes."

"That's not the way your grandmother tells it."

A welcome smile lifted my spirits for a moment. "Well,

she's not an impartial storyteller. Matt used to hide things for me to find when I was little. He spent more time with me than an annoying little sister deserved."

"So he helped you develop your skills? Sounds like a good brother to me." Mason's warm tone turned my insides gooey. Too much of a distraction. Shaking my head, I breathed out a sigh. "But I get where you're going with this. I'm not gonna be much of a help finding the flask if I don't have something of Tipper's."

A flap of feathers and a familiar squawk alerted us to Biddy's presence as she circled overhead. How the bird always knew was beyond me, but I couldn't say her instant appearance didn't fill me with relief.

"You've got to be kidding me." Mason watched the crow break through the ward and land on the bench. "Okay, how did it do that?"

"Hello, old girl," I called out to her, testing the ward protection with my finger and still finding it impenetrable. "I don't know. Maybe because of her deep link to Tipper?"

Pursing his lips and furrowing his brow, Mason held up his hand and murmured a few words. The pressure of the ward dissipated and he stepped forward. Biddy hopped on the back of the bench, tilting her head to get a better look at the two of us.

With careful deliberation, I approached the bird and addressed her. "Biddy, we could definitely use your help."

"What are you doing?"

"Talking to her."

Mason's face soured. "It's a bird. It's not like it can understand you." He flinched when the crow beat her wings and chastised him with an annoyed squawk.

I stifled a chuckle at his naive big-city assumptions. "Didn't anybody you encountered before have a bird for a familiar? Or at least a pet? Of course, she understands me. Besides, you need to learn that old Southern saying. You definitely get more flies with honey."

Before I could talk to Tipper's crow again, she hopped off the bench and in a flutter of dark feathers perched herself on my shoulder. A squeal of surprise rose in my throat, but I did my best not to scream out loud since she'd cut to the chase.

"I've never seen anything like that," Mason uttered in awe. "Can she really help you find the flask?"

Since we were shooting from the hip with no plan in place, my brain hadn't made it that far. Normally, I'd hold an object or person with my hand, but that didn't seem like a viable option.

With a shift in her weight, the crow squeezed my shoulder and sunk her talons into me, just piercing the skin with a sting. A gasp of shock and pain stuck in my throat as my arm ached and my vision blurred. A buzz of recognition and intent bound me to the bird. Before I could stop myself, my body turned to the right, and I took a faltered step in that direction.

"Whoa, hold on there. Wait for me," insisted Mason. He reached out to help me from stumbling.

"Don't touch me," I warned. "Whatever's happening, I don't want it to break. Just make sure I don't hurt myself."

My right arm throbbed, and the distinct line of connection to an object somewhere nearby fizzled a little bit. Biddy tightened her grip, the intentional pricking pain refocusing me. Wanting to use the advantage while I had it, I quickened my steps.

The allure of the desired object beckoned me forward. Never before had the link been as potent in all of my childhood nor the past year or so of learning and practicing. Nothing else existed except the pot of gold at the end of the golden tether that drew me forward. Closing my eyes, I gave in, allowing myself to be pulled forward like a piece of metal unable to resist the draw of a magnet.

An unknown force in the dark stopped my trajectory. I pushed against it, the need to keep going outweighing anything else. A violent yank on my body caused the glowing tether to waver. With a piercing screech that shocked me out of my semi-trance, Biddy released me. Flapping her wings, she launched herself into the air, and the connection completely died.

"Why'd you do that?" I blinked my eyes, adjusting to the real world. With a jerk, I wrenched my sore arm out of Mason's grip.

A pained look passed over his face before he shook it off. "Oh, I don't know, maybe to save you from smashing your face into that." He pointed at something behind me.

When I turned in defiance, my body stood inches away

from a large metal lamppost that definitely would have taken out my nose without Mason's help. "Oh."

"Yeah. Oh. I tried calling out your name, but you ignored me."

The connection had taken hold of me more than I thought. "I didn't even hear you," I marveled.

"Which is why I had to grab you. You're stronger than you look."

"You were getting in my way, and I needed not to stop." My brain did its best to figure out why. "It's never been like that before."

Mason stared at me, and heat rose in my cheeks. "What? You think I'm a freak, don't you?" I could add him to the list of people in my life that barely understood my magic. Myself included.

"Not at all. I told you, I've worked with other trackers up North. There was one guy who was like a bullet out of a gun. Much like you just were. We had an entire team devoted to keep him from killing himself in pursuit of his mark."

Hearing about someone with talent like mine reassured me. "So he was successful?"

"Yes." Mason's tone darkened. "But it always came at a price."

I frowned. "What price?"

He shook his head. "Never mind."

"No, don't wimp out. I can take it. What price?"

He glanced into the distance, avoiding my glare. I reached

out and brushed the back of his hand with mine. "Mason," I insisted in a quieter tone.

Looking at our hands, he frowned. "You have to understand, he was incredibly powerful. One of the best trackers, from all accounts. But ultimately, his power consumed him. The more he succeeded, the more he needed to use it. The more he used it, the more it ate him up. And if he didn't find what he was looking for?" Mason looked up at me, his eyes boring into mine. "I don't ever want to see that hollow expression on your face. Ever."

The silence stretched between us as we both weighed his words. Before I could come up with some joke to lighten the moment, the sounds of conversation interrupted us. Two people rounded the park path and made their way in our direction. I stifled a smirk as I recognized my aunt walking with the guy who claimed to be Tucker's best friend.

"Detective Clairmont, what a pleasant surprise. I see you're keeping *very busy* doing your job, investigating the untimely demise of my uncle." Aunt Nora's resting witch face looked extra puckered with her sarcastic remark.

Mason stood up straighter and adopted a more professional tone. "Of course. We're following every lead we've found so far."

"I wouldn't think you'd have very far to look, considering that the last person a victim sees tends to be the one who committed the crime." My aunt eyed me up and down with outright contempt.

To his credit, Mason recovered faster than I did and

placed a hand on my back to stop me from mouthing off at my aunt.

I shrugged out of his touch and flashed my biggest *bless your heart* smile. "And a happy good morning to you, too, Aunt Nora."

Her unlikely companion shifted in his stance, trying his best not to show his discomfort. He studied my face for a long enough beat that my ears burned. As if suddenly aware of his rudeness, he smiled and presented his hand to shake. "My deepest apologies. I don't believe we've met. I'm Ashton Sharpe."

Aunt Nora touched his arm. "This is my niece, Charlotte Goodwin. Ashton here is one of the up and coming bright stars of Honeysuckle. He and Tucker will be making this town into a place to be reckoned with. A rival to other cities like ours, if it's allowed to grow the way that it should." She batted her eyes at him, and I was pretty sure that if she could switch places with her daughter, she'd have chosen the man currently at her side.

"Pleased to meet you." Relying on deep-rooted politeness, I gripped Ashton's offered hand.

A lightning shock of pain bolted down my arm. Gritting my teeth, I ignored it. "Friends usually call me Charli."

Ashton furrowed his brow, but his annoyingly perfect smile remained plastered on his face. "A beautiful girl like you deserves a prettier name than Charli."

I let go first. The desire to punch him in his perfect teeth rose to the surface. "Thanks."

Aunt Nora cleared her throat. "Don't let us keep you from your *thorough* investigation, detective." She shot me one last glare.

Mason's curt nod spoke volumes. "Thank you."

With a smug smile spreading on her lips, Aunt Nora slipped her hand through the crook of Ashton's arm. "Excellent. We have other business to attend to, if y'all will excuse us."

"It was a pleasure to meet you, Charlotte. Detective." He nodded at Mason, and I watched a bead of sweat trickle down his temple. Ashton did his best to hide the quick swipe of his hand to wipe it away. As he and Aunt Nora walked away, the words *incompetent* and *flake* were spoken loud enough to hear.

Mason whistled. "That aunt of yours is a real—"

"I know. As my brother has said many times, she puts the *B* in witch." Placing my hands on my hips, I bit my lip. "And as per usual, she's interrupted something important. How in the world am I ever going to find the flask now?" I searched the sky for Biddy but couldn't see her.

"Is your connection to the object completely gone?" Mason asked.

Closing my eyes, I checked. When my arm throbbed again, I rubbed it in irritation. For a brief second, the golden thread presented itself again, wavering, its connection thinner than before.

I gasped in shock. "I've got it."

"You do?"

I nodded. "I think so. But let me try something first."

Concentrating, I reached out with my will to access my one last sure connection to Uncle Tipper.

"If I can use it, then I bet I can find the flask," I muttered out loud.

"Use what, Charli?"

With determination, I pointed my finger at Mason. "Whatever you do, whatever happens, do not touch me or stop me." My death curse could finally be of use instead of a hindrance. "Here goes nothing."

Like plugging my will into an overcharged socket, a dark and murky power surged through me, almost blowing all my circuits. The pain I'd grown far too used to crept over me until my head threatened to explode from each painful pound. I moaned in agony but found the golden tether back to full strength.

"Charli, stop this. Whatever it is you're doing, you have to stop," demanded Mason.

The object lay somewhere nearby. If I could concentrate hard enough to get my feet to work, I could find it. Taking stumbling steps, I made my way forward. The closer I got, the more everything hurt. From somewhere far away, I heard my name being called. But I couldn't be distracted. Not until I completed the task. Not until I found it.

The golden tether buzzed and beckoned, but the curse muddied my mind. Pain racked my entire body. My knees buckled, and I fell to the ground. So close. Almost there. I crawled inch by inch on the ground, grasping at clumps of grass and dirt to pull myself forward. Darkness threatened to swallow me whole, and I wanted to give in. Just as soon as...If I could just reach...

The tips of my fingers brushed metal, and the connection shattered. I collapsed on the ground in a sweating, gasping heap. Voices repeated my name over and over again, but a cloud swallowed me whole and pulled me under.

Chapter Ten

My body floated in midair, carried by a strong current. No, not a current. Something with arms, hands, and fingers held me up like a life preserver.

Opening my eyes, I adjusted to the scene around me and stared straight up into amber eyes glaring at me.

"She's awake," Dash commented, a slight hint of a growl rolling at the end of his observation.

"Then you can put her down now." Mason glared at the man holding me, hovering close by.

When I tried to speak, my lips, moved but nothing came out of my mouth. I cleared my throat. "Hey, guys, you know I can hear you, right?"

Dash's chest rose up and down against me as his breath quickened. "I think that I should take her back home now. Her grandmother sent *me* to find her at just the right time. If

I hadn't shown up when I did, there's no telling what *you* would have allowed to happen to her."

Mason shuffled even closer. "She was fine up until that last point. I had no clue what she was going to do until it had already happened."

"That doesn't mean you're not culpable in hurting her. If I didn't have to take care of her, you can bet I'd take care of you," snarled the wolf shifter.

"That sounds like a threat to me, Mr. Channing." The detective leaned in. "I could take you in just for threatening a warden. Especially with your record."

"Leave my history out of this." The growl in Dash's voice reverberated through me.

Rolling my eyes at the two testosterone-filled cavemen, I pushed against the rock-solid body of the shifter. "You can put me down now. Hey!" I yelled with as much strength as I could muster, kicking my legs. Both men stopped and stared at me.

Dash blinked, emotions warring in his eyes. "I don't think that's a good idea, Charli. Your grandmother would kill me where I stood if I let any more harm come to you. As it is, your current condition may get my furry butt zapped anyway."

I gave him my best *I'm not kidding* glare right back. "Yeah, well, I'll hex your hiney right here and now if you don't drop me. That goes for both of you." I shot a similar threatening glance at Mason.

"I don't think she's bluffing," the detective said, taking a step back.

Dash snarled his displeasure and set me down with gentle care. As soon as my feet hit solid ground, my head swam, and the world tilted. Both men reached out to catch me, and their immediate reaction tickled me. My laughter stunned them both.

"Do you think that she's in shock?" Dash asked Mason.

The detective eyed me a little too personally. "I don't know. Maybe we should take her to the doc first?"

While they conversed with each other and ignored me, I placed my hands on my knees and leaned over, doing my best not to faint. "My ears and my brain are still functioning. I think I can decide what needs to happen on my own."

With determination, I straightened and took a few steps. The world blinked out of existence again, and when I finally opened my eyes back to reality, I stared up into two very differing faces.

Disheveled scruff covered a rugged face, and the eyes that regarded me could not hide the animal inside. The other hovering person was a clean cut guy who carried the weight of the world on his shoulders that lifted in rare moments to show a real person with real emotions hidden underneath. Taking them both in, I broke into uncontrolled chuckles.

Mason's lips pursed in frustration. "See, I told you. She's in shock. We need to get her to the healer now."

I covered my mouth with my hand and gave into the giggle fit, the burst of giddy merriment shaking my entire body. "I'm fine," I choked out between laughter. "The problem is that I feel a little like the fairytale princess who has not one but two princes determined to rescue her."

"Well, I could have told you that I'm no royalty." Dash winked, adding a brief moment of levity.

"No kidding," taunted Mason.

Before Dash's snarl could return, I held up my hand between the two. "That's enough. I think it's clear that I'm no princess, and I can save myself."

Taking my time, I rolled over onto my side and pushed myself into a sitting position. Even on my behind, the world still spun around me too fast. As much as I wanted to be my own hero, my body had other plans. The final efforts to find the flask had burned up all the energy in my body. By my guess, there'd be no way I could make it home on my own.

"Dash." I patted the wolf shifter's arm, garnering a look of hungry anticipation. "Go find Flint at the Harvest Moon. Discreetly. Ask him to get Gossamer here as soon as possible, please."

His eyes shifted to Mason, full of suspicion. "Are you sure?"

I nodded. "Need her help if I'm going to make it."

"I swear to you that I will keep you safe from harm if you let me escort you," insisted Dash.

Mason shook his head. "No, I should be the one to get help for her."

I held up my hand to stop them. "Mason, if I'm remembering correctly, you have another task to perform. At least I think you do. Because I found it, right?"

He frowned at me and shook his head just enough for me to know not to ask any more questions. Dash looked between the two of us in confusion.

"But your safety is more important," protested Mason.

"If I risked myself for nothing, I'll—"

"I know," the detective cut me off with a huff. "You'll hex my hiney as well." He grumbled under his breath something about the stubbornness of Goodwin women.

Dash caught the throwaway comment and snickered once in agreement. With a nod to both of us, he took off in the direction of Main Street.

Despite Mason and I being alone, I lowered my voice. "So did my last ditch effort work?"

Mason produced the flask, holding it with a handkerchief. "Yes. But that doesn't mean I'm not angry with you."

"Why? I got the job done." I cringed at the whine in my voice, but it hurt my feelings a little bit that I was getting scolded instead praised.

"But at what cost? I can't tell you what it was like watching you struggle and debating whether or not to stop you." He ran his fingers through his hair.

"But you, of all people, understand why I had to sacrifice the way I did. Why I had to try. If it's our only lead, then I had to do it. By the way, you're welcome." I held out my hand. "Can I see it?"

Mason's eyes darted around the near vicinity. Finding ourselves still alone, he nodded and placed the metal object nestled in the handkerchief in my hand.

The last time I'd seen the flask was with Tipper. It seemed small and insignificant instead of the most important clue we'd found. Any adrenaline I had leftover from my victory dissipated in a puff of sadness. "Now what?"

The detective kept a watchful eye on the flask. "I take it back with me and see if we can dust it for prints and test the insides to find out what the contents were."

I snorted. "Chances are it will pop positive for alcohol. It's what he used to carry with him almost all the time."

"I hope it's that simple." Mason furrowed his brow. It's more than helpful that you found it. But I'm not sure how much good will come of it."

"Why?" There I went again, whining.

"Because when you touched it, you dislodged it from where it was laying. The flask tumbled and fell into the creek. Any chance of retrieving evidence from it has decreased significantly." Taking the container back, he hid it away in his pocket again. "I'm sorry."

"So all of what I just went through was for nothing? And now the biggest clue to solving Tipper's murder is useless." Failure washed over me like an ocean wave, dragging me under.

He placed a hand on my shoulder. "I didn't say it was hopeless. But I think it might be beyond the capabilities of what we have here in Honeysuckle."

I picked at a blade of grass, willing the tears pooling in my eyes not to fall. "You should check with Nana before determining that. This town has secrets that only a few know.

There might be a possibility that someone here can help unexpectedly."

A thoughtful expression broke on the detective's face. "I'll take that into consideration. In the meantime, I'll make some calls to some former colleagues. Call in a few favors I'm owed."

That minuscule glimpse into his past piqued my interest. "Are you sure you want to burn those on this case?"

"Absolutely," he replied in such a soft voice, it caught me off guard.

When I glanced up, the stoic wall that he routinely hid behind was gone. Nothing but warm care beamed back at me. I didn't have enough strength to interpret what that meant. Or why an odd excitement bloomed in my stomach.

I coughed in an attempt to cover my wonder and confusion. "After all, it is your first murder case in town. It might not go down well if it goes unsolved, right?"

"Sure," he said, distracted by something in the distance.

Dash returned with Flint, who did his best to keep up with the wolf shifter's mighty stride. If I had more strength, I could appreciate the situational comedy of the scene. But I was far worse off than I wanted to reveal to them.

Gossamer flew directly to me, leaving a trail of pink fairy dust in her wake. "Charli, you look terrible," she squeaked.

"That's what a girl wants to hear." I did my best to attempt a smile, my ability to stay conscious waning.

"I can open the fairy path right away. But unless she can

walk through, then I don't know how she'll manage the travel." Goss's wings fluttered in agitation.

"I'll carry her," insisted Dash.

Gossamer gazed at him in surprise. "Mr. Channing, I'm not sure if you can. I've never heard of one of your kind using the path before. It might not work, or worse, you could get both of yourselves lost."

Dash spoke before Mason could protest. "I'm taking her, and I will guarantee her safety at whatever cost, Mrs. Hollyspring."

The fairy bobbed up and down in the air, a look of wonderment and admiration spreading on her face. "Very well. But I think I should escort the two of you to make sure."

Unable to waste any more time, I put an end to any argument over who would take me. "It's settled then. Mason, go do what you need to do. Make sure that what happened here wasn't in vain. Okay, Dash. Goss. Whenever you're ready."

Chapter Eleven

The shifter lifted me up as if I were as light as a feather. Dash cradled me in his arms with more care then I thought he possessed.

"I've got you, Charli," he whispered into my ear.

Steadying myself, I nodded. "Goss, let's get 'er done."

Dash hesitated for a second, his muscles tensing underneath me. Could it be that the big scary wolf shifter feared the path of the fairies? I threw my arms around his neck to hold myself as upright as possible.

Leaning in, I whispered back, "One step at a time."

His chest vibrated with something between a growl and a chuckle. He took a deep breath and stepped forward through the shimmering doorway in front of us. At my best, the fairy path discombobulated my senses. Now at one of the worst times I ever felt, I thought I might lose my lunch.

"Hurry up," I pushed.

"I'm trying." Dash grunted under the strain. "It feels like thousands of bees buzzing around and stinging me," he gritted through his teeth.

When I turned in his grasp to check on him, his appearance sent shivers of nerves down my body. Sweet honeysuckle iced tea! His dark stubble was growing longer and thicker. Thick hair, or possibly fur, was sprouting out all over him. His grunts turned more violent through gritted fangs.

"Keep it together, Mr. Channing," warned Goss. "Do not bring any harm to Charli while here, or I will make sure *you* do not make it. Trust me when I tell you that you do not want to stay stuck here."

"I'm trying." His voice sounded more like the bark of an animal.

"He'll make it. I trust him." I squeezed my arms around his neck tighter, willing my words to be true.

"There it is," Goss cried out. "Prepare yourselves."

With a push of energy, we emerged from the path as if breaking the surface of water, gasping for air. My family's house stood in front of us, the afternoon sun bathing the porch in a warm glow.

Dash dropped to his knees, breathing hard but never letting go of me. His hair receded, and his teeth returned to normal with great effort. Sweat poured down his temples, and he continued to cradle my body in his strong arms.

Nana rushed out the door. "Stupid child. Risking yourself like that."

Rolling my eyes would take too much effort. "I'm fine, Nana."

"She's lying," retorted Dash. "If I had to make a guess, she's in pretty bad shape."

"Thank you, Gossamer dear. You." Nana pointed a finger at Dash. "Bring her inside." My grandmother directed her alarm at me. "You just ensured a huge dose of gray sludge, young lady. And I don't want to hear one peep of defiance from you." She swung the screen door wide and let it slam behind her, muttering about hexing me if she thought it would do any good.

Dash chuckled. "You Goodwin women are all the same. I better obey."

"Hold up, Mr. Channing," Goss said. "I wanted to say that what you did for her was very..."

"Necessary?" he asked.

"I was gonna say brave, but I'll bet that will just embarrass you. Let me say thank you on all of our behalfs. You showed your true character today, and your actions will speak well for you here in Honeysuckle." Her wings sprinkled pink dust down on him in approval.

His brow furrowed. "I'd rather this stayed between us. It's nobody else's business."

Goss's delicate laugh tinkled in the air. "Good luck with that. It's a small town, in case you haven't noticed. Not much is kept secret. But I give you my word that no one will hear anything from me."

Dash relaxed a fraction. "Thank you."

"And you, Miss Charli. I don't know what we're going to do with you." She stared at me, a tinge of sadness in her eyes. "But I know you well enough not to tell you to stay out of trouble. So, here."

She produced her pink wand from goodness-knows-where and flourished it in the air. In a cloud of sparkles and dust, a shiny object formed in her tiny palm.

With excitement, she flew around me and clasped something around my neck. "There."

I lifted up the necklace to find a small key at the end of the chain. A giggle bubbled out of me. "It's even in your signature color." A tiny, sparkling pink key rested in my palm.

"Of course," she sniffed.

"Does this mean we're going steady?"

She smacked me lightly on my head with her wand. "Don't sass me. I just gave you a very useful gift. You seem to be getting into situations where you need a little extra help. Consider this an emergency backup. If you need it, and let me say I hope that you really don't, just hold it in your hand and concentrate with intent. It will open a door to the path."

My mouth dropped open. Fairies rarely gave gifts like this. "Goss. I don't know what to say."

"It's nothing," she shrugged. It took little effort to detect the lie in her high-pitched voice.

"Thank you." I fingered the key. "For everything."

She kissed my forehead, and I was pretty sure she left a tiny pink lip mark there. "I gotta get back to my Flinty. Take care of her, Mr. Channing."

"Call me Dash, Miss Gossamer." The wolf shifter nodded at the tiny fairy, who blushed and rocketed off.

"Are you two determined to watch the grass grow, or what? Move it," Nana called out like a drill sergeant.

"Yes, ma'am." Dash snapped into obedience, carrying me inside.

I needed to remember the exact tone my grandmother used for future reference.

⚜

I sat on a rocking chair on the front porch, my third glass of sludge in my right hand, gazing out at the late afternoon sun dappling through the trees. Moments like this made me glad to be alive on a normal day. On a day like today, it made me sad that I might not get that many of them anymore.

The screen door creaked, and heavy footsteps stomped on the old planks of the porch. "Your grandmother said I was to make sure you'd finished that glass." Dash held the fourth one in his hand. "Don't make me have to force-feed it to you."

"I'd like to see you try."

He chuckled, a rare smile spreading across his lips. "You think you'd be any trouble for me to take care of? I've taken down scarier monsters than you."

His statement reminded me of something Mason had said. "Is that so? I don't suppose that has anything to do with the past that Mason spoke about?" I knew I stood on shaky ground, but if ever there was a chance where he might take pity on me in answering some of my questions, it was now.

His smile faded. "I don't like talking about my past."

"If you don't tell me something about yourself, how can we ever become friends? Here, I'll show you." I pointed out to the nearby live oak dripping in Spanish moss in our yard. "See that tree yonder? That's the tree that my brother Matt swore up and down he'd seen pixies in. I was pretty young, so I hung on his every word and never thought once to question him. He was so convincing that one night when I saw sparkling lights in the branches, I decided I wanted to go capture one. I snuck out of the house and climbed up only to find that the lights were fireflies, not pixies."

Dash's smile lit me up on the inside. I swallowed hard and continued. "Yeah, climbin' up the tree was not the problem. Gettin' back down was, especially at night for a young girl in a nightgown. I made it part way before my foot slipped and I fell the rest of the way. Broke my arm." I pointed to a specific line on my skin. "Right here. My mom and dad were furious at Matt, but it ended up getting me a whole lot of attention and sympathy as my arm healed. Also, I got to eat all my favorite foods for weeks, so I couldn't stay mad at him for too long."

"Sounds like he wasn't that great of a brother." Dash frowned as if he might go find Matt right now and give him what for.

"Actually, he was. But siblings don't always get along, do they?"

A dark shadow crossed Dash's face, and he gazed out at the tree. "No, they don't."

Silence followed as I waited for an explanation. When nothing but the evening cicadas answered, I drank the rest of the sludge in the third cup and held out my hand for the fourth.

"Sounds like there's the story behind that statement," I dared. Nothing but cicadas chirped. "How about you give me a memory in trade for cup number four?"

"No deal. You don't have a choice about drinking that. But I have a choice about giving you any details about myself. It's better that way. Trust me. You already said you did," he added in a quieter tone.

"I did." The truth surprised me. "But if you give me a little more of yourself, that trust will solidify and grow. As far as I've been able to observe, you're a wolf shifter without a pack, living in a small country town that has specific protections for those in the magical community. So I don't believe you chose Honeysuckle randomly. You are handy with your tools. And that's about all I know." I skipped the part about him being a huge support to me. Not a Prince Charming. Maybe more like a superhero.

"So you've been observing me, have you?" The corner of his mouth crooked up despite his attempt to stay serious.

I rolled my eyes. "Don't take it as a compliment, Mr. Channing. Goss is right. In a small town, there really are no secrets. Not for long anyway."

"And when it gets to that point, what if my secrets are scary?"

"Scary is in the eye of the beholder, Dash. Don't you know by now that you're stronger in numbers rather than alone?"

He gestured his finger back and forth. "Between the two of us, Ms. Goodwin, which one understands the concept of a pack more?"

"Touché." I stopped my nagging and enjoyed the buzz of the cicadas and the rustle of leaves and Spanish moss.

After a minute, Dash spoke in a faraway tone. "I didn't use to be alone. I had a family. Well, technically, they may still be alive. But I don't know what's happened to them."

Instead of drilling him with the multiple questions that popped into my head, I waited patiently. My silence paid off, and he continued.

"I can't tell you everything. Pack rules. But I can tell you that sometimes, families can be the best things in the world. And sometimes, they can be your downfall."

After a few quiet moments, I spoke. "Have you met my Aunt Nora?"

A low chuckle rumbled in his chest and turned into real laughter. "Touché, yourself."

"So what you're saying is that after some things have happened to you, you chose to come to Honeysuckle Hollow in order to build a life, find peace, and maybe be able to live with yourself?"

Dash lifted his eyebrows. "Pretty much."

"See, Mr. Channing? You and I have more in common

than you thought." I paused, considering my next move carefully. "You know why Nana's making me drink this nasty stuff?" I guessed that she had told him something since she'd been the one to send him to me.

He rocked in his chair, not answering but waiting for me to continue.

"When I found Tipper, I guess I picked up a death curse. So, she's trying to slow down its effects." If that didn't show Dash how much I trusted him in that moment, I didn't know what would.

With genuine compassion in his eyes, he nodded. "I know."

"Nana told you?"

He shook his head. "I could smell it on you that morning you brought me sweet tea on this here porch."

I stared at him. "You've known all this time and kept it to yourself? It's pretty juicy stuff that could be good currency in a small town that thrives on gossip."

His eyes captured mine with that smoldering amber glow. "Not their business. Nor my place to tell."

Butterflies took wings in my stomach, and a warm mushy feeling oozed through my veins. The screen door crashed, breaking the mood, and my grandmother stood in front of me with yet another glass.

"You're falling down on the job, Dashiel Channing," scolded Nana.

The wolf shifter sat up straighter in his rocking chair.

"Deepest apologies, Ms. Goodwin. I'll do my best to make sure Charli stays out of trouble from here on out."

"Good luck with that," Nana scoffed, leaving the fifth glass of sludge sitting on the porch next to me.

"I'd like to see you try," I joked.

"I'll make you a deal," Dash dared. "I'll keep you out of trouble, and you can attempt to do the same with me."

I stuck my fist out at him. "We misfits have to stick together."

He bumped my knuckles with his. "Charli, you know nothing about being an outsider. And I hope you never do."

The evening played its Southern melody in the air, and we rocked to the rhythm of it in companionable comfort.

"Your grandmother called me by my real name," Dash said in a low voice, breaking the silence.

I smiled. "Be glad she doesn't know your middle name, too. By the way, what is it?"

After a pause, he covered his face with his hand. "It's Thaddeus," he admitted.

Laughter bubbled out of me. "Oh, man. That would sound awesome if my Nana middle-named you. Dashiel Thaddeus Channing. It's a mouthful."

"You better not tell anyone," he fake snarled.

I placed my hand on my heart. "I swear, I'll take it to my grave." The ill-timed joke fell like a lead balloon.

His hand touched my arm. "Not if I can help it." He pulled away when Nana checked on us again.

She placed her hands on her hips. "You're falling down on the job, boy."

I gave in to a fit of giggles as Dash covered my mouth while I tried to tell my grandmother his middle name. The lighthearted game bolstered me more than any gray sludge, and the night ended with a note of victory and laughter instead of sadness.

Chapter Twelve

The Founders' Fair didn't hold a candle to the State Fair, but all of us in Honeysuckle loved it. We'd use any excuse to break out fun games, have small booths, and enjoy food with each other. I couldn't be happier that I'd recovered enough to enjoy myself tonight.

For most of the games, any means of magic were fair use. I stood to the side, watching Lily attempt to use her very limited telekinetic powers to beat Lucky at popping balloons with darts. Problem was, he ran The Rainbow's End, the only bar in town. Taking on a leprechaun who shot darts on a regular basis probably hadn't been the best idea. He didn't even need magic to beat Lily.

"I'll take the unicorn." Lucky pointed at the limp stuffed animal hanging in the prize section. He added it to the growing pile beside him. "Thanks for trying, Lily. You come down to The End sometime, and I'll teach you my secrets."

Lavender giggled beside me. "I think he'll share more with her than that. He's all pink and fuzzy." She pointed at the aura that only she could detect.

Lily shot her cousin a dirty look. "You'd better be talking about the unicorn and not who I think you are. Hey, there's Lee." She waved at someone behind us.

A short, stocky guy with thick glasses sitting on his nose sauntered his way to us. "Y'all want some boiled peanuts?" He held out a soggy bag.

Lily and Lavender dug in, but I shook my head. "No way."

"What? You don't like 'em?" Lee popped a couple in his mouth and chewed. "They're a Southern delicacy. You're betraying your own tribe."

I stuck out my tongue. "They're slimy and mushy. Y'all enjoy my share."

"So, I've been working with my dad on your motorcycle." Leland Chalmers, Jr. had worked on and off at his dad's shop since middle school. "Pretty sure it's more a mechanical issue than a spellwork one. And we're gonna need to scrounge for some parts, which will take time."

How ironic could life get? "Time is all I've got left." The words gritted like sand on my tongue.

"You know, Bennett's back in town, right? I say we gather the whole gang for an old time get together like before." Lee finished the last of the boiled peanuts.

Lily's scowl disappeared. "You know, that sounds great."

Lavender batted her eyes and nudged her cousin. "How about we all head to The End after the fair?"

"How about you go replace Sassy at the Kissing Booth? I heard there's a line of trolls waiting." Lily's sneer dripped with venom.

We walked past other carnival games and enjoyed the general atmosphere. Alison Kate met us at the table with baked goods from Sweet Tooths, where she worked. Sprinkle and Twinkle, the two retired tooth fairies that owned the bakery on Main Street, handed out mini cupcakes to all of us. Alison made sure to give one directly to Lee, her cheeks brightening the same color as the strawberries in the treats.

Next to the sweets table, Boyd hustled to distribute the baskets of strawberries to everyone. Behind him, a display of all kinds of vegetables advertised the weekly farmer's market.

"Boyd? What in the heck is that?" I pointed at the enormously oversized green veggie.

The farmer tipped his straw cowboy hat at me. "That there's my pride and joy. This year's monster. I named it Biggus."

Lee spit out some of the tea he'd been swallowing. We all laughed and admired the magically-enhanced zucchini. Alison Kate arranged to pick up four baskets of strawberries to take home at the end of the night, and Boyd set them aside for her.

Our group continued meandering around, tasting more food and drinking tea and lemonade. My sister-in-law beamed when she saw me and beckoned me over by holding up a kitten. The other girls squealed with delight and ran over to the wire fencing that barely contained a wild bunch of fuzzy beasts-in-training. Luckily, no cat would ever capture my heart. Ever.

"Why Traci Jo. Whaddya know?" I greeted Matt's wife with a quick hug.

"We found this group of souls abandoned in the woods. They're looking for their fur-ever home." TJ held up a tiny black beasty squirming in her hands. "Maybe this one's your familiar. Care to try?"

"No, thanks." I crossed my arms to hide my hands. "Try some other sucker."

Lee nudged me with his elbow. "Heads up. Incoming." He nodded his chin toward the two guys ambling our way.

Tucker had his eyes trained on me with purpose. Beside him, his bestie Ashton walked as if he owned the very grass we all stood on. Nerves shot through me, and I did something I never thought I'd do. With mock enthusiasm, I joined the others at gushing over the animals.

Inside the flimsy containment area, one kitten stood out from the rest of them. Tinier than the others, its striped orange fur made it the outcast from the rest with black or grey markings. Instead of meowing in sadness for being left out, the little thing wriggled its butt and pounced on the others with utter fearlessness. My hands moved on their accord and picked the tiny freak up.

"She's a fighter, that one." TJ nodded in approval and moved to wrangle a stray kitten trying to climb its way to freedom.

"Hey, Charli Bird." My ex's deep voice spoke a little too near to my ear for comfort.

"Hey, yourself." I focused all my attention on the tiny fur ball in my hands that intermittently licked and chewed on me.

"I thought you didn't like cats," Tucker said.

Needing a distraction, I brought the kitten up to my face. Looking at its bright yellow eyes that stared directly into me, a part of my heart thawed. "I don't like *most* cats. Especially Nana's. But that's because she gave hers a terrible name that it had to live up to." I scratched the orange beast on its head, and the darn thing purred.

"So a name's important? Guessing I should have taken yours a little more seriously then, huh, Bird?"

Frosted fairy wings, Tucker intended to row with me right here in the middle of the fair? Where was his current intended that he could pay attention to?

"You know what I'm gonna name her?" I continued, ignoring his comment. "I'm going to give her a name that will make her as sweet as sugar." Giving it some thought, I came up with a brilliant title. "From now on, you shall be called Miss Peach Cobbler Yum Yum Fuzzy Pants." As if on cue, the kitten nuzzled my chin, its tiny purrs growing fiercer.

Pixie poop. Pretty sure I'd just gotten suckered.

"That's a long name for something so small," added Ashton, joining Tucker's and my conversation as an unwelcome addition. With a look of haughty disdain he must have picked up from my aunt, he kept his distance.

"True," I admitted. "Of course, I'll call her Peaches for

short. But she'll know that even though she's small, her name makes her mighty. Isn't that right, Peaches?"

The orange kitten nestled underneath my chin, its tiny needle-like claws digging into my skin as it made biscuits with its paws on my skin.

"Oh my," Alison Kate exclaimed. "There's something I never thought I'd see."

The rest of my friends turned their attention on me. I wished down to the soles of my feet that Blythe were here instead of working tonight. She'd place herself between Tucker and me.

"Where's Clementine?" Somehow, having a purring animal burrowing into my nook made talking to my ex a little easier. "I would think she wouldn't let you out of her sight." *Or be happy that you're talking to me.*

He shrugged, his indifference surprising. "Clem's somewhere around here. Listen, is there a chance that you and I could get together and talk?"

The immediate anger that bubbled up inside my chest startled me. Thankfully, having the animal resting on me kept the emotion at bay. "I don't think there's anything to say. We've both moved on with our lives. Isn't that enough?"

Something akin to pain flashed in Tucker's eyes. "Charli, please." He reached out to touch me, but I maneuvered away.

"Give me some time to think about it, okay?" Since my days might be limited, there might be no reason to talk at all.

With a look of dejection, he gave in, allowing Ashton to

pull him away from me. I joined the others in their conversation.

"What's wrong?" Lily asked her cousin.

"My head. I don't normally get headaches." Lavender rubbed her temple.

Alison Kate held out her a drink. "Here. Maybe you're dehydrated."

"Is that sweet tea?" Ashton passed the cup to Lavender. "A little caffeine might give you some immediate relief. But if it turns into something more serious, a little tea brewed with feverfew works wonders, although its taste is a little bitter."

Lily brightened. "I'll bet Grandma has some."

"You can also rub some concentrated peppermint oil on your temple. But try the sweet tea first and see if caffeine does the trick," Ashton added.

"Thanks," Lily said. "Where did you learn all this?"

"My mom taught me." A speck of sadness rested in his eyes.

He leaned in to speak to Lavender in a low tone. Whatever he told her, it made her grimace disappear, and her cheeks flush. He touched her arm for a second, a satisfied smile growing on his lips. While I appreciated his advice and attention to her, something about him still nagged at my insides.

When he caught me watching him, he gave me a curt nod and joined Tucker as they headed toward the concession area.

"Well, that went as well as could be expected." Lily patted my arm.

"Tucker wants to speak to me. Alone." Plucking the sleepy kitten from my chest, I handed her back to TJ with a promise to pick her up at the end of the fair.

"Do you think that's a good idea?" Lavender asked. "Also, do y'all think it's a good idea if I attend the barn dance with Ashton?"

We all exploded with surprise and then apologized because of her headache. She smiled with shy wonderment. "He just asked me out of the blue. I mean, we haven't even talked all that much."

"What did his aura tell you?" I asked.

A little wrinkle formed between her eyebrows. "You know, that's funny. I didn't even notice or think to look for one."

"That is unusual," agreed Lily. "But hey, at least you've got a date for the dance. At this rate, I shall be going alone."

I placed my hands on my hips. "Hey, what am I? Chopped liver? No one's asked me yet either. I say that we attend like we used to. As a group."

"Oh, I don't know," ventured Alison Kate, her eyes flitting in Lee's direction. "I think going with someone might be a good idea."

When my bespectacled friend didn't catch the hint, I elbowed him. He rubbed his ribs in confusion, still not getting it. Boys. Lily and I rolled our eyes while Alison Kate looked at the ground in abject dejection.

Wherever I went, people stared and whispered. My friends stayed loyally by my side, but nothing quieted the dramatic air that surrounded me. My ears perked up to try and catch more potential clues, but detecting anything specific was almost impossible with all the hustle and bustle of the fair.

We made our way to the main stage, where Deacon "DK" King, the editor-in-chief of *The Honeysuckle Holler* made some announcements.

"Of course, I hope all y'all are enjoying tonight's event. A big round of applause to everyone for making it happen in light of recent tragedies."

More eyes burned in the back of my head, but I clapped along with everyone else. Because I stayed focused on the stage to ignore those around me, I didn't notice the wet presence that joined me at my right elbow until the person ran their fingers through their hair, flicking drops of water at me.

Mason practically buzzed with glee, but his face remained stoic and professional. He nodded at my friends, who offered him polite acceptance, but who I knew were scrutinizing the two of us like gossipy old hens.

"For mermaid's sake, how did you get so wet?" I asked under my breath.

"It's your fault," he accused.

"What?" I turned my head to him.

"Well, you're the one that said I should try and fit in. So I volunteered for the dunking booth."

Disappointment burned my insides. Had I known that, I'd have spent every penny I possessed to take a shot at drowning him. "Looks like somebody hit the bullseye." His wet shirt clung to his chest, outlining his athletic physique.

"There seemed to be an unending line once I crawled up on the hot seat. Even your brother bought a few tries."

"Tell me he dunked you." At least one of us Goodwin's should have had that pleasure.

Mason smiled. "Second try."

I bumped him with my hip and then regretted the friendly move. When he nudged me back, my heart skipped its record for a second.

Big Willie took the stage to loud cheers from the crowd. He basked in his moment, blowing kisses to us. "All right, y'all. It's time for the main event. This year, our talented Sassy has gone out of her way to make the pies for this year's contest. How about a big hand for our little pie queen."

The fairy's green head bobbed up and down at the front of the crowd. No doubt, she loved every second of worship.

"What was it you called her?" asked Mason in a whisper. "Queen of Flaky?"

A snort escaped me, and when heads turned to look, I pointed at Mason.

Big Willie continued. "Since this year's big spellcasting event happens on the night of the Strawberry Moon, Sassy here has provided us with a slew of her famous strawberry cream pies." He held one up for the audience to ooh and ahh over. "We also owe big thanks to our farmer extraordinaire, Boyd, and his family for providing the berries so late in the season."

The shy farmer stood next to his wife and kids, his cheeks red. He only waved at the rest of us when Kelly forced him to.

"There are four seats up here that need to be filled. First, I'd like a volunteer for the first one."

A voice I didn't care to hear called out. "I'll take that seat, Sheriff." Tucker strode up on stage, shook Big Willie's immense paw of a hand, and stood behind the first chair.

"And now, for the warden department's representative. Give a big hand for our newest edition, Detective Mason Clairmont." Big Willie pointed at the soaked man beside me.

Unable to get out of it now, Mason sighed and made his way to the stage. He bypassed Big Willie and stood next to Tucker.

"Now, we've got two strappin' fellas up here. How about one of you ladies take a stab at it. I've seen the way some of you can put away some pie. Who's up for a challenge?"

"Right here," called out Lily.

Looking up, I noticed three different fingers pointing at my head. Traitors, all of them. "No way," I protested.

"Charli Goodwin," Big Willie called out, a tiny bit of caution in his eyes. "You willin' to live up to the challenge?"

I shook my head with violent determination.

"Oh come on, Charli. You afraid of losing?" teased Tucker.

"No. Are you?" The words flew out of me.

"Not to you." His arrogance grated my nerves.

My violent determination morphed into fierce competitiveness quicker than lightning. "Bring it on, T." Nobody else in town dared to call that man anything close to that. He'd be best to remember I knew him better than most. No doubt my aunt and cousin were shooting daggers at me from somewhere in the crowd.

When I made it to the chair next to Mason, he spoke to me out the side of his mouth. "I guess laying low isn't in your DNA."

I shrugged, not having a snappy comeback out of the sheer shock of being on stage.

Big Willie strutted in front of us. "That leaves one final seat. Does anybody—"

"I'll take it," a loud voice snarled.

Dash pushed his way to the front of the crowd and hopped up from the ground directly onto the stage with a crash. He strode to the seat on my left side. Without a word, he took his place next to me, his eyes burning into mine when he glanced my way.

Holy unicorn horn, how had I managed to get in the middle of a hot guy sandwich?

"Contestants, take your seats," Big Willie instructed.

The four of us sat down. I gripped the table to steady my shaking nerves.

The sheriff continued. "Each of you will have a helper, who will tie your hands behind your backs. They will also be responsible for replacing your consumed pies and keeping track of the emptied tins. Helpers, please take your places."

"Good luck, Charli," Gossamer offered through her giggles.

"Goss, do me a favor and try not to dust my pies. If I

sneeze in the middle of this, it ain't gonna be pretty." No way did I want to make a bigger fool out of myself in front of everyone. *Definitely not in front of the guys. Or my ex.*

"I'll do my best," she promised.

Lily, Lavender, and Alison Kate gave me thumbs up and whooped my name. Lee crossed his arms and focused on Dash with a disapproving scowl. Huh. Since when were those two acquaintances?

"Care to make this interesting?" Dash growled.

"I don't have anything to pay with," I whispered back. The helpers placed the first pies in front of us.

"If I win, you can pay me with a date." He eyed the pie and smirked as if it were a tiny morsel.

My, what big fangs he might have behind that smile. "A d-date?" I stuttered.

"And what if I win?" Mason leaned forward and stared down the other guy. "Do I get a date?"

"Deal. If either of you wins, you can go on a date with each other," I nodded with mock bravery.

Before either of the guys could protest or my ex could throw his hat in the ring, Big Willie raised his hand. "On your mark. Get set. Go!"

I slammed my face into the pie tin, strawberry goo and whipped cream going up my nostrils as my mouth worked its best to devour the first pie.

"Done," grunted Dash.

Mason followed next before Tucker asked for another pie.

No matter how fast I swallowed, my first tin never seemed to be finished.

When the three men moved to their third pies, Gossamer finally replaced my first empty one with a new pie. Through the haze of whipped cream, I glimpsed at my Mt. Everest of strawberries. Knowing that I didn't have a unicorn's chance at winning, I decided to play the game my way.

Scooping up bits of pie in my hand, I added content first to Mason's tin and then to Dash's. The crowd erupted in laughter and cheers. I wiped off the mess from my face and licked my fingers in delight.

Big Willie roared with laughter. "By my count, Dash holds the lead with Detective Mason hot on his heels and Tucker Hawthorne bringing up the rear. Our dear Charli has decided to maintain her reputation as a troublemaker, adding an additional obstacle to the contest."

In cahoots with Gossamer, we took my remaining pies and added to the other tins so that none of the boys truly held the lead. When Dash doubled his efforts to pull ahead, I plopped a larger amount of pie in his tin. Sassy hovered with her arms crossed in annoyance, her green head practically steaming at our disrespect to her masterpieces.

"And we're coming to the end in three. Two. One. Stop eating," called out Big Willie. "Time to count tins."

All three guys lifted their faces covered in strawberries and whipped cream. Tucker seemed less than pleased, but Mason's shoulders shook from snickering. He wiped a massive glob off his face and chucked it at me. It missed and hit Dash upside his head.

The wolf shifter growled, wiped both hands down his face, and flung even more pie fragments in Mason's direction. It never made it that far, splattering on my face. I took the remains of the tin in front of me in both fists and shoved my hands in each of the guy's faces, smearing the red and white glop around. By now, Tucker had removed himself from the carnage.

Big Willie stared us down. "Pull yourselves together." He turned to the crowd. "Well, this may go down as the most memorable pie eating contest in Honeysuckle history. What do you say, folks?"

Cheers rose from the crowd until someone yelled out, "Who won? I've got a fiver ridin' on this."

Sassy pouted. "Isn't Charli disqualified?" Every party needed a pooper.

"Yes, I would agree that Miss Charli cannot be the winner, although she is the most entertaining." The sheriff pointed at me.

I stood up and took a bow, pie fodder falling off my face and onto the table.

"So that leaves us with Detective Clairmont and Dashiel Channing. And by my calculations, this one turned out to be much closer. Again, because of our girl, Charli, here. But if I had to call this one..." he paused, looking back and forth at the two men who stared each other down. "I'd have to call it a tie between the two."

Boos floated up from the crowd, and Big Willie held up his hands. "However, since I am judge and jury in this competition, I have to say that due to Charli's interference, I must disqualify the tie. Which means we have a winner in Mr. Tucker Hawthorne. Let's give the man a big hand."

Tucker walked back on stage, his face already clean and shining. He waved at the crowd. "On behalf of my family, my business with my partner, Ashton, and my soon-to-be wife, I thank y'all for the support."

Before he left the stage, he came over to shake hands with the losers. He left me for last and pulled me into him. "So what do *I* win, Charli Bird?"

Since the sea of nosy townsfolk could see us, I slapped a polite smile on my face. "How about a big bag of nothing?"

"At least give me a chance to talk to you," he pleaded.

"I think the lady made herself clear." Dash approached with his hands closed in fists.

Tucker let me go and backed away. "At least think about it, Charli." He turned and gave another wave to the crowd and left.

"You cheated," accused Mason, bumping into me again.

"Did not." This time, I kept my hip to myself. "And think about it this way. Since neither of you won, you don't have to go out on a date with each other. So it's a win-win-win, if you ask me."

Unwilling to let them argue with me, I bolted from the stage, ready to never see another pie or strawberry for the rest of my life. However long that might be.

Chapter Thirteen

Crickets chirped their echoing chorus in the night air accompanied by croaking frogs. After parking on the side of a back road on the border of Tipper's land, our little gang walked through the woods to our old hideout.

"There better not be any snakes out here." Lily held up a lantern to light the way. She shrieked when Lee snuck up behind and grabbed her by her shoulders. "I'll hex you seven ways to Sunday, Leland Chalmers, Jr."

A strand of Spanish moss hit my face, and I spluttered. Peaches squirmed against me, but I held her close. I should have taken her to Nana's, but no way would I introduce her to her new nemesis, Loki, without being there to referee. For the time being, she'd have to be a witness to tonight's purpose.

The woods gave way to a field, and our destination came

into view. The old dilapidated hut defied its age and definite tilt in its structure. Nearby, a shed of similar age sat like a faithful companion to the bigger wooden structure. Growing up, our perfect place to meet had been the lean-to that the local 'shiners stayed in when they made their moonshine. For tonight, it needed to keep even more secrets.

"I can't believe we decided to come here." Lily ran her fingers across a filthy tabletop and placed the glowing lantern on it. Shadows danced on the walls surrounding us.

"Wow, this place hasn't changed a bit." Alison Kate stepped carefully into the one-room structure. "We should have gone to Lucky's."

"I can't believe that the younger Honeysuckle generation wouldn't want to hang out in our palace," added Lavender. "And ask Lily why we couldn't go to The End."

I sniffed the air around her. "You know, you smell like peppermint." The cloying scent fought the dank smell of must and dust in the hut.

Lavender grinned. "I took Ashton's advice before we came here. The oil seems to have done the trick since my head no longer hurts. Ick, is that a nest of spiders?" She flinched away from the corner.

I set my new orange kitty down on the wooden floors, and she proceeded to stalk around the place, inspecting every inch with no fear. Only her occasional sneezes marked her location.

Footsteps pounded on the creaky steps. "So what's tonight's password? I solemnly swear I am up to—"

"Don't finish that," I warned. "And get your behind over here, Bennett."

Our other friend entered the hut and caught me up in his arms. "How ya doin', pal?"

I'd forgotten how tall Ben had grown. "I think the bigger question is, what the blazes are you doing back in Honeysuckle? Last I'd heard, you took your foo foo law degree from the College of Charleston and headed up north to some fancy schmancy place to gain your advocate's license."

"Yeah, out of all of us, you're supposed to be the success story." Lee clapped him on the back.

After Ben had completed his law degree from the College of Charleston, he'd pursued his dream to obtain extra qualifications to defend and represent the magical community. Ever since he was young, he'd been the first to defend anyone who suffered injustice. He'd honed his argumentative skills convincing all of our parents at some point and time how the trouble we were in was worth a lesser punishment.

Using his height as an advantage, Ben curled my head in the crook of his arm and gave me a head noogie. "I did. I'm certified a Class One Advocate."

"Don't you mean Class A unicorn's behind?" Lee smacked him, and Ben let me go so that the two boys could embrace in a manly hug.

Lily stayed quiet and out of the way, watching Ben with wide eyes, her old torch for him still burning steady. Alison

Kate held a close second in the crush department, mooning over Lee.

Lavender watched her cousin and friend with barely contained amusement. Catching my attention, she shook from holding in her giggles and mouthed at me, *"Pink. So-o-o pink."*

It took us long minutes to properly greet Ben and settle down. Blythe stormed the door in a huff, her conjured ball of light popping like a soap bubble. She pointed at me in between hard breaths. "What did you do to tick off Sassy?"

Holding up my hands, I widened my eyes in faux innocence. "Nothing, I swear."

Alison Kate chimed in, "She ruined the pie eating contest."

"Did not," I countered. "What was there to ruin? And the town's golden boy walked away with the win in the end."

"I didn't see you complaining about being caught in the middle of those two yummy guys." Another giggle escaped Lavender.

"What guys?" Ben asked. "I've been gone too long."

"The new detective. Mason Something. He came from a warden's department somewhere up north, too. And Dash Channing." Lee stopped his explanation and stared at the floor.

"Who's this Dash person?" Ben lifted his eyebrows.

Lily snickered. "Some brooding bad boy that our Charli here is crushing on."

"You know, I'm not sure which one she likes." Lavender

tapped her lip. "The glow about her didn't dim no matter which one she talked to."

I searched for my new kitten, desperate not to be the subject of this particular henpecking. Catching Peaches mid-pounce in attacking an unknown mass of something in the corner, I pulled her in to nuzzle. "The only crush I have is on Miss Peach Cobbler Yum Yum Fuzzy Pants here. Isn't that right, Peachy Poo," I cooed at my new best friend, who outranked every single person in the room at the moment.

Everyone exploded in guffaws and disbelief at my turn from cat hater to kitty mama. Peaches purred in great satisfaction at gaining the room's attention. When I sat down cross-legged on the floor, she happily plopped down in my lap and proceeded to lick her body parts with no shame. The kitten had more bravery in her swishy stubby tail than I possessed in my entire body. If I wanted a chance at beating my odds, I needed all the help I could get.

"Sit your behinds down. We've got things to discuss." I patted the floor and waited for the rest to obey.

Lily plunked herself down next to Ben and failed at attempting not to glance at him every two seconds. Her cousin narrowed her eyes as she watched me and missed Alison Kate sitting as close as possible next to Lee.

With a nervous sigh and bolstering myself by scratching the orange fur ball with my fingers, I poured out the long tale of everything that had happened since my return. When I got to Tipper and the death curse, more than one swear word exploded into the dingy room.

"So that explains it." Lavender dashed a tear away from the corner of her eye. "There's been a dark smokiness hovering around you. It fights with your other colors. I've never seen anything like it." Her lower lip trembled, and her cousin reached over to rub her back.

"What can we do?" Lily couldn't manage a glance my way.

"Not a lot," Ben answered faster than me. "When I worked for the High Advocate's office, we dealt with a high profile case of something like this. Although in that instance, it was the person who'd caused the death that had the curse on him. The only thing we could do was to help him get his affairs in order." He pushed himself off the floor and paced to the window. "That blasted old fool."

Unable to stomach much more discussion, I scratched Peaches and worried. The mood in the room plummeted, and silence filled the vacuum.

"Well. I think we all need a little something to help. Be back in a sec." Lee moved too fast for us to ask him where he was going.

What had I thought I could accomplish by revealing the curse to them? All I'd managed to do was upset my friends and burden them with the knowledge of a tragedy they couldn't change.

Blythe slapped her legs. "Well, the first thing we're going to do is to stop calling it a death curse. Talk about a serious downer." She crawled across the space in the middle and cupped my cheek for a second. Out of all my friends, I needed her to be strong. For all of us. Patting Peaches on the head, she knelt on her knees in front of me. "Let's call it...Bob."

"That's the worst idea ever," Lily muttered between a few hiccupped chuckles. "Besides, we have an Uncle Bob, and I don't want to have to associate a curse with a family member."

Alison Kate raised her hand. "What about something cute? Like Daisy. Or Pinky."

"We could call it...Tim?" Ben offered.

"How about Tucker? Then every time I got mad at it, I could say, 'Stupid Tucker.'" My amusement didn't alleviate the heaviness around my heart.

Lee returned, shaking a mason jar of liquid in the lantern light. "Here, this ought to take the sting off the news of the curse."

I sniffed. "We've decided to name it something else. Like that will help." The wet blanket of depression dampened my mood.

"It might," Lily insisted. She listed off the possibilities so far, and Lee dismissed each one.

He added in a couple of well-known villain's names, but none of them worked. Peaches turned three times in my lap after her self-inflicted bath and settled down into a curled ball. Her general sweetness gave me the only glimmer of hope for good in the world. See, names *were* important, so we couldn't waste the opportunity. Either we could give the curse our fear and make it stronger, or we could take that away.

I snapped my fingers. "Let's call it Doozy."

"Wait. Why?" Lee asked.

"Because who can be afraid of something called Doozy? Plus, I get to say things like, "Ooh, she's a Doozy,' or, 'Be careful of that last curse. She's a Doozy.'" My friends stared at me slack-jawed. "Okay, fine. At least you could carve on my tombstone *Here lies Charli, Her curse was a Doozy, So let's celebrate her life, By getting all boozy*."

"That's not funny," Blythe uttered through hysterical cackles.

"Not at all." Lily wiped tears of laughter from her eyes.

"Speaking of boozy." Lee unscrewed the lid on the mason jar. "I say we christen Doozy with a little of this special batch of moonshine."

"Where did you get that?" Something about the liquor nagged at me.

Lee jerked his thumb behind him. "From Pappy's still next door in the shed." Lee's family had a long line of moonshiners in it. But when his grandfather passed, so did the spirits production. Or so I thought.

"You're making it again?" Ben took the jar and unscrewed it, sniffing the contents and coughing.

Lee puffed up his chest. "Yep. Back in business with a new partner. He works the process, and I add the old magic touch. This particular batch is specially made. We distilled it using the phases of the moon to give it a little kick. According to Tipper, it's the best we've done yet."

An all-too-familiar zing of ice flashed down my right arm. "What did you just say?"

Lee's face dropped. "I know. The old guy always demanded

first taste as his payment for the still being hidden on his land."

A thought took root in my head as the ache in my arm throbbed again. Since being inebriated was like breathing for Uncle Tipper, I'd dismissed such an important detail of our last time together. "Lee, what do you mean that Tipper tasted the moonshine? Did he just sip from the jar?"

"Well, yeah. More than sip. If we left him to it, we'd have nothing left."

"Have you had any yourself?"

He shook his head. "No. There wasn't much to the batch, and what we had has already been promised."

"And Uncle Tipper didn't take any jars with him?" I pressed.

"No." Lee crossed his arms. "Why the third degree?"

I breathed a sigh of relief. "Good." And yet, frustration settled on my brow.

"Except...he did take his usual payment," added Lee.

I swallowed hard in anticipation. "And how did you pay him?"

"He filled a flask to the brim. Look, let's stop talkin' about the stuff and get to drinkin' it." Lee took the jar back from Ben and raised it in the air. "To good ol' Tip. And to gettin' rid of Doozy."

"Don't," I yelled, and smacked the jar from his hand. It shattered on the floor, its liquid contents draining through the cracks in the floorboards. Peaches jumped in my lap, her tail fluffing out in fuzzy fear.

"Oh my stars." Alison Kate covered her mouth.

"What did you do that for?" demanded Lee.

Blythe knocked him upside the head. "Can't you connect the dots? Tipper drank some of your special moonshine. And shortly after that, he was no longer alive. You know. Gone home. Passed away. Dead, you moron."

The ghost of my meeting with my great-uncle haunted my memory. If my current suspicions turned out to be true, then maybe I had a chance at solving things and breaking the curse.

I pointed at my surprised friend. "Lee, you can't let anyone touch the moonshine. And you can't get rid of any of it. Not until it's been tested."

Ben closed his eyes. "Do I need to leave?"

"Why?" Lee asked.

"Because I'm both a lawyer and an advocate. If you're about to reveal something illegal, you're gonna have to hire me to earn client privilege. Or keep your behind out of jail."

Panic filled Lee's face. "But I'm not the one who makes it. It's just my Pappy's still."

"And *your* magic," I observed.

"Oh. Right." Lee kicked a piece of shattered glass on the floor.

"Who's the unnamed partner you're talking about?" Blythe crossed her arms.

"Um, not sure I should say." His eyes bounced between Ben and me.

"Spit it out," Blythe pushed. "We'll claim friendship first, and Ben can pretend he's not a high fallootin' advocate for two seconds until we decide what to do. Together. Now, who is it, Junior?"

With a sheepish glance at me, Lee frowned. "It's Dash."

That wolf shifter's secrets ran deep. Not that I'd had a whole lot of time to mine them from him in the first place. But now, if I went to Mason with my new suspicions about the tainted moonshine, it could jeopardize both Lee and Dash.

All of us could vouch for my old friend, but who would stand for the wolf outsider? And the last thing I wanted was to pit the detective against a man he barely tolerated.

Still, the blasted tingling demanded me to follow the current clue to its end. If I wanted a chance to break the curse, I had to take the next step.

"You really are a Doozy," I muttered, rubbing my arm and hatching a plan.

Chapter Fourteen

"What in the world do you think you're doing, Charli?" Ben watched me from outside the shed door.

Using the light of the lantern, I scanned the entire space of the other hut. The smell of fermenting mash and strong alcohol filled my nose. Careful not to disturb too much, I searched the place for random stuff lying around, picking up small objects to test them. A book of matches, an old newspaper...nothing possessed the right flavor.

"If you told me what you were looking for, maybe I could help you," Lee offered.

"You need to stay right where you are. You're in enough hot water as it is," Ben advised. His volume raised. "And someone else should really get out of there before she disturbs a potential crime scene."

"Crime scene?" protested Lee. A heated debate followed,

and I shut them out, spotting an item of interest on the floor.

An old red bandana lay scrunched up and trapped under a wooden crate, long forgotten. Picking it up, I willed my magic to test it. A brief image of the tall and mysterious wolf shifter appeared in my mind. "Gotcha." I crumpled it up and stuffed it in my pocket.

Stepping back into the night air, I hid my intentions. "Well, nothing obvious here to incriminate you, Lee. At least from what I could see." Not that I knew what might be there to be seen in the light of day.

Lee replaced the chain and lock around the door, and we walked through the woods. Once back at the cars, Ben convinced Lee to go with him to the warden station to establish his side of things first. Lavender insisted that Lily should accompany them for solidarity, flashing her cousin an insistent glare. Alison Kate looked torn, the keys to her car shaking in her hand.

"I can drive it if you want to go with him, Ali Kat. I'll drop off Lavender and Blythe first, and then park your car at your place." And with the use of her vehicle, I could confront the person whose face burned in my brain.

When I took the keys, Alison Kate thanked me and told me to drive it to her place in the morning. Ben helped Blythe get her bike into the trunk as she jumped in the front seat while Lavender climbed in the back seat.

Ben ran his fingers through his hair and blew out a breath. "Can't say I was prepared for things to go so sideways as soon as I returned to Honeysuckle."

I smirked. "Join the club. You think he'll be okay?"

"I don't know for sure. But I'll do my best to facilitate what I can tonight, and we'll go from there." He pulled me in for a quick hug. As he turned to head back to his car, he called out. "Oh, hey, Charli. I almost forgot that I need to talk to you. Can I come by your Nana's place tomorrow?"

"Sure." I furrowed my brow. "Why?"

He waved at me, eager to get in his car. "I'll fill you in in the morning."

We followed the tail lights of Ben's car back into town, slowing down to wave at them as they turned into the warden station. My nerves tightened again with worry for my friend, with curiosity if I'd found the key to solving Tipper's murder, and with burning questions for a wolf shifter.

Lavender yawned. "Not to diminish what Lee's gonna go through tonight, but I kind of hope that he and Ben figure out that they've got dates to the dance."

"I don't know why everyone's so concerned about pairing off." Blythe stared out the window.

"Right? I mean, there's nothing wrong with going with friends." I nudged her to get her out of the quiet mood settling over her.

Leaning forward, Lavender tapped me. "Oh, I don't know. I think you might be able to get not one but two dates."

I allowed myself the temporary distraction, my stomach twisting with hope and dread. She couldn't be right. But if she were, which would I prefer to ask me? Or maybe I shouldn't think about it since there were more important things to figure out. Like how to end the curse and give me a chance to find a date for next year's dance.

After dropping off Lavender, we drove in silence to Blythe's house. When we pulled up to it, I helped her struggle to get her bike out of the trunk.

"B, you've got to learn to drive, sweetie. You shouldn't have ridden all the way out there on your own," I scolded.

She rang the bike's bell. "It's got a light on it. Plus, me and mechanical things equal a lot of trouble. What do you expect me to do, ride a broom?"

"Do you think you on a flying object would be a good combo? I have no desire to scrape you off the ground like common road kill." My attempt at making her laugh failed.

Blythe gripped the handlebars and regarded me, her face souring. "I'd like to believe that everything's gonna turn out fine. But for the life of me, I can't pull that hope from anywhere." She dropped her bicycle and grabbed me around my neck, crushing me in tight. Her sobs racked both our bodies.

I patted her back, swallowing down the lump of sorrow rising in my throat. "Hey, you're the strong one out of all of us. You can't break."

She buried her face on my shoulder. "Frosted fairy wings, my best friend's got a curse that might kill her. You can't expect me to be stone." She backed away and wiped the back of her hand under her nose.

"Something named Doozy has no chance at taking me down." I summoned up all my strength to remain positive.

Blythe sniffed. "Doozy. Right. So what's our next move?"

I straightened. "Well, there's not much we can do for Lee tonight. He's got the rest of the gang there to help him, and I know that Ben will do what he can to keep things from getting bad. Best thing to do is for both of us to go to bed and get some sleep. And that's about as far ahead as I can plan."

Blythe narrowed her eyes. "So you're heading home?"

"Yes."

"Straight there?" She tipped her head in suspicion.

I hugged her and turned to the car. "Yes, Mom. I'm gonna head straight home." If there were no curves in the road on the way, then technically, I was telling the truth.

"We're gonna discuss more tomorrow." Her bike clicked as she walked it towards her house. "Night, Charli."

From the driver's seat, I made sure she made it inside okay. Peaches climbed out from underneath and jumped up beside me in the passenger seat.

"Buckle up, Peaches. This might get bumpy tonight." I pulled out the dirty bandana and held it tight in my hand.

It had never been easy for me to describe how my magic worked to those who didn't possess the same skills. I'd gotten called things like *bloodhound* or *divining rod* all my life. Dad liked to call it *Charli Bird doggin'*, but for the most part, I didn't have an official name for it. Those who I'd found in my travels for the past year had different terms. Tracker. Finder. Hunter. But they were not easy to locate because those who had talents to find things seemed to know the best ways to hide themselves.

Concentrating, I pushed magic to the fabric. "I want to find Dash."

A tingle buzzed inside me for a second, and an image of him flashed in my mind. But the connection fizzled when my arm throbbed. Stupid Doozy. This might take a little extra rhyme to focus me.

I took a deep breath and let it out slowly, giving my brain a chance to compose on the fly. "*Come on, bandana, I want to find Dash. But do me a favor and don't let me crash.*"

I switched the object to my left hand and tried again. A general sense that I should head straight in front of me tugged on me. Starting the car, I drove off down the road with slow deliberation. If I missed a turn, the direction of the connection jerked at me to turn around. Although I was stronger in finding objects rather than people, I managed to roll the car to a stop in front of a house isolated from other properties. A perfect place for someone who didn't want to be found.

I rolled down the window and checked out the house. Dark windows. Grass that needed mowing. No lawn decorations to personalize the place. The only mark of a tenant came from the music floating in the air and light streaming from a structure behind the house.

"Stay here, Peaches," I whispered.

She squeaked a defiant mew and followed me out my open door, her fuzzy behind circling my feet. I placed her back in the car again, but she zoomed past me and sat on her haunches in the middle of the driveway.

"Fine, but stay close," I commanded. She cocked her head and waited for me to follow her.

When I caught up with her, she turned and trotted toward the light, her tail swishing in the air. We rounded the back corner of the house and found the source of the glow streaming out of the open garage doors. Inside, a black, shiny motorcycle sat parked next to another one in pieces with parts strewn all about it. One that had a tank very similar to...

"Old Joe," I cried out.

"You suck at being a spy, you know," a gruff voice startled me from behind.

I straightened my back and turned to face him, ignoring the heat in my cheeks. "Wasn't trying to sneak up on you. I intended to come see you, Dash."

His left eyebrow quirked up. "Really? That sounds promising." He looked down at my feet, where Peaches jumped around, trying to swat a moth out of the air. "Looks like you brought me a snack."

I whipped my orange kitty into my arms. "Hey, don't talk about Peaches like that. She might take you seriously."

"She's named after fruit. Sounds like food to me."

"Talk about eating my precious girl one more time, and..." I looked around, trying to find something to threaten him with. I walked over to the pristine motorcycle. "And I'll kick your motorcycle."

A growl rumbled in his chest. "Touch my bike, and you might not make it out of here alive."

Peaches didn't take kindly to the threat. She clawed out of

my hold and worked her way to my shoulder. From under my hair, she poked her little orange head through and hissed at Dash.

The scary man smiled despite himself. "Feisty thing."

I narrowed my eyes at him. "Which one of us?"

"Both." He held up his hands in surrender. "So what can I help you with tonight? Did you come to help me fix that old wreck?" Dash pointed at Old Joe.

"I didn't even know you had it. Come to think of it, why do you?"

He walked over to survey all the pieces laid out on the floor of the garage. "Lee asked me to help him out with it. They don't work on bikes that often at his dad's place. If I can get it back in general mechanical working order, then those two can work on all the woo-woo magic stuff. Wanna beer?"

"What? No. Stop distracting me."

"Distracting you from what?" Dash took a long swig from his drink, and his muscles underneath his tank top flexed. When he finished the bottle, he licked his lips.

"Hmm?" There used to be a reason why standing in such close proximity to the beast of a man had been a good idea. A flirty Dash was a distraction I couldn't afford.

"Why. Are. You. Here. Charli?" He waved his hand in front of my face.

"Ow, you little tiger." Tiny kitten claws dug into my skin, bringing me back to the here and now. "Oh, right." I set Peaches down. "I wanted to ask you some questions."

He frowned. "Like what?"

"Like, how long have you lived in Honeysuckle?"

"Long enough."

I did the math from my absence. "It's been at least a year or less. And where were you before you came here?"

His flirtatious nature evaporated. He squared off with me. "In different places."

Secrets, secrets, and more secrets. His evasiveness meant he still didn't trust me, and I needed at least a kernel of faith in me to complete tonight's mission. But that might take time, and we didn't have much of that.

"How long have you been in the moonshine business?"

The atmosphere around us changed in a split second. The grumpy, standoffish Dash returned. "Why do you care?"

"Answer my question." I pushed. "How long have you and Lee had your set up?"

"For about six months. And again, why do you care?"

"I have my reasons." I rubbed my arm. "How did the two of you become partners?"

He frowned. "You make it sound like some sort of formal business thing. I overheard him talking about his grandfather's moonshine one night at Lucky's bar."

"The Rainbow's End."

"Is there another bar in town?" he sneered.

"Less sarcasm and more explanation, please." I crossed my arms.

He mimicked my stance, not backing down. "When he left the bar, I approached him about starting it all back up again. I have some connections on the outside that pay good money for the stuff."

"Legal connections?"

His eyes flashed, and he spit on the ground. "I'm not answering anything else until you tell me why it matters to you."

Unable to come up with a quick explanation that didn't give too much away, I stammered. "Be-because."

He stepped forward, closing the distance between us. "That's not an answer." Another inch closer.

"It's all I'm giving at the moment. So, did anyone other than you and Lee go out to the shed in the woods?" I swallowed hard as the air pressure around me thickened.

"How do you know about the shed?"

I chuckled. "Because I grew up here. Everyone knew about it. Didn't Lee tell you anything?"

Dash's face grew thoughtful. "He's told me some. But I don't ask a whole lot of questions. Unlike some. And to answer your last one, just me, Lee, and occasionally Tipper were in that place. Only Lee and I have a key to get in."

He confirmed Lee's information, which was both good and bad. It meant that he'd probably told me the truth. But it also had a substantial consequence.

Time to take a chance. "Listen, you could be in real trouble. I need you to come down to the warden station with me. Now."

At the mere mention of the word *warden*, he snarled at me. "What are you talking about?"

"Lee is down there right now telling them what he knows. You need to get ahead of this before it becomes a bigger problem."

Before I could say anything more, he picked up a wrench from the floor and flung it against the wall. The alarming crash and loud swearing scared Peaches, who scurried back to me. I picked her up and protected her from his wrath.

"The night that Tipper died. He'd been drinking," I called out over the cacophony he made while he threw things, flinching at every thunderous noise.

Dash stopped for a second. "So what?" His voice sounded more animal than human. He hid his face from me.

"It occurred to me that he'd offered to spike my drink. By using what he had in his flask. He poured the contents into his drink right in front of me."

Another enraged roar, and Dash proceeded to fling anything not nailed down into the walls. When he picked up the tank to Old Joe, I yelled at him to stop, but he ignored me in his rage. The crash of the beloved pieces of metal broke my heart. Maybe I should let this uncontrolled man fight his own battles.

He ran his hands down his face and growled with great force, "How could I be so stupid? Why didn't I see it?"

His whole frame shook with tension, and his back flexed with quick pants. Power crackled in the air close to him, and I backed out of the garage with unsteady steps.

Dash bowed his head in my direction, still hiding his face and clenching his fists. "You smell like fear. I swear, Charli, you don't have to be afraid of me. Ever." Although he sounded gruff, his words matched the man I'd been getting to know before.

"I'm not afraid." I didn't know which one of us needed convincing more. Despite his assurances, I still didn't trust the wolf in him. My feet widened the distance between us. "Listen, I didn't connect the dots, either. But the line from point A to B is clear enough that you've got to go to the station on your own. Talk to Mason and get ahead of things."

"So it's Mason and not Detective, is it?" he grunted.

"Detective Clairmont. Or my brother. But you've got to volunteer to go if you want to stay out of trouble."

"Trouble seems to find me, even when I do my best to stay away from it." He turned to confront me head on, his eyes a glowing amber and his fangs glistening. "I didn't kill him, Charli. I swear it. On my mother's grave."

Dash's sincerity shot through my heart like an arrow. "You don't have to convince me. Just the authorities."

He took a step in my direction, and I stumbled backward. Regret shadowed his face, and he closed his eyes. "You're the only one that matters."

Even Peaches seemed to take his side. She mewed and pawed the air in his direction. Against the advice in my head that I knew everybody would give me, I steadied myself and held out my free hand. "Come on. I'll go with you."

The squeal of wheels and a flood of lights interrupted us. Car doors slammed, and Mason ran around the corner followed by my brother and another two wardens.

The detective called out in a clear voice, "Dashiel Channing, you are under arrest by the authority of the wardens. Come out with your hands up."

The wolf shifter stalked out of the garage, his eyes flashing bright yellow and his muscles rippling underneath his skin. He stood in between the wardens and me, shielding me from them. A growl ripped through him. The man risked giving in to his animal.

I touched him on his shoulder, his skin burning like a fever. "Dash," I implored.

He slumped forward, fighting his shift with exerted grunts. Sweat dripped off him when he stood straight again. He turned one last time to glance at me, a deep sadness resting in his glowing amber eyes.

Without another word, he walked around Mason and offered himself to the others. My brother let the other wardens deal with Dash while he shot me a look that resembled the one that Dad used to give me before I got grounded. I'd be getting an earful sometime soon.

When they escorted Dash away, I took in a deep breath. Not quite the outcome I'd wanted. Not even close. I hit a button on the wall, closing the garage doors ducking underneath to head back to Alison Kate's car.

Rounding the corner of the house, I bumped into the tall frame of Detective Mason Clairmont.

"Charli, what do you think you were doing? I should arrest you right here on the spot."

Chapter Fifteen

P eaches squirmed in surprise and almost made it out
of my grip. Not wanting to lose her in the wilderness
around Dash's place, I struggled to keep her under
control.

"That's the second time in less than a week that someone's
threatened to arrest me." Hitching my arm over the kitten, I
held her in place.

"Yeah, well, maybe then I could keep better tabs on you
and make you stay out of trouble."

"I'm not a child. And you heard what Nana said. I have
every right to break Doozy on my own. After all, it's my life
on the line." Not willing to listen to a lecture from him, I
pushed past Mason down the driveway.

He followed after me. "That doesn't mean you take
unnecessary risks. And who the blazes is Doozy?"

"It's what we're calling the curse," I yelled back at him.

When I made it to Alison Kate's car, I opened the door and placed the kitten on the passenger seat. Turning the key over, I rolled the driver's window closed. With strict instructions for Peaches to stay put, I slid back out of the car, shutting the kitty inside and facing Mason.

"It doesn't matter what you call it because the curse *will* do its job unless we solve the case. And as far as I can tell, Dash is our best lead. But that doesn't explain why you would go and put yourself in harm's way by sharing the same space as an angry werewolf."

"Shifter," I corrected. "Why can't you get that right? What do you have against him?"

Clouds cleared away from the moon, and its light beamed down on Mason's disapproving countenance. "I have my reasons."

More secrets. My level of trust, especially in exasperating men, dropped a few more notches. "You said that when you thought you detected the curse on me that I could have been the killer. But you gave me the benefit of the doubt. And tonight, did you arrest Lee when he came into the station?"

The detective pursed his lips. "No. At least, not yet." he uttered.

"Why? Because he voluntarily came in? Or because he's a witch and not a shifter or vampire or anything else you hold a grudge against?" I held up my hand to keep Mason quiet. "I was here trying to encourage Dash to go to the station with me so he could add his information. But you and your cowboys came in guns blazing, and you arrested Dash."

"There weren't any actual guns." He avoided my stare. "Besides, how do you know he's not guilty? Because you think he's hot?"

In all my years, I'd only ever hit my brother. And that was because he's my older brother. But my fingers curled into fists at my side. "So that's all this was? It's some sort of pissing contest between the two of you?"

"No."

"Lie."

"Charli, it makes sense that Dash is involved. Tipper drank a lot. According to Lee, he had some moonshine, and you'd told him that he'd poured some in his drink that night with you."

His detective's brain didn't protect him from the anger boiling inside of me. "And you leaped from that info to Dash being guilty? What about Lee? No, that's just going down the wrong path. Here's the bigger question. What have you found out from Tipper's flask?"

Mason's mouth pursed. "Not much. I'm still waiting on my favor."

I threw my hands up in the air in exasperation. "Exactly."

"What does that mean?"

My groan echoed in the still air. "It means that we don't know squat yet other than some suspicions. And I've given you the best leads so far. Test all the moonshine left to see if there's anything in it that could have killed Tipper. Also, maybe my uncle wasn't the only one to touch the flask? Maybe someone else laced it with something? Frosted fairy wings, you're supposed to be the detective here." I drew in a slow breath.

Mason stepped closer to me. "Exactly. It's supposed to be *my* job to approach a dangerous suspect. Not. Yours."

I shook my head. "Dash isn't dangerous."

"How would you know? Have you ever been around an angry were—"

"Don't you say it."

"Fine. Shifter." He grabbed me by my shoulders, his fingers digging into my skin. "You have no idea, do you? That there are some beings out there that cannot control what they become and what they do to others."

"Mason," I complained.

"And what if something *had* happened? How would that have helped? How would it have affected everyone around you? Your grandmother. Your brother. Haven't they lost enough?" His breath panted on my face.

I stared at him, scared to answer. He blinked at me, a sudden awareness waking him up. With a sigh, he loosened his grip but didn't let me go.

"I've been through it. Lost someone that I cared about," he said.

"To a werewolf," I finished.

He nodded and swallowed hard. "I was still a warden at the time, not a detective. By the time I made it to the scene, there was hardly anything left to identify her. But I knew."

My brain itched to ask him who his *her* was. But I gave him the space to share what he wanted.

Mason released me from his hold. "He could have hurt you, Charli, and no one would have been here to stop him."

"He wouldn't hurt me. I know he wouldn't. He promised," I uttered in a quieter voice.

Mason's shoulders slumped. "Yeah, well, sometimes we make promises we can't keep." Grief and anguish rolled off of him in waves.

My frustration waned just a fraction. "I appreciate your concern, Mason. I do. But I've been taking care of myself for a while now. I somehow managed an entire year all on my own. Doesn't that count for something?"

"And how's that working for you now? As soon as you return, you get cursed. And no, I won't call it anything other than what it is. A death curse, Charli. Do you get it? Death. This isn't a game."

Anger rose inside me for a second time. "Yeah, I'm living as best I can with it. Do you expect me to do nothing when my own life—"

"I expect you to live!" His voice echoed in the night air.

The tension between us buzzed like bees. He wanted me safe, and I wanted a say in how my life would be lived for however long I had left.

Taking a deep breath, I rolled my shoulders back. "I want to live, too. But not tucked away somewhere hidden from the world. I have to actually *live* my life for it be a life."

Mason took a step away and rubbed the back of his head. "That's not what I meant. I'm not good at this."

"At what?"

He gestured his fingers between the two of us. "This. Talking. Making sense."

"You do." I sighed. "And I could do a better job at not jumping into the deep end first. Maybe just the waist-deep water."

The moon lit up his small grin. "There's probably no chance I can convince you to stay out of the water altogether, is there?"

I lifted my eyebrow at him, unsure if he could see it in the dim moonlight. "About as likely as me not drinkin' sweet tea on a hot summer's day."

He lifted his hand, and my breath caught in anticipation of his touch. Instead of cupping my cheek, he brushed a strand of hair behind my ear. "Aw, Charli. What am I gonna do about you?"

I closed my eyes, willing my body to stop trembling from all the extra adrenaline coursing through my veins. Just adrenaline. Nothing more.

"Do your job. Help me solve Tipper's murder and end the curse." I rubbed my arm where it throbbed again and ventured to look at him.

"Don't you mean Doozy?" Mason's attempt at a joke broke the tension between us. "We need to get you home. You want me to follow you while you return that car and then take you home?"

What I needed was some distance between frustrating men and me. "No, I'll take care of it in the morning."

A wall descended between the two of us as I walked back

to Alison Kate's car. Mason waited for me to get inside and closed the door for me. He tapped on the window, and I rolled it down.

"Get some rest. That's an order."

With a bang on the top of the car, he dismissed me. His headlights followed me back down the road but turned in the opposite direction toward the station.

Peaches stretched on the passenger seat next to me and climbed into my lap. She turned in a circle a few times and settled down.

I scratched her little head. "I'm exhausted, too, Little Peach. Let's get some shut-eye tonight and see what tomorrow brings us."

Chapter Sixteen

When I made my way down to eat in the morning, I almost tripped over an orange and grey mass of tangled kitty cats asleep on the small carpet at the foot of the stairs. My new kitten's charms worked on more than just me. Maybe she'd be the surprise cure to no more bitten ankles.

Nana poured a mix of coffee and her newest concoction to keep the curse as dormant as possible into my mug. It looked more like mud, but I'd take any help I could get. Taking a sip of the mixture, I did my best to keep the foul-tasting sludge down.

My brother stormed into the house, calling out from the foyer. "Birdy, I'm gonna kill you."

"Get in line," I snarked back. "And what for?"

Matt joined us in the dining room, and Nana disappeared into the kitchen to, no doubt, fix the jerk a plate of food.

"What were you doing out at Dash's place last night by yourself? Are you stupid or what?" He sat down in the chair next to mine and leaned in.

"I was trying to convince him to go to the warden's station, if you must be all nosy about it. Would have gotten him to do it if you hadn't ruined my efforts."

Nana returned with a loaded plate and cup of coffee for my brother. "What's this about Dash?"

We both yelled our version of the story at the same time, and Nana's eyes flitted back and forth between us. She waited until we finished, fingers pointing at each other, narrowed eyes glaring.

She crossed her arms with a sniff. "Best I can tell, you're mad at your brother for being worried about you because you put yourself in harm's way with Dash. And he's not entirely wrong. A shifter can be a might dangerous if he or she is not in control. It's the human side that keeps the animal in check. You know as well as I do that the animal side is wild."

"See," Matt said. I waited for him to stick his tongue out at me like he was ten years old or something.

"And you, young man. You should have more trust in your sister to judge a person's character. Sure, I know that Dash is a relatively new addition to our town. But he's here and under its protection. If her gut tells her she was safe, then I would say that speaks volumes to who he is deep down inside. Now. You two. Make up with each other." She smacked us both upside our heads and walked back to the kitchen.

Matt picked up a piece of bacon and stuffed it in his mouth. "Sorry," he mumbled while chewing.

I cupped my ear. "What was that?"

"I said I was sorry," he enunciated. "But you can't be too mad at me, Birdy. I mean, you're already dealing with the curse and everything. If I lose you..."

My heart softened, and I grabbed his hand. "I know. I get it. I'm sorry, too." To show him how much I loved him, I stole a piece of bacon from his plate.

"Thief," he accused with a grin.

A knock on the door interrupted our moment. "That better not be Mason here to yell at me again. I got enough of that last night. And this morning."

"Can't be him. He's gone," said Matt.

I stopped in my tracks. "What do you mean gone? Gone where?"

Matt shrugged. "I don't know. He left a message at the station that he needed to go somewhere to retrieve something and would be back as soon as possible."

He must be picking up whatever favor he called in. Still, it unsettled me that he left in such a hurry. The fact that he took off without saying anything to me probably meant he was still mad at me. Pixie poop.

Ben waved at me from the other side of the screen door when I went to answer the knock. He held a small box in his other hand.

"Mornin', Charli."

I beamed at my friend. "I completely forgot you wanted to

stop by. Come on in."

"Did I just hear Bennett Raynor?" Nana called out before making her way to the foyer. "You handsome devil, get your behind in here and give me some sugar."

Ben pulled open the squeaky screen door and joined us. "Hey, Ms. Vivi." He kissed her cheek and wrapped her up in a tight hug.

"Boy, I think you've grown." My grandmother took a good gander at my friend. "Seems to me you've turned into a right good lookin' young man. Wouldn't you agree, Charli?"

"Yes, ma'am." She wasn't wrong, but she *was* barking up the wrong tree. Ben occupied the same space of love in my heart that I possessed for Matt. My friend might be handsome, but thinking of him in a romantic way made me grimace.

"Whatcha got there in your hand?" Nana asked.

Ben cleared his throat. "Well, that's one of the reasons why I'm here. While I'm in town, I'm helping Jedidiah Farnsworth get organized."

"Such a nice boy, helping out Old Jed with his practice." Nana beamed at my old friend. "I heard tell that he was thinking of retiring after all these years."

Ben nodded. "He is."

"You considering taking his place?" Barely contained glee rolled off my grandmother.

"It's a possibility." His eyes turned wistful, and I'd give anything to tell what he was thinking about. Or *who* he was thinking about. Maybe Lily would get her girlhood wish after all. "Why don't we go have a seat so I can fill you in on a couple of things."

Despite his protests, Nana set a place for him and brought in a plate of ham and jelly biscuits. He took one to be polite but didn't eat it.

Placing the box on the table, he slid it in Nana's direction. "This is for you. I think you know what it is."

My grandmother stared at the box. "Tipper's treasure. I was gonna go into town and ask Jed if he'd left anything. This year's founding ceremony is gonna be interesting to navigate."

Matt stared at the box. "You gonna open it?"

"It's tempting, but no," declared Nana with a gasp. "All the founding members choose an item that has both personal worth and is a sacrifice to give. If Tipper were here, I might ask his permission. But it feels wrong to open it without him. How'd you come by it, Ben?"

My friend folded his hands in front of him on the table. "I'm trying to gather everything for Tipper's estate together. I found a package in Jed's office that had been recently delivered there. Inside, there was a note with strict instructions to give the box to you."

"Tipper sent his advocate instructions of what to do in case he died?" I asked. The enormity of my great-uncle's paranoia bloomed in front of me.

Ben nodded. "Looks like it. I've verified the handwriting against some other papers we already had on file." He looked around at the three of us. "And that means there's also another problem that's come to light."

Nana got up from the table. "This doesn't sound good. Let me get some more food and coffee to bolster my spirits."

Taking advantage of our grandmother's absence, my brother and I got down to business.

"Did *you* open the box?" Matt asked.

Ben shook his head. "I was tempted to, but I'm a professional as well as a little superstitious. Remember those stories we were told growing up about what would happen if any of the sacrificed treasures were messed with? Like I want to walk around with the head of a donkey on my shoulders."

"That's from Shakespeare, you dope," I teased. "And besides, it's not about what happens to the person who steals the treasure that's important. It's what will happen to Honeysuckle. Remember Mrs. Kettlefields and her dramatic warnings?"

Matt stood up, hunched over like old Mrs. K, and shook his finger at us. "The skies will darken. The waters will rise. And the tree of life will perish," he croaked in imitation of her shaky voice.

Nana joined us. "That old witch had no business teaching history to you children."

"Come on, Nana, tell us," I cajoled. "What would happen if one of the founding member representatives didn't bury a treasure?"

My grandmother touched the box in front of her. "We haven't had to test that theory yet, and I have no intention of trying. So, let's leave it."

"What are you using this year?" asked Matt.

"That's something I was gonna talk to the two of you about," she said in a soft voice.

"Do you want me to leave?" offered Ben.

She touched his arm. "Of course not. I know I can trust you as a close friend of the family and as a professional advocate."

Our friend blushed under the immense trust Nana placed in him. "Honored," he muttered, tipping his head at her.

"I was thinking of sacrificing your dad and mom's rings. If that's okay with the two of you." Nana's eyes searched ours.

"Their wedding rings?" clarified Matt.

She nodded. "I know that means neither of you will get to wear them. I've been selfish and keeping them in my jewelry box, although I guess I should have offered your dad's band to you, Matthew."

My brother fingered the band already on his finger. "I'm good with the one I have. TJ special ordered our bands so that they match."

"And what about you?" Nana looked at me for permission.

I'd always thought it would be nice to wear Mom's ring if I ever settled down. She'd never wanted a separate engagement ring, so Dad had gotten her a band with small diamonds encrusted in it. When I was engaged to Tucker, I was supposed to wear a gaudy family heirloom of the Hawthorne's, which broke my heart. Clementine could wear it for the rest of her life, for all I cared.

"I think it would mean more if I had someone who wanted to marry me first." I tried to joke to ignore the weight of sadness when remembering my parents. "But Nana, I thought the family tradition was to sacrifice something that represented knowledge?"

My grandmother looked at me in confusion. "What do you mean?"

"Blame old Mrs. Kettlefields again. She said that the first treasure that sealed the pact and created the town was a valuable piece of jewelry from the Hawthorne descendant. That represented wealth or good fortune. The Walker descendant sacrificed a pink ribbon from her deceased daughter that she carried with her always to represent the heart of things. And the Goodwin descendant buried a valuable book of some sort to represent knowledge."

"Y-e-s," dragged out Nana. "That's true. To an extent. And then all of the gifts from each year are known within the families or are passed down to the next family member who takes the place on the council. But it's absolute hogwash that the chosen items have to represent specifically wealth, heart, or knowledge. That old witch had a few too many bats loose in her noggin'."

"Who's going to take Tipper's role in this year's ceremony?" Matt asked the crucial question I'm sure most of Honeysuckle gossiped about.

"Probably Aunt Nora." I couldn't hold back an eye roll of disgust.

Ben cleared his throat. "That actually brings us back to why I came here this morning. Leonora Walker has started some procedures that will affect the ceremony. She's demanding to be instated in the Walker council seat as soon as possible."

"Over my dead body," I declared, then winced when I saw the looks of fear in my family's eyes. "I mean, nothing could be worse than *her* on the council."

"But it's a smart play on her part," mused Nana. "If she takes Tipper's role in the ceremony, then it will solidify her as the heir apparent. And I am not ready to make that an official decision yet, no matter how much pressure I'm getting."

"That's not all. Your aunt's also on the verge of invoking the *heredis intestatus* clause." Ben looked to my grandmother apologetically.

Nana leaned back in her chair. "That's clever. A little too clever. No way that empty-headed fool thought of that on her own."

Matt crossed his arms. "Any chance you two wanna share what that means?"

Ben sat up straighter in his chair. "In advocate terms, she is challenging magical and human laws to proclaim that all of Tipper's possessions will be passed on to her with immediacy. The procedure was created in medieval Europe by the last descendant of Cornelius the Mage upon his untimely passing. Without a will in place, all of his possessions, including very valuable magical objects and grimoires, could have been claimed by those unworthy or even those who would seek to destroy them."

"So it's a legal form of stealing?" I asked.

Ben shook his head. "Not necessarily. The person who

invokes it must be a proven relative that has a clear and proven path to being the next descendant."

"Which could have been Mom," Matt uttered.

"But now it's just Aunt Nora." The chair underneath me squeaked and groaned as I slunk back into it. "You're right, Nana. She didn't come up with this herself. I'll bet Hollis Hawthorne is involved since I'd guess that he's one of the ones that's pressuring you to make a quick decision about the council. Or maybe not." The memory of Aunt Nora with Ashton Sharpe in the park replayed in my mind, and I wondered if he were the type of person to come up with a strategy like this.

Matt waved his hands in front of him. "Hang on. I may be a bit slow here, but all of this doesn't matter. Nora can only invoke the hereditary clause thing if there's no will. You've got Tipper's will, right Ben?"

My friend's silence spoke a little too loud.

"Holy unicorn horns. Have you searched all the files in the office?" I asked.

"I have, but I found nothing but older versions. In Tipper's note with the box, he specified details about a new will that he and Jed had created very recently," Ben stated. "And Jed's out right now."

Nana slammed her hands on the table. "Where is that old fool?"

"He's off on a fishing trip with Wayne and a few others. They're supposed to be back the night of the pig pickin' and tree ceremony. And I can't hold off Nora. If she wants to invoke, I can't prevent her."

My mind raced to put all the pieces of the puzzle together. "So if we want to stop her for the time being, we need to find this new will Tipper wrote about."

"If it exists," Matt added.

"How much time do we have, Ben?" I asked. "It can't go through the advocate system in an instant. We should have the opportunity to challenge her, right?"

"This is old law, meant to ultimately pass on familial power in whatever form. Any delay was seen as a threat to that power, so that means when she does invoke it officially—"

"Everything goes to her," I finished. "The house, the land, who knows what else. But if that's the case, why is she waiting?"

Matt snapped his fingers. "Because she's worried that there *is* a will out there that would negate it all." He looked at me with enthusiasm. "You know what this means."

I fist bumped him. "Time to go *bird doggin'*." The chair scraped on the floor as I stood up from the table.

"Hold on," interrupted Nana. "Exactly what is the plan?"

Matt tipped his head at me with confidence. "To let her do her thing. If anyone can find something, it's our Charli Bird." He got up from the table as well.

"We should start at Tipper's house," I suggested.

"But it's under warden protection," countered Matt.

I knocked him upside the head. "And what are you? Duh."

"But it won't be an official investigation. I could get into a lot of trouble."

"Since when did you become such a scaredy witch? Come on, what's more important? Following the rules or bending them a teeny tiny little bit for us to try and save the day?"

Nana spoke in a low voice. "What if you using your magic affects the curse?"

Her words cut into my excitement. She didn't have to elaborate because the same worry kept me up at night, too. But I couldn't stay at home and risk losing.

"Don't worry about Doozy. This won't be a hard task. And who's the best at finding things?" I batted my eyes, trying to cheer her up. Taking a dutiful sip of the mixture in my cup, I did my best to keep the foul-tasting sludge down.

"You are," she admitted. "Although right now, I'd give anything that you weren't so I could keep you right here with me." She pushed away from the table and approached, wrapping me in a close embrace. She felt like warmth, love, and home all at once.

"Use the rings for the ceremony, Nana. Mom and Dad would love that." I sniffed to keep from snotting on her. "I think we've all learned a lot from missing them."

She patted my back. "Thank you, sweet girl. You be safe. And you." She pulled my brother into the massive hug. "You watch out for your sister."

"I always do," Matt mumbled against her head. He ruffled my hair in confirmation, and I batted his hand away.

On the porch, we told Ben that if we found anything, we'd bring it to him immediately. If we didn't, we'd stop by his office to let me search there as a backup. Taking Alison Kate's car, he drove off.

Nana stood in the doorway waving at us, her smile unable to hide her worry. "Do me a favor. Try *not* to use your gifts, Charli."

"But Nana," I whined.

She held up her hand to stop me. "Think about how many glasses of my cure you *won't* have to drink."

"She has a good point," Matt said.

"She plays dirty," I grumbled as we walked down the porch stairs. Waving at her, I got in the car beside my brother. "So, we have a missing will to find."

"On top of a murder to solve," he added.

"And a curse to stop."

Matt blew out a breath and gripped the steering wheel. "You sure you're up to this?"

I shrugged. "What's the alternative? I told Mason last night I couldn't just stay locked away safe somewhere and not try to help."

"I understand." Matt avoided my gaze. "I don't like it, but I get it. When Mom got sick, she used to tell us to live each day to the fullest because—"

"You never know what day might be the last," I finished.

He took my hand in his and squeezed it three times. Dad's silent signature way to say *I love you.*

I squeezed him right back. "Let's do this."

Chapter Seventeen

"If Big Willie found out I was here right now, I might lose my job," Matt said, releasing the warden's protection with a flourish of his hand and unlocking the door to Tipper's house.

The thick wood creaked open, flooding the darkened house with sunlight. The breeze from outside stirred the dust particles floating in the stagnant air.

The size of the house used to delight me as a child. So many places to explore. Antiques and dark wood furniture lined walls and decorated rooms covered with a fine layer of grime. The sheer number of hiding places that a man like my great-uncle might use could be endless.

Matt shut the door behind us. "We need to stay as stealthy as possible." He spellcast a simple ball of light. The eerie glow cast strange shadows.

"Where exactly are we supposed to start?" I sneezed and wiped my nose.

"I don't know," said Matt. "Maybe an old desk somewhere or a drawer?"

The downstairs foyer we stood in had at least five potential starting points packed in the small space. One look to either side of me into other rooms unveiled the vast undertaking we had before us.

Hope drained out of me. "It could take us an entire year if we search every nook and cranny."

"What choice do we have?" Matt directed the light ball around him.

I lifted my eyebrows, pointed at my chest, and rubbed my hands together in anticipation.

"No. No way," he whispered. "Nana was very clear about the potential consequences."

"Why are you whispering? She can't hear you." My louder tone echoed in the empty house. "If I can tap into my magic just a little, it might save us a lot of time."

"Or it might affect the curse."

"We don't know that," I countered.

"I'm not willing to risk it. Not your life, and definitely not Nana's anger. Stick to the plan and let's search on our own. I'll take the downstairs, you take the upstairs." My brother shook his head when I attempted another protest.

I gazed up into the darkened hallway of the second floor. "Oh great. There's no telling what he has in all those bedrooms up there."

Matt nudged my shoulder. "When I'm finished down here, I'll help you upstairs," he promised.

"And how am I supposed to see?" I pointed at his light ball.

His eyebrows furrowed as he debated with himself. With a click of his tongue and a sigh, he gave in. "Fine. But just a small one. Don't burn up any more of your magic than you have to."

"Yes, Mom," I mouthed at him.

Finding the creak of each wooden step, I climbed the stairway. The afternoon sun filtered through the drawn curtains of the house, but not enough to help me see clearly. However, why waste my magic on a ball of light when I could find the will myself?

Drawing a tiny bit of energy from inside and palming a button I'd snatched from a bowl on a table near the front door, I prepared myself and concentrated.

After a few seconds, I concocted my rhymes. *"Help me lock away this curse before it manages to get worse. Let me access all my skill and find the path to Tipper's will."*

The tiny effort drained me faster than I'd anticipated, and I doubled over in pain. I sunk to the floor of the hallway. Squeezing my eyes shut, I bit my forefinger to keep myself from moaning. We had enough to deal with without my brother dragging me back home and putting me under house arrest. And I would endure anything to find that will and stop Aunt Nora from her little power-hungry trip.

Afraid Matt could finish patrolling downstairs any second

now, I pushed up off the floor and made it to my feet, the world tilting a tiny bit. I braced myself against the wall, allowing my eyes to adjust to the dim level of light and taking a few seconds to recover.

A rustling sound followed by a crash startled me, and I stood stock still. Crawling against the wall, I slunk toward the noise. My heart jumped at another dull thump and groan.

"Frosted fairy wings," uttered a wheezy male voice. One that I'd heard before.

Rounding the corner and staring into the room, I spotted the culprit. "Beauregard Pepperpot," I exclaimed.

The elderly vampire I recognized from the re-enactment play gasped in surprise and transformed into a tiny but plump bat fluttering in the air in wobbly circles. With another poof, the bat turned back into a petrified Beauregard.

"You startled me, Miss Charli." He clutched his chest over his non-beating heart.

"I startled you? What are you doing here?" I hissed at him.

My brother bounded up the stairs and crashed into the room, pushing me aside. "Stop, under command of the wardens." Power pulsed at the end of his hand.

Beauregard's wrinkled face drooped, and he lifted his hands. "I wasn't doing anything bad, I promise," he said in a voice dripping with pity.

"What are you doing here?" my brother demanded.

"I already asked him that," I said.

"Has he answered?"

"No."

"Then he needs to answer the question."

"He would if you would just shut up," I insisted.

The vampire's eyes bounced between the two of us squabbling, and he kept his hands in the air. He waited until Matt and I stopped bickering. Clearing his throat, he proclaimed, "I live here."

"But this house has been warded off from anybody else entering. How are you here?" Matt asked.

"Because I *live* here," Beauregard insisted.

My brother lowered his hand and placed it on his hip. "You mean you broke in? You're squatting? What?"

The vampire continued to stand with his hands in the air, confused.

"Put your hands down," I demanded.

"Hey, that's my job to say," complained Matt.

I waved my brother off. "What do you mean you live here, Mr. Pepperpot?

"Call me Beau, please." He shrugged. "I've been living in one of the extra rooms for ages now. I don't know. I guess that Tipper took pity on me or something. At least that's what he always told me."

"So this is his current residence. Is that why the protective ward doesn't work on him?" I asked my brother.

The puzzled expression on Matt's face didn't reassure me. "I guess. Maybe. I'm still stuck on why you were living with Uncle Tipper."

A slight smile revealed Beau's fangs. "Because he was my best friend. But...I think it was more than that."

"Like what?" interrogated Matt in a calmer tone.

Beau glanced down at the floor. "I think he was lonely."

Guilt rose in my chest and squeezed my heart. My great-uncle and I had a relationship different from anyone else in the family or even in Honeysuckle. He had doted on my mother with all his heart, and perhaps he thought of me in much the same way. Like Matt and Nana, I had abandoned him, too.

A quick glance around the room revealed no bed or anything that made it look lived in. Stacks of old newspapers, old broken furniture, and things one might find that yard sales cluttered the space.

"If you live here, then why does it look like you don't?" I asked.

"Oh, I don't stay in this room," Beau explained.

Suspicion rose in Matt's eyes. "Then what are you doing in here?"

A sheepish shadow crossed Beau's face. "Cleaning?"

I shook my head. "Try again."

His eyes darted to the wooden drawers on the floor, the contents from inside scattered about. "Doing some restoration?" he offered.

"Beau," I insisted.

The vampire gave up. "Fine. I was trying to find something."

"Of yours?" clarified Matt.

"Yes?" The vampire attempted. His face dropped again

under my brother's stern stare. "No," he admitted. "I imagine I'm looking for the same thing that brought you here."

I narrowed my eyes at the pudgy vampire. "You mean, you're looking for Tipper's will, too?"

"Charli," barked Matt.

"We're running out of time to beat around the bush. And if he's already done some of the legwork for us, then what does it matter? It'll be the talk of the whole town if it isn't already. You can't keep something like a lost will a secret for long."

"It's not lost. Tipper told me where it is," exclaimed Beau.

"What? Where?" my brother and I shouted at the same time.

The vampire grimaced and scratched his head. "That's the problem. I don't rightly remember."

I clenched my hands to keep myself from strangling the kindly but doddering old fool. "Think. Hard."

"I-I-I have been," Beau stammered. "It's all I can think about. Where Tipper told me he hid it. But my mind isn't what it used to be. I'm over three hundred years old, you know. And after losing him, I'm having more trouble concentrating."

My brother stormed toward the vampire, but I stopped him. Anger and insistence wouldn't pull the information out of Beau's sieve of a brain. We needed honey to get the flies.

"I miss Uncle Tip, too, Mr. Beau. But it's very important that we find the will. We're not the only ones looking for it, and the sooner we find it, the better," I crooned in a soothing tone.

The vampire offered me a sad smile. "He always talked about you. Was real proud you took off on your own. Said you reminded him of his favorite sunshine."

The mention of Tipper's nickname for our mother softened Matt. "So, how much of the house have you searched?"

"All of the downstairs. Including inside the kitchen cabinets and the oven, which I know doesn't make sense." He chuckled and covered his mouth in shock at the jovial outburst.

Beckoning us closer with a crook of his finger, he leaned in and spoke in a dramatically hushed tone. "I was supposed to go to you if I couldn't find it. But I tried my best to remember where it was on my own. And then he up and died, and I got busy putting on the play in his honor. Now Tipper's no longer here. I miss him." His voice became squeakier by the second, and by the sounds of his sniffs, the poor old vampire was crying.

Matt mumbled under his breath in frustration, but I put my arms around Beau. I let Tipper's friend purge himself in weeping sobs on my shoulder and patted his back, uttering reassurances. What would happen to him if Aunt Nora got her hands on the house and all of my great-uncle's property? No doubt Beau would be out on his own in no time flat.

Once the sobs turned into light whimpers, I ventured

more questions. "How many of the bedrooms have you searched?"

Beau took out a hankie from his pocket and blew his nose. He opened his mouth and pointed at the drawers, but a loud creaking of the front door interrupted him. All three of us cringed.

I shot a glance at Matt. "Pixie poop. Who could that be?"

My brother frowned. "I don't know. It could be another warden here to check on the place, although I'm not aware of any patrols scheduled for today." He put his finger to his lips and maneuvered to the door to listen.

With a high-pitched squeak and a quiet poof, Beau turned into a bat again and flew into the open wardrobe, hanging himself upside down on the clothes rail.

As I closed the door to the piece of furniture, I whispered to him, "I'll let you back out when this is all over." I hoped he understood that I meant when the intruders were gone, not when we found Tipper's will or figured out his murder.

Joining Matt next to the door, I strained to hear the voices. My rapid heartbeat thrummed so loud in my ear that at first, it was hard to identify anything. But as whoever it was advanced toward the stairway, their voice echoed up.

"I thought it would be harder to get inside. Isn't there supposed to be some sort of warden protection in places?" asked a female voice. "Of course, I'm not surprised that a small town operation like we have here could screw up something like that."

Matt and I exchanged glances. "Aunt Nora," we mouthed at each other at the same time.

"I don't know. But we can't take too long. I'm not sure I agree with the plan," a deep male voice countered. One that I had intimately known at one point.

"That can't be..." Matt whispered.

I held up my finger to my lips, wanting more confirmation before I stormed down there and confronted my ex-fiancé.

"That will is the one thing that stands between you and your development. Once I take the seat on the council, you'll have the votes of me and your father on your side," admonished my aunt as if she spoke to a child.

"You'll probably get the seat regardless. Why do you need to find his will?" asked Tucker.

"Because what's the Walker seat on the council without the Walker property that goes with it? And what if meddling old Vivian Goodwin attempts to put her grandson on the council? He may be my sister's son, but that does *not* make him a Walker. He's a Goodwin through and through, and then what power will you and your family wield in this town?"

Anger boiled in my veins, and Matt's muscles tensed like a cat ready to pounce. I kept a hand on him to keep him steady.

We heard the sound of a drawer being pulled open. "There are too many places the old fool could have hidden it. This is a flawed plan," said Tucker.

"Keep searching," my aunt hissed. Something like glass shattered on the floor. "And try to be more careful. I figured you'd be more enthusiastic. You need access to his property in the long run. Think of it as poetic justice, that you could get some of the land back into the Hawthorne name. That could be the legacy you leave your family."

"Father would like that," admitted Tucker.

Aunt Nora continued. "We've got to find that will and destroy it so that I can invoke that witch clause thing."

Tucker's voice rose in volume. "But what about Charli and her family? Don't they deserve to know if Tipper bequeathed them anything?"

I listened, stunned at my ex's concern. My disappointment in him wavered for a brief second.

"Don't mention her to me again." The chilly vitriol that dripped off her voice could freeze a lake of lava. "You are marrying *my* daughter, bringing the bloodlines of the Walkers and Hawthornes together. Besides, she was never one of the family. She was a stray that my sister and her husband took in."

"That's it," gritted Matt. He emerged from the room. "Who goes there?"

Our aunt squawked. "Matthew. You scared the devil out of me."

"As if," I muttered, scooting part way into the hall so I could hear but stay out of sight.

"What are you doing here?" Her voice had melted into sugary sweetness.

"I think the same could be asked of you, Aunt Nora. What business do you have here?" my brother clipped.

"Don't take such an impertinent tone with me, young

man. I have more right to be here than you. After all, I'm his surviving niece. This house is practically mine," she huffed.

I crawled to the edge of the banister and looked down. Matt stood at the bottom of the stairs, standing up straight with authority. Aunt Nora's nose pointed in the air like usual while Tucker stood off to the side, guilt shrouding his entire demeanor.

Matt shooed them toward the door. "This house is under the protection of the wardens for now," he explained. "It's still part of the investigation."

"Is that why you're here, Matt?" asked Tucker.

"Of course," my brother bluffed. "It's my job to check on the property to make sure nothing has been handled or messed with. I'll report that a small vase was broken when I searched the house. How does that sound?" He ushered them onto the porch.

"What would we do without conscientious wardens like yourself, Matthew," purred our aunt. "Come, Tucker."

"Thanks, Aunt Nora. You take care now." My brother stood in the open doorway for a while.

After an interminable wait, he closed the door again and rushed upstairs to find me prostrate on the floor. "I thought I told you to stay put."

"Like I ever listen to you." Pushing myself up, I dusted off as best I could.

"We need to get out of here," Matt insisted. "No telling if they're watching the house or what they'll do. I don't think I was all that convincing."

I started to make my way downstairs before I remembered. Running back to the room, I opened the door to the wardrobe. Beau flew out in a rush and hit the wall with a dull clunk. He poofed back into himself before his little bat body landed on the floor.

Wringing his hands in concern, he rocked back and forth on his feet. "Who was it? Was it that angry guy again?"

"What angry guy? It was Tucker Hawthorne. Is that who you mean?" asked Matt.

"Or do you mean someone else?" I followed up.

Beau glanced back and forth at us, becoming more and more agitated. "I don't know."

Matt rubbed his forehead. "That's a problem. Because now it seems there might have been multiple breaches of the warden's protection, which is something we need to know about if we're going to fix that."

"Focus," I reminded him.

"Right. Not the time. Beau here got inside because he was already living here."

"Not through the doors," offered Beau.

I stared at him, puzzled. "Then how?"

His fangs grinned at us. "Flew down the chimney."

Matt blinked. "That's a new one."

"Then how did Tucker or whoever else it was get inside?" I asked.

"Perhaps there's some other way to get in here," surmised my brother. "Which is more worrisome. I think I'd better report this to the warden station."

I grabbed his arm. "No, don't."

"That's not your call, Charli."

"Think about it carefully," I insisted. "If you tell the wardens, then more people will suspect that the will is somewhere here at the house. If one person can break the ward, then chances are there are other ways. Do you want all of Honeysuckle ransacking Uncle Tipper's place?"

My brother pondered my logic. "You have a point."

"Sometimes I do, you know."

He nodded in resignation. "Fine. I won't report anything. For now. Mr. Pepperpot, as much as I appreciate your efforts, I think it's best if you leave the house."

The old vampire whimpered. "But it's *my* home. Where am I supposed to go?"

"You know, it might not be a bad idea to keep him here. He could keep up the search for the will. And he can watch over the house and stay out of trouble. By himself. Not talking to anybody." I hoped Matt picked up on my hint how we needed to keep things as quiet as possible.

My brother groaned. "Okay, he can stay. As long as he keeps searching."

Beau brightened. "I will. I know it's here somewhere, although I don't know why you aren't using your powers that Tipper talked so much about, Miss Charli. Unless you can't because of the curse."

My jaw dropped at the same time Matt's did. "How do you know about it? Did Tipper tell you he was spellcasting it on himself? And how did you know I'm affected?" The questions came tumbling out of me.

Beau covered his mouth. "I don't want to say. I don't want to get anybody in trouble or get taken into the warden station. We vampires have already endured enough."

"But nobody's supposed to know about it," Matt complained.

I shook my head at the two of them. "It doesn't matter if he knows about Doozy. More than enough people do. But Beau, I need you to promise me you won't tell anybody else. And to keep searching for that will. Can you do that?"

The old vampire nodded with sincerity. He made a mark with his finger over his undead heart. "I promise. For Tipper, right?"

I gripped his shoulder in agreement. "For Tipper."

Chapter Eighteen

My grandmother hovered over me and placed her hand on my forehead for the hundredth time. I batted it away in frustration.

"I don't have a fever, Nana. And I feel fine." The first statement was true, but the second was a bold-faced fib.

Time was not my friend anymore. The lack of progress in solving the murder plus the curse drained me, adding to the overall miserable mess of the situation. As much as I didn't want to stay at home and rest, I needed to. But I didn't want to be treated like an invalid.

Nana touched my cheek with the back of her hand again. "I know, I know. I just wish there was something I could do for you, sweet girl."

"You mean other than mixing the gallons of nasty dark sludge?" I joked.

"Don't knock the stuff, Charli. It's the best thing that I've got for you. Believe me." The dark circles under her eyes told the story of how hard she must be working to find another way to get rid of Doozy.

"I know, Nana." Obediently, I took another sip. "I just wish you could make it taste better. More like sweet tea. Or maybe chess pie in a glass." I wiped my mouth off with the back of my hand. "I don't suppose using honeysuckle syrup would help?"

Nana frowned. "I did add some. But judging by the scrunching of your face with every sip, it never helps. Now tell me again about what happened at Tipper's house."

Peaches jumped up into my lap and demanded rubs as I recounted the entire story of our failed mission. When I got to the part with Nora and Tucker, she raised her eyebrows but remained silent in that scary way that used to give me the willies. Like standing in the eye of a hurricane, knowing the storm was swirling around, ready to hit with powerful force at any second.

Nana narrowed her eyes at me. "What else happened?"

"Nothing," I lied.

"You know, you and your brother think too little of me if you haven't figured out by now that I can always tell when you're telling a fib. Let me guess, you attempted to use your magic to find the will against my explicit instructions."

I nodded, feeling like a scolded child with her hand caught in the cookie jar.

"No wonder you look a hot mess today. I can't emphasize this enough, Charli." She took both my hands and her warm ones. "You cannot, I repeat, you cannot tap into your magic anymore. I fear that if you do, it will fuel the curse even more. And you know what that means."

"I understand," I whispered, my bottom lip trembling.

"Do you?" She lifted my face with her finger on my chin. "You don't get how precious you are to me, and I would do absolutely anything to keep you safe. Even if that means I have to work a sleeping spell over you to slow the effects of the curse down."

"Nana," I protested.

"Promise me you won't use your magic again."

Without my magic, who would I be? In a town full of magical beings and supernatural creatures, I would stick out like a sore thumb. Would I have to live the rest of my life that way? Of course, who knew how long my life would last anyway if we couldn't solve the murder?

"Drink it all down," Nana ordered. "I should get started on the food for tonight. I wish that I didn't have to do anything other than take care of you, but in my position, it's important that I be there."

I drained the glass. "I would never ask you to miss anything, Nana. And I won't, either. The pig pickin' will be too good not to go, and I don't want to skip out on barbecue with all the fixin's. And then there's the official Founders' ceremony."

My grandmother took the cup from me. "Charli, I think that you should stay home tonight."

Scooching my behind on the couch, I sat up. "No way.

There will be people there I need to talk to, like Jed. I'm not missing out on tonight." I crossed my arms and hoped that Nana bought my confidence.

She stared at me for a few seconds until her gaze softened. "I suppose there's no use in arguing with you. We'll just go round and round. And against my better judgment, I won't cast a sleeping spell on you to keep you safe. You're a Goodwin woman, and that means you're as immovable as a gargoyle. So, I'll let you go to the pig pickin'."

"What about the ceremony?" I'd never missed one yet, and this year's would be extraordinary.

She shook her head. "With the absence of Tipper, I'm not sure how controlled the ritual will be. And with the addition of the strawberry moon to boot, I can't rightly guess how much power will surge tonight. Or what that might do to you."

"I can't live with *what if's*, Nana."

She grabbed my chin in her hand. "And I can't live without you, sweet girl."

Her words of anguished love crashed against me in harsh waves. Of all the people in my life, she and my brother tethered me to it. I tried to tell her how much I loved her, too, but the words caught in my throat.

She threw her arms around me, careful not to squish Peaches, and rocked me back and forth, crooning sweet words in my ear and rubbing my back as the built up emotions broke the wall I'd erected and spilled out of me and onto her shoulder in the form of tears and sobs.

A heavy knock on the door startled the two of us. Nana produced a lace handkerchief from out of nowhere and instructed me to clean myself up. She returned to the living room with Lily and Lavender in tow. I brightened in the presence of my two friends, but my hopes sank the second I glanced at their expressions.

"What's wrong?" I asked.

Lavender held something behind her back. "I swear, she will get more than she deserves."

Confused, my gaze bounced between the cousins. "Who will get what now?"

Lily sat down next to me. I couldn't read auras like her, but it didn't take magic to know something devastated her. "I swear, she didn't hear it from either of us. Nor do I think that any of our group told her. I don't know how she got the information."

"Show me what you brought with you, Lavender," Nana said with a chill in her voice.

My friend looked like she'd rather do anything else in the entire world, including cleaning up an acre's worth of unicorn manure, but she handed over a newspaper with reluctance to my grandmother.

After a quick reading, Nana folded the paper in half, her face turning the color of cooked beets. "The nerve. I can't believe DK would print this. Even your Uncle Philip shouldn't have allowed this to go to print, even if he is married to that awful woman. How do they think that it was a good idea to run with the story? Gossip, more like."

"Okay, what story?" I asked.

Relief flooded Lily and Lavender's faces that they were not the ones to hand me the newspaper. I opened the fold, and sucked in a breath as I read the headline: *Death Comes to Honeysuckle: First a Murder, Now a Death Curse*

I didn't have to find the author of the article's name before knowing the exact culprit Lavender had meant. "If I survive any of this, I will hex her hiney into the next millennium, I promise."

"Get in line," Lavender stated with more anger than I'd ever heard come from her soft soul. "Good luck getting me to cleanse her aura anytime soon. Granny has already made enormous threats to her current health."

I smirked. "But I guess in the end, she got her story, didn't she?"

Lily winced. "But at your expense. And I still want to know who gave her the information. There is more accuracy there than speculation."

Starting over, I read through the article twice while Peaches batted at the wrinkly paper. Lily was right. The details of the curse were spot on. The speculation had been saved for Tipper's demise and proposing possible causes. But it didn't take a genius to figure out that a big finger pointed at the person affected by the death curse, based on the imaginative narrative.

"When I get two seconds free," my grandmother spit out, "I will work up a spell so heinous that whoever the *anonymous source* is will rue the day they spoke their first word."

"Calm down, Nana," I insisted. "Linsey was just trying for her first break. Besides, everyone in town is bound to find out and talk about it anyway. Remember, small town, big mouths, no secrets. She just put it in print."

Lavender snatched the paper from me and closed it, placing it next to her. "The fact that they didn't even contact you to give you a heads-up is worse than her writing it. I can't believe your Uncle Philip would do that to you."

"I'll bet your Aunt Nora had something to do with it. Her husband may own the newspaper, but I'm pretty sure that underneath her flowery dresses, she wears the britches," accused Lily.

A nagging thought that had been planted since the trip to Tipper's house knocked on my brain. Aunt Nora was mean, but she was never that smart. Someone else had to be encouraging her from behind the scenes. Tucker? Maybe. I needed to go to the pig pickin' tonight more than ever.

Lavender stood up, taking the paper with her. "We need to get back and help our families get ready. Are you gonna be able to come?"

"Count me in," I said. "Nana and I have come to an understanding. I plan on eating as much barbecue as possible until my belly explodes. And I call dibs on at least one serving of cracklin'. Crispy tails and ears for me."

"As far as I'm concerned, you can have all the cracklings. We'll make sure you get them," promised Lily. The two cousins bid their goodbyes with hugs and kisses.

After my friends left, I rubbed my temple. Nana rushed to

my side. "What's wrong? Should I make up some more potion?"

I stroked Peach's head and took comfort in her tiny purr. "No. It's yet *another* mystery to solve, and they're all connected. But I can't see how. Or Why. And who was Linsey's source about the curse?"

We counted off the names of all the people who were in the know. For the most part, we could say with confidence that it wasn't any of them.

"Mason?" Nana asked.

I shook my head. "He's not even here right now, and he's a detective and a professional. I don't think that he would talk to a reporter."

"Dash?"

I fingered the pink key around my neck, remembering the night it was gifted to me. Would the wolf shifter betray my trust? "No." A small amount of doubt flavored my answer.

"Is there anybody else not in your inner circle who knew about the curse?"

Only one possibility popped up in my memory. She wore blood red shoes and had been the first to speculate what was wrong with me from the beginning.

"Bring me another glass of sludge, Nana. I guess I have a new reason to attend the picnic in tonight."

Chapter Nineteen

The smell of barbecue permeated every molecule of the air. The annual pig pickin' stood out as the most anticipated food event of the year. Other than fueling everybody for the night's founding ceremony, it was a good time for everybody to fill up with outstanding food and indulge in an immense amount of fun.

As soon as we arrived, Nana checked with me one last time before splitting off to talk to others. The decorating committee had gone all out with sparkling lights floating in the air that resembled strawberries of various sizes. Based on their twinkling pink color, I bet Goss had a hand in it.

I searched the crowd for my friends, but my growling stomach drove me to the line at one of the large grill cookers to get a heapin' help of shredded pork smothered in spicy vinegar-based sauce. After getting my fair share, I worked my way through the side dishes, scooping up spoonfuls of tangy coleslaw, sweet baked beans, Brunswick stew, and stacking golden squares of cornbread until my paper plate threatened to collapse.

It took great effort to ignore all eyes watching my every movement as I weaved through the crowd. Some people scattered out of my path so I wouldn't even touch them. All the whispers, stares, and general pointing did nothing to help me feel that welcome.

When the crowd parted, I caught a glimpse of Linsey across the way. Lily's sister stopped in her tracks and turned as bright as a ripe strawberry. She darted her eyes away from me and sprinted in the opposite direction.

"Yeah, you better run," I mumbled under my breath, shoveling a victorious forkful of barbecue in my mouth.

The words *murder* and *curse* floated in the air around me. Maybe coming to the picnic hadn't been the greatest idea. But what were my alternatives? Should I have stayed at home, counting the seconds until Doozy...no, scratch that...the *curse* took me? Or should I be out eating some of the finest barbecue in the South and drowning my sorrows in sweet tea? With stubborn resolve, I made my way toward the refreshment area.

As I got to the end of yet another line, somebody jostled me into a nearby figure. A dollop of coleslaw smeared down the back of the innocent bystander in front of me. Before I could wipe it off, the person turned around.

Raif glared down his nose at me with disgusted

recognition. "My deepest apologies, Miss Goodwin," he sneered, flinching away from me.

Lady Eveline flashed me an apologetic glance from her spot in front of him, and the pieces fell together. I knew that Raif was supposed to stop by her house the same night I visited her, and she definitely knew about the curse. It had never occurred to me that she might have shared the information, but that would make sense as to why Beau knew about it as well.

"I would think that a young woman in your condition should not be attending an event such as this," Raif uttered in his impeccable British accent. He tightened his grip on the bedazzled leash that led down to a little pug sitting dutifully at his feet, tail wagging and tongue panting. "After all, if these be your last hours, should you not be spending them with those you love?"

I glanced around at everyone surrounding me. Maybe he was right, and I shouldn't be here. But if I were to drop dead at that very second, I would wish to spend it with as many people as possible. After all, why else had I returned Honeysuckle?

"I am, sir," I replied, standing up straighter.

"But are you not afraid that you could pass the curse on to someone else?" The vampire picked up and snuggled his beloved pug even tighter, making kissy faces and speaking in baby talk. The longer it went on, the more I was losing my appetite.

Lady Evangeline touched his arm. "Raif, darling, you know that's not how this works."

He ignored his friend's reprimand. "I know nothing of the sort. As you keep trying to reassure me, your friend here is not the one to blame for Mr. Walker's demise. That is, *if* we are to believe that the one with the curse did *not* genuinely commit the murder, against all properties of any death curse I've ever heard of."

A crowd had gathered around us, and my cheeks flamed under all the attention. "That's because she understands I would never have killed my own kin."

Raif stopped doting on his beloved pet long enough to dismiss me. "So you say. Come, Sir Barkley. Let us find more suitable company."

He set his pug on the ground, and the two sashayed their uptight behinds away in practical unison. I kept my mouth shut about the unsightly smear on his back. Served him right to have his perfect image dirtied up a little bit.

Lady Eveline stayed behind as if she wanted to say something more to me. However, when Raif beckoned, she seemed torn. Mouthing an apology to me, she joined her fellow vampire.

Having witnessed the minor kerfuffle, my friends rallied around me. They held out plates of food and cups of sweet tea as shields against any more accusers. With the music playing loud and too many people milling close by, I didn't see how I could fill them in about the will or ask about Lee or Dash without allowing too many curious bystanders to hear.

When the music came to an end, Nana approached the microphone and waved to the crowd. "Hey, y'all. How's everybody doin'?" She waited for the various cheers to die down. "How about that good food sittin' in your bellies provided by our mighty fine team? Let's give them a round of applause for sitting with the pigs in their grills overnight."

As I scooped up some barbecue, I noticed the slight shake in my hand. The throb that I'd grown accustomed to in my arm radiated across my entire body. Sudden dizziness threatened to overtake me, and I shut my eyes for a second.

Blythe touched my shoulder. "You okay?"

I nodded and plastered a smile on my face. "Sure." Maybe Nana had been right about me not coming out tonight.

An exit plan formed in my head until I spotted Wayne, the proclaimed pirate who'd been on the fishing trip with Jed Farnsworth. Downing the last of my tea to bolster my energy, I handed my plate and cup to Blythe, who shot me a puzzled look but took my trash with a shrug of her shoulders. While the audience clapped and responded to my grandmother, I used the opportunity to weave through the crowd undetected.

"I'm so thrilled to introduce tonight's band," Nana continued. "It's their first debut in Honeysuckle, and we couldn't be any prouder. Y'all give a warm round of applause to our very own Jordy and the Jack-O'-Lanterns."

The crowd whooped and hollered as a young lady with some of the longest hair I'd ever seen approached the mic, wielding a bass guitar. It had only been a year since I'd been gone, but I recognized her in an instant. I followed the loudest hollering to a nearby table where her proud papa stood up, cheering for his daughter.

"Wayne," I clapped the jolly pirate on the back. "Don't tell me that's your daughter."

"It sure is," he exclaimed with great pride in his eyes.

"I can't believe how grown-up she is."

"It happened so fast," admitted his lovely wife, Greta, wiping a small tear from her eye.

After an amazing cool bass intro, the band broke into a country blues song. The second Jordy wailed on the mic, I knew she was the daughter of a siren. She sang about the trouble that people can get into because of moonshine, the lyrics of the song a clever play on words between moonlight and alcohol.

"Want to buy a T-shirt?" Wayne asked.

"Absolutely," I shouted over the song. "But I'll have to owe you one. I didn't bring any money with me."

"That's fine as long as you put it on right now." He handed me the shirt, and I obliged.

By the third time Jordy sang the chorus, the whole crowd knew the words, and we all sang along. At the end of the song, everyone burst out in gleeful cheers. The talented young lady flashed a smile at her parents and bent her head so that her hair covered her face, hiding her slight embarrassment from all the positive attention.

"She's awesome," I told her father over the racket.

"That she is." He beamed at his beautiful and talented daughter.

I waited for things to quiet down for a moment. "Hey, Wayne. When did you get back from your fishing trip?"

"This morning. We brought in a huge haul." His eyes remained glued to the stage.

"So that means that Jed's back, right? Any chance he's here tonight?" I asked.

Wayne shrugged as his daughter started a new song. "I guess," he said. "Isn't everyone here?"

I let him be so he could enjoy his daughter's performance and moved through the excited crowd, looking for the town's head advocate. If Jed was here, then maybe he could tell me where Tipper's will was hidden, and we could stop Aunt Nora. That mission fueled my search, and I ignored the ache in my body.

As I snuck around the edges avoiding the attention from others, a warm hand touched my arm, and I turned. Tucker glanced at me with hope and determination. "Charli, I'm glad you're here."

I *so* did not have time for him. "Shouldn't you be with your fiancée?"

He stepped closer to me. "She doesn't matter right now. You do. Can we talk?"

I tried to walk away, but he grasped me harder. "Let me go, T."

"But Charli, if we don't talk now, it may be too late."

"It's already too late." My sharp words made him grimace.

I couldn't help my conflicted emotions about him. Once upon a time, he was supposed to be my Prince Charming. I knew I'd walked away from him for a reason, but never in my life did I think he'd end up being the villain and not the hero.

"There are things I need to say to you," he insisted.

Like telling me that you broke into Tipper's house? That you're helping Aunt Nora? That maybe you're a part of my great-uncle's death? Questions swirled in my head and turned my stomach. "What kind of things, Tuck?"

He opened his mouth to say something but closed it again. Releasing my arm, he ran his hand through his hair. "I've thought about what I wanted to say to you if I ever got a chance for over a year. And now that you're here in front of me, I honestly don't know where to start."

Typical Tucker. Full of promise, but in the end, he could never follow through. I narrowed my eyes at him, "Is there something you need to confess or get off your chest?"

My question took him by surprise. "What?"

The song ended at the same time that I spotted Jed standing around not too far away, eating barbecue. Two choices plagued me that I had no time to consider—stand here and see if my ex had the integrity to own up to his actions or pursue a more direct line of information we desperately needed.

"I've got to go," I insisted.

Tucker grabbed my hand. "Wait."

The applause died down, and my grandmother returned to the stage. "What a great way to cap off this year's pig pickin', wouldn't you say? Now, y'all finish what you're eating and let us all head to the tree for tonight's ceremony."

With a twist, I yanked out of Tucker's grip. I looked at him in disappointment. "Bye, T."

Hustling to catch Jed, I pushed my way against the flow of the crowd. By the time I arrived at the spot where he'd just been, he was gone. I'd have to wait until after the ceremony. Or maybe I could catch him before it all began? If I were there before everything started and then left, I, technically, wouldn't be breaking my grandmother's request.

Keeping a low profile and attempting to avoid Nana, I searched for any of my friends and found Alison Kate standing with Lee. I gave my spectacled friend a huge hug.

"I thought you were rotting away in a cell." I clapped him on the shoulder.

He shook his head. "I'm not under arrest."

"That's good." I wiped the beads of sweat from my brow, trying to stay upright on my unsteady feet.

"But I'm not supposed to leave Honeysuckle, either," he added, frowning. "Neither was Dash, but he took off anyway."

My stomach curdled. "You mean, he left? Temporarily or for good?" That crazy wolf shifter better not have done something stupid.

"I don't know," Lee admitted. "I told him to stay put and wait things out, but he wouldn't listen. He said something about trouble always finding him, and that everyone would be better off if he weren't here."

My friend leaned in and gave me another hug. He turned his head so only I could hear him. "He also told me to give you this and to tell you that he's sorry."

I pushed Lee away. "You've got to be kidding me."

Alison Kate tugged on Lee's sleeve. "Guys, we're gonna be late. We need to go."

Disappointment weighed on my heart. Finding out Tucker's insides weren't as pretty as his outsides didn't surprise me. Learning that Dash was a coward did.

Bitter anger burned away my dismay. In fairytales, the men swung the swords and defeated the monsters. In reality, Tucker might be on the side of the monsters, and Dash tucked his tail between his legs and ran away.

Well, those two men might not be capable of doing the right thing, but I definitely was. Although my inner gas tank was almost on empty, I would use up all my reserves to fight until the end.

"Lee, take me to the tree."

Chapter Twenty

The Founders' tree stood in the middle of an open field. Like many others in our region, it was a massive live oak, growing taller and wider than its relatives that beat it by hundreds of years. Town lore stated that it expanded to its current height within five years of the original three founders planting their first treasures.

Its branches twisted and spread out wide in all directions that dipped as close to the earth and stretched high in the sky. The thick green canopy of leaves hosted long strands of Spanish moss. Benevolent energy radiated off of it on a normal day. On a night like tonight, the entire atmosphere of the area crackled with magic.

Once we arrived, I ignored the increasing pulse of pain in my body and enlisted Lee and Alison Kate's help to look for Jed. With all the chaos before the ceremony buzzing around us, it didn't take long for the two of them to be pulled aside or distracted. Trying to stay hidden from my grandmother didn't help my ability to openly run around asking questions, either.

While walking backward, searching the faces around me, I stumbled into someone and lost my balance. Strong hands caught me and kept me upright.

I turned to apologize to my savior and found myself in the arms of Ashton. "Thank you," I managed.

Instead of polite acceptance, he pushed me away from him, his hands fisting at his side. "Sure."

"Ashton, darlin', there you are." Aunt Nora approached him and hooked her arm around his. When she noticed me, her smile disappeared. "Oh, you."

"Yes. Me." My irritation with her extra-puckered countenance flamed my anger over her entanglement in the entire mess.

"Why are you here, Charlotte? I would think in your current condition it wouldn't be safe for you to participate tonight. If I looked as disheveled as you do, I wouldn't step a foot out the door," she challenged.

For once, I wished with all my might that I *could* pass on the curse. "Gee, thanks."

Turning her attention back to Ashton, Aunt Nora's face lit up. "I've secured you a perfect spot so you can watch me take my place as the Walker founding member." Her eyes flitted back to mine in triumph.

"Since when?" I blurted.

A malevolent grin spread across her face. "Since your

grandmother realized the necessity of all three families being needed to complete the ceremony."

"But Nana already has Uncle Tipper's treasure. Why would she need you?"

She held up her fingers as she counted. "It took a Hawthorne, a Goodwin, and a Walker in the beginning. I imagine your grandmother realized how much she needed me."

The world flashed in and out for a second, and my legs threatened to give out. I took a deep breath, willing myself not to faint. "For the ceremony only. That seat isn't yours permanently."

"Not yet. But soon." She pulled on her companion's arm. "Ashton, are you coming along?"

The young man looked about as good as I felt. Sweat trickled down his face, and his color resembled more that of a ghost. He hid a slight cough behind the back of his hand. "If you don't mind, Leonora, I'm not feeling all that well. I believe that I will have to miss out on tonight's events." He unhooked her arm from his. "Charlotte, if you need an escort home, I would be happy to take you with me."

Ashton's dismissal of my aunt and attention to me shocked the bitter witch. Her tone chilled. "I'm sure my niece can find her way back to where she belongs on her own. You run along home and feel better." She took my hand in hers and held me in place so that I couldn't leave if I wanted to.

"Listen," she hissed. "I saw you talking to Tucker at the barbecue, and now you're after Ashton. I don't know what plans you're making, but you will not ruin mine. Clementine, who is a *real* Walker daughter, will be marrying the Hawthorne heir."

I yanked my hand from her frosty grip. "What about *your* plans, Aunt Nora?"

The sound of Nana's voice interrupted our confrontation. With determined haughtiness, Aunt Nora made her way to the center to stand next to my grandmother and Hollis.

Nana addressed the crowd with great solemnity. "Every year, we go out of our way to celebrate the founding of our small town because what we've accomplished is worth celebrating. Three families came together to form one place where any and all could live without judgment and without fear in a world where both exist rampantly.

"Tonight, we come to the tree that grew out of sacrifice and promise in the place of the first pact to renew the protection and purpose of Honeysuckle Hollow."

Hollis raised his voice. "Please take your designated places, and we'll get started."

Everyone who would contribute their magic to the ceremony surrounded the founding members in a large circle. Those with wings lit up into the sky around the tree. Four experienced witches from an older generation rode broomsticks high in the air to take their places at the cardinal points.

I walked my way to the edge of the grounding circle. My eyes spotted Jed on the far side, and I refused an offered spot in between Lily and Lavender. Leaving my confused friends, I broke through to the outside, the circle enclosing and shutting me out.

For the first time, I joined others who could not be an active part of the ceremony but still came to watch. Big Willie nodded at me, his hands full with a very hairy baby he rocked back and forth. Lucky chewed on a toothpick, focusing on his fingernails rather than the ceremony that he couldn't see. Still, he remained here.

The ground trembled a bit, but I couldn't tell if it was the gathering of magic or my legs failing. With dragging steps, I did my best to make it closer to Jed so I could catch him after the ceremony.

Pain rocked through me, and I reached out to grab hold of anything to steady me.

A pair of kind eyes regarded me from the person who held me up. "I have you, Miss Charli."

"Beau, what are you doing here?" I asked.

"Can't miss tonight. It was one of Tipper's favorite events. He said it was the most important thing. And, I think it's very pretty." He pointed at the light sparkles shimmering around the form of the tree.

I wanted to ask him about whether or not he'd found the will, but I wobbled again, the proximity to so much magical energy taking its toll on me.

Another pair of cold hands held up my other side. "It is different when you stand out here, is it not?" Lady Eveline asked.

My grandmother's voice rang out from the center as she

called out the ritual. I knew the words by heart, and yet they sounded different from this distance.

"I never considered how the ceremony looked from this perspective," I admitted.

"Now you can understand Raif's campaign a little. Sometimes it takes walking in someone else's shoes to fully grasp the situation. To see who wields the power," Eveline tipped her head toward the inner circle, "and who does not."

Those who formed the circle chanted words of promise and intent. The edges of the Founders' tree glowed brighter. The ground shook underneath me again and rocked the three of us.

"I think tonight's power will be at a much greater magnitude," Lady Eveline observed. "Also, I must apologize profusely for my part in the article. I told Raif that information in the strictest of confidence."

"No secrets amongst us vampires. For our security, he says," added Beau.

I didn't have time to dive neck-deep into vampire politics. Magic swirled and surrounded all of us. It tugged on me, demanding to thread my reserves in with the collective. And I had nothing left to give.

I fingered the pink key around my neck, but didn't think I had enough energy to activate it. "I need to get out of here."

"What's wrong?" Lady Eveline turned her concerned attention to me.

Raif appeared at her elbow. "I believe she may not have

taken into consideration the effect of tonight's ritual on what she holds inside her."

"We do not have time for your reproach right now," Lady Eveline admonished the tall vampire.

Nana's voice rang out strong and true as she finished weaving the spell. The radiance around the tree bloomed as bright as the sun until it bathed the field and all around in light as bright as daytime. A vacuum of power pulled around us like the tide being sucked out all at once, leaving the ocean floor dry before the first destructive wave of a tsunami.

"Take me out of here. Please," I begged all three vampires.

"Here." Raif handed his precious pug to Beau. "Be careful with him." With polite intent, he gathered me into his arms and turned to take me away.

A bright flash and a sonic boom ripped through the air. A column of power burst out of the tree and into the air high in the sky as if it rocketed all the way to the slightly pink moon. A mighty force teeming with magic radiated out, penetrating through every single being in the blast zone.

With his vampire speed, Raif had managed to carry me further away, but not far enough. The wave of energy struck us, and he stumbled in its overwhelming wake.

For a second, the world stopped, and an eerie calm descended over the two of us. I took a deep breath, the hole of energy inside of me filled to the brim. I hadn't felt this good, this alive, since before I'd come home to Honeysuckle.

In surprise, I gazed up at Raif, still holding me in his arms. "You helped me."

"Contrary to what you may believe, I do not wish any harm to come to you, Miss Charlotte. I value my position as a citizen of this town." His tone did not hold any friendliness in it.

I pondered whether or not he meant to be kind to me or whether or not he wanted to garner favor with my grandmother by helping. Either way, he'd helped.

"I feel much better now," I ventured. "In fact, maybe you can put me—"

A throb of agonizing pain wrenched through my body, cutting everything else off. All sense of well-being fled, replaced with a black hole of nothingness, sucking my very essence into its gaping jaws and attempting to swallow me whole. I clawed to stay out of its reach, but I sunk further into its murky shadows with every attempt to fight.

In the dark, only my screams remained.

Chapter Twenty-One

Voices echoed from someplace I couldn't see. They surrounded me, called to me, ordered me, yelled at me, and cried for me, but I couldn't answer them. A cold embrace of nothingness wrapped me in its cocoon, and for once, I had no will to fight against it.

With great effort, I attempted to surface out of the gloomy depths. Searching, I tried to find a speck of light, a glimmer to guide me out of the glacial pool that threatened to drag me under. With hope leaking out of me, I did my best to listen.

"Give her some of that yucky drink," a female voice said.

"How can I when she's still unconscious?" Nana countered.

"I'll open her mouth, and you can pour it down her gullet. I don't care. This is not how her life ends," argued a male voice that sometimes irritated me and sometimes brought me great comfort.

I strained to pluck his name from my memories but found myself sinking back into the bleakness again.

"Doc, can't you fix her?" gritted the same man.

"I'm not sure how much more she can take. I have found no cure for this in my searches," the voice of the town healer explained. "My guess is that the blast from last night's ceremony fried her circuits like a chicken leg in hot grease."

Another determined voice wavered when he spoke. "No, I refuse to accept this. There's been enough death. Enough loss." He gripped my hand and squeezed three times.

Matt, I recognized. I called out to him, but no sound came out.

Real life waited on the other side of the water's surface, tempting me to break through and breathe clean air. I could sense everyone, hear them, but they couldn't see that I was there. Trying hard not to give in.

The heavy weight of the dark wrapped itself around my body and pulled me under again, and I lost the connection.

"Not yet," I begged it. "I'm not ready to go."

A smokiness whirled around me, and I swore I heard the voices of two people that I missed with all my heart. The first of their whispers told me to go.

"I don't understand," I called out. "Go where?"

As if speaking in a vast cave, the words echoed around me. "Go back. You have to go back." The soft voice tinkled in the familiar tones of my mother.

"Finish it, Birdy," the voice of my father pushed. "Finish it and be done."

Tears sprung from my eyes. "Where are you?"

A spark of warmth and comfort bloomed in my heart, guarding me against the surrounding despair. The word *here* resounded over and over.

"Can't I stay with you?" I implored.

"You're choice," they both said, the last word reverberating.

It could all end now. No more pain. Reunited with my parents. But what about my brother? My grandmother? My friends? There was something left unfinished that nagged at me, but the longer I pondered, the more it didn't matter.

A warm presence touched my shoulder. It slid down my arm until it felt like fingers wrapped around my hand. With three squeezes, my father's energy permeated me.

"You are so much stronger than you think. We're very proud of you. Be my Birdy and *find* your way back home. You have things to do."

His words resonated in me, but I still didn't know which choice to make. "What should I do, Dad?"

The warmth slipped away, and nobody answered me.

"Mom? Dad?"

My time to take action grew short. If I chose to stay, maybe I would be reunited with my parents forever. But when had I ever given up without a fight? According to many, we Goodwin women were stubborn to a fault.

The final decision made, I concentrated on locating what

I wanted most. A tiny pinprick of light pierced the dark, and a thin glowing thread extended to me like a lifeline. I grabbed onto it and let it pull me forward, reeling me out of the nothingness.

Gasping a deep breath, I broke through the surface and into the bright sunny day. Familiar faces surrounded the couch I lay on. Matt sat on the edge of the coffee table, still holding my hand.

Nana wiped the sweat from my brow with a shaky hand. "Welcome back, sweet girl."

My fuzzy little orange kitten jumped up into my lap with a little chirp, purring and rubbing her head against my hand. Alison Kate clapped her hands, and Lee hugged her around her shoulders. Lavender clung to her cousin Lily, who stood next to Ben, all of them watching my every breath. Blythe waited on the edges, a mix of emotions swimming in her eyes.

Relief rolled off my friends and family who crowded around me. A bit too close. I squeezed my eyes tight and burrowed into my grandmother's chest to be cradled.

"Y'all give this girl some breathing room right now," Nana demanded.

"Somebody, get her some sweet honeysuckle iced tea," Mason said. He stood close behind Matt on the coffee table, staring at me with too much concern in his eyes. "I heard it does wonders." He winked.

"I'd rather she down some of Nana's sludge, just to be on the safe side." Matt squeezed my hand one more time and let me go, attempting to hide that he wiped a tear away.

I groaned, but Nana patted my back and got up to fetch me a glass. Settling back on the couch, I struggled not to fuss at all of them staring at me like an animal in the zoo. The uncomfortable quiet scrutiny made me squirm.

Peaches hopped off my lap and took a seat on the edge of the couch. Spreading her striped legs, she proceeded to clean herself in the most undignified manner. The awkward display broke the tension, and we all laughed.

"What's so funny?" Nana asked as she came back in holding two glasses. "One sweet tea. Then you'll need an extra dose of my concoction, and we'll see where we go from there. In the meantime, y'all say your peace and skedaddle. We can't have you hovering around her all day."

Protests flew around the room, and I held up my hand to quiet them down. With as much effort as I could manage, I pushed myself to a sitting position on the couch and faced my friends and family.

In a shaky, quiet voice, I attempted to lighten the mood. "Hey, it's not like it's my funeral."

Nobody laughed.

"I promise I'm not dying today. I've been ensured that there's something I have to do first." My eyes darted to my brother, but how could I tell him who had given me the reassurances without him thinking I'd gone crazy?

After a lot of hugs and way too many kisses, my tribe of friends left. Doc promised to come back the next day. Only Matt, Mason, and my grandmother remained. The three of them stared at me with unspoken scolding in their eyes.

"Go ahead. Let me have it." I braced myself.

"What were you thinking, going to the ceremony?" Matt cringed at his harsh tone. "I mean, you should have known better. And why did you let her?" he asked our grandmother.

"Don't blame her," I insisted. "Nana told me not to. I was supposed to go home after the pig pickin', but I saw Jed there and wanted to catch him before things started."

Nana sighed. "And I got too caught up in my role to mind you."

I faced my grandmother. "Remind me some time that we need to talk about how things are run here in Honeysuckle. Someday, you should experience the ceremony from outside of the circle. It might help you make decisions as you sit in the high seat."

She stared at me dumbfounded. "What are you talking about?" The expression on her face told me that she thought I hadn't quite recovered yet. "Does it have anything to do with Raif being the one who carried you here?"

My eyes widened. "He did?"

Mason spoke up. "He wouldn't let anyone take you from his charge. Said it was important that he deliver you."

Clever vampire. Whether out of kindness or out of ingenious manipulation, Raif had earned the admiration of others and placed my grandmother, the High Seat on the town council, in his debt.

Too many thoughts and questions crowded my head, and I closed my eyes to concentrate. Nana took the glass of sweet tea away and forced the other one in my hand. Taking obedient sips, I waited for the blurred edges to clear.

"When did you get back?" I asked Mason.

"Earlier today. I would have returned earlier, but there was a delay in procuring the package." He frowned. "If I'd have known you would be foolish enough to attend, I would have insisted on a guard to make sure you stayed put."

"I don't need a babysitter," I whined.

He gestured his hand at me. "The evidence says quite the opposite. I swear, you don't go looking for trouble. You hunt it down, tackle it to the ground, and claim it as yours."

"Welcome to my world, Detective Clairmont," Nana complained. "Can I fix you somethin' to eat?"

Mason shook his head. "I need to get back to the warden station. I've got a phoenix feather waiting for me."

Matt whistled. "Those are beyond rare and hard to come by. Expensive too, if reports are to be believed. You better hope Big Willie has approved that requisition."

"This time, it's not on the Honeysuckle warden station." Mason clapped Matt on the back. "Like I told Charli here before, I called in a favor."

"That had to be some big favor, Detective," my grandmother said.

"It's one that was overdue." Mason furrowed his eyebrows but dismissed his concern when he caught me looking.

"Maybe one you shouldn't have burned on us," I said.

If we pooled together all the money in our small town, I'm not sure we'd be able to afford even half of a single phoenix feather. Hunted into extinction, anyone who obtained any part of the mythical creature possessed a priceless treasure. I wondered what Mason had done to earn him the ability to procure such an item?

"It was the only way I could think of to try and get those fingerprints off the flask. A last-ditch effort, you might say," the detective explained.

"Are you sure?" I pressed. "With something as rare as that, you could buy your way onto a more prominent warden force anywhere. Get out of our little town and make a name for yourself."

"I don't know," Mason said. "I'm starting to like the small-town vibe." He regarded me with a vulnerable look for a brief moment before the wall of professionalism descended again. "I should go."

Nana patted him on the back. "I knew you were good people when I first met you, Detective Clairmont. Now, you get to work so that maybe we can fix things, you hear?"

"Yes, ma'am." With a tiny salute to her, a handshake to my brother, and a nod to me, Mason left.

My brother took a seat next to me on the couch and tapped the glass of goo. "Drink up."

"I don't need you hovering over me, Matt. I'm sure TJ is waiting for you."

"I'll wait until you finish at least two glasses worth." He raised his eyebrows, daring me to disobey. "And then, I'll go to the station to see the phoenix feather at work. It may be the last hope to find the faint fingerprints on the flask. Once we have them, we might be able to match them to someone in the system."

"Or it might melt the flask, destroying it," Nana warned.

"It might," admitted Matt. "But it'll be cool to watch."

I had to admit, I wished I could go with my brother and see the feather at work. But even I knew that leaving this house was impossible at the moment, no matter how many glasses of sludge my grandma brewed for me.

"Go ahead and go," I told him, not hiding my jealousy. "I'd be right there with you if I could."

"You sure?" My brother looked at our grandmother for permission.

I squeezed his hand. "I know you have my back, Matty D. Now go."

Without any more protests, my brother left, leaving me alone with Nana. Loki and Momo tussled in the middle of the floor with growls and hisses. Without any extra strength, I had nothing left but to give in to my grandmother's care.

Her silence scratched my nerves until I couldn't take it. "I'm sorry, Nana. I know I should have gone home after the barbecue, but I didn't want to miss out on a chance to question people. We're running out of time."

Despair cracked her polished veneer. "You don't think I don't know that? Of course, I do. Every single day, I do my best not to show it, to be strong for you. I know well enough what this curse is doing, and there's nothing I can do about it. No spell, no amount of wishing, and certainly no amount of love seems to be able to save you."

I threw my arms around her, giving her a fraction of the comfort back that she'd provided for me for years. We both crumbled against each other in heaping sobs.

When we'd both quieted down to gentle weeping, I murmured into her shoulder, "It's not your job to save me."

She squeezed me harder with a sniffle. "Pixie poop, yes it is."

"Language, Nana," I scolded.

"Oh, hush up." She clung to me until our tears ran out.

I drank enough of the foul concoction until my stomach couldn't take anymore. When my grandmother offered me real food, my stomach turned. Sleep threatened to drag me under, and I fought against it.

Nana escorted me upstairs. "Give in, darlin'. No use fighting the little extra kick of sleeping spell in that batch. You need your rest."

I made it to the edge of my bed, unwilling to lay down in it. "What if I don't wake up?"

"You will. I promise." My grandmother covered me with my quilt, and I snuggled under its comforting weight.

Staying by my side, Nana brushed her fingers through my hair and hummed a lullaby until I couldn't fight sleep anymore.

Chapter Twenty-Two

At least while I slept, I didn't have to swallow more of those disgusting concoctions Nana forced on me. But I couldn't play Sleeping Beauty anymore. I needed to find out as much about Tipper's will from Jed. Tonight, everybody in town would be at the barn dance, the final Founders' week event.

Rummaging through the large wooden wardrobe in my room, I couldn't find a single thing to wear that would be appropriate. Despite the dance taking place in Boyd's largest barn, we still treated it like the fanciest social outing. I dismissed outfit after outfit.

When I got to the end of the wooden clothes rack, my fingers wrinkled a plastic clothes bag. Pulling it out and unzipping it, I discovered an old dress of Mom's. Memories pushed everything else out of my mind, and I touched the delicate fabric.

I hadn't told Nana about the conversation I was pretty sure had really happened with my parents. That would remain between the three of us. I missed Mom and ached for Dad. How could my life have gone so terribly sideways? If the curse had its way, I'd be joining my parents way sooner then I'd ever intended.

A yellow tag wrapped around the hanger caught my eye. Turning it over, I read the cursive handwriting.

Dear Charli, I'm sure that you'll remember that this dress belonged to your mother. I miss her every day, but seeing the woman you've grown into reminds me a little of her and heals my heart. Her store is ready for you when you are ready for it. Until then, I hope you like this gift.

The note was signed by Mom's best friend, Patty Lou. She'd waved at me the other day through the window when I had shown Mason around town. Maybe it was past the time that I needed to stop ignoring the aching sadness any longer and give myself a chance heal before all my chances ran out.

I undressed and slipped the silk over my head. Sliding my arms through the delicate capped blue sleeves, I pondered how I'd manage the zipper. Before I could fumble for it, a tingle tickled my ribs. The dress conformed to my body in perfect precision, and I heard the metal sound of the zipper rushing up my back.

Standing in front of the mirror, I marveled at the dress which now fit me like a glove. I may not have been my mother's biological child, but her dress provided the illusion of a slight resemblance, to my delight. The reflection in the mirror captivated me, but I needed to get my hustle on if I wanted to make it to the dance.

Grabbing an acceptable pair of heels, I opened the bedroom door and peeked outside. Peaches waited for me in the middle of the hall. She stretched, wrapping herself around my ankles. Shushing her, I strained to detect any other movement in the house.

"Nana?" I called out in a weak voice. Clearing my throat, I tried again with a little more force. "Nana." Only my orange kitty replied with a mew.

Grasping my shoes and finding my courage, I tiptoed down the hallway, following the exact path of footsteps I'd memorized as a teenager to miss all the creaks and incriminating squeaks in the floor. I peeked over the banister and strained to hear the sound of someone still rummaging around. Nothing.

I took careful steps down each stair but forgot to skip the fourth one from the top. The second my foot hit it, a loud groan of wood echoed in the air, and I winced. Frozen in place, I waited. Still no reaction from anybody. Blowing out a sigh of relief, I hurried down the rest of the flight, scurried across the foyer, and made it to the front door.

"Where do you think you're going?" My brother revealed himself from his hiding place behind the grandfather clock.

My nerves jangled at the surprise. "I'm just going out to get some air."

"Right. In one of mom's dresses, which looks good on you, by the way." Matt crossed his arms. "I guess I owe

Nana some yard work. She told me you'd try to make a run for it."

I dropped my shoes. "You know why I have to go. Jed. The will." Out of all people, Matt should understand.

He refused to budge. "You need to stay home and rest."

"What good is staying in bed if I'm never going to make it out of it."

"Don't say that." My brother frowned.

"It's true, and you know it. So let's finish this." I pleaded with him. "You can help me."

"I'd rather eat a pound of unicorn manure than to put you at risk again." He crossed his arms. "The answer is no."

"But you can take me to the dance and let me ask my questions. Then I'll go home quietly." I held my hands up like an incarcerated criminal.

Matt shook his head. "No can do. I'm not under just our grandmother's orders."

I scowled at him. "Don't tell me that Mason has you putting me under house arrest?"

A funny look crossed my brother's face. "Okay, I won't tell you that then. Let's call it under wardens' protection then."

"You've got to be kidding me. How many times do I have to point it out? We are. Running. Out. Of. Time."

He pointed at the stairs, summoning all the authority he could in his voice and did his best imitation of Dad. "March upstairs now, young lady."

"In your dreams."

"Listen, little Bird, one way or another, you're staying

here. Don't make me have to hog-tie you." He took steps toward me, and I backed away, holding up my fists like I used to as a kid.

"Try it, and you'll come away with a black eye. Remember that one time?" He would always regret that he'd taught me how to throw a proper punch.

"Lucky shot."

"You wish."

A loud knock on the door interrupted our childish exchange. "Matt, are you in there?" called out a male voice that I couldn't quite place.

My brother rushed past me and opened the door. "What's up?"

A tall warden stood on our porch. "Detective Clairmont has found something, and wants you down at the station."

"But I have to watch my sister," complained Matt.

"I'm not a child," I sung out. "I don't need a babysitter."

Matt looked between the other warden and me. "Can you watch her for me, Zeke?"

The other guy shook his head. "I was sent here to get you and come right back. I think it's all hands on deck."

Mason must've found something. Curiosity got the better of me, and I wanted in on the action. "I could go with you."

Zeke wrung his hands. "Um, you look real pretty, Miss Charli. But Detective Clairmont also gave me another directive. Under no circumstances were you to come along. Or go to the dance."

That sneaky detective. I didn't need anybody else in my

life telling me what I could or could not do with the last moments of my life. Time to play possum.

"Fine, everybody else wins. I'll stay home." I slumped my shoulders in defeat.

Matt cocked his left eyebrow. "Like I should believe you. Maybe I should lock you in your room and spellcast a warden's protection to keep you there."

"No need to go treating me like a criminal. I've learned my lesson. And I'm not feeling too great." I faked feeling dizzy. "Going back to bed may be a good idea."

My brother spoke under his breath to the other warden and held up his finger for him to wait. He came over to me and took both of my hands in his. "No kidding, Birdy. I know you mean well. But put a little trust in me to do the job. I promise you, I won't let you go. I'm not about to lose you, too." His voice cracked at the end.

My confidence wavered when I answered his pleading gaze. He'd been through as much as I had and lost just as many people. Losing me would be a bitter result of my plans. For once, maybe I needed to be obedient instead of making choices that could hurt others. My shoulders slumped in earnest. "I promise, I'll stay here. You go and figure things out. But if you don't mind, could you please hurry?"

Relief spread on my brother's face. He kissed my forehead. "You got it, Birdy."

"Don't call me that."

"I will because I can." He gave me a quick hug and bolted out the door.

Once they were gone, I had my chance. The only thing that stood between me and the dance was my promise. The weight of the whole situation rested on my shoulders, and exhaustion hit me. Maybe I could let my brother take this one just this once. I closed the door and shut out the chirping cicadas.

Just because I wouldn't be going to the dance didn't mean I couldn't eat. Heading to the kitchen to raid the fridge, I found a plate of barbecue and Brunswick stew with all the side fixings waiting for me.

"Thanks, Nana," I called out to the silent house.

When half the plate of food sat in my belly, I decided to go upstairs and get out of my mother's dress. I made it halfway up the stairs when another knock startled me.

"Frosted fairy wings, yes, I'm still here. I didn't need you to come back and check on me." Irritated, I yanked the wooden door open. "Tucker? What are you doing here?"

My ex-fiancé stood on the porch, wearing a tailored suit and looking ever the Prince of Honeysuckle.

He looked me up and down with admiration. "Charli, we have to talk."

I shook my head. "Go to the dance, Tucker. Don't disappoint Clementine."

"Since when did you care that much about your cousin?" he asked.

"She might not be my favorite, but I can tell that you mean a lot to her. Also, you're the one that asked her to marry you."

"I also asked you. Or don't you remember?"

"Of course I remember, T. But we weren't a good fit." I squirmed where I stood, my skin crawling with unease. "I explained it all in the note I left you."

"I never read it."

My heart dropped. "Never? Why?"

"Because I burned it."

I stared at my ex-fiancé in disbelief. "Why would you do that?"

Pain shadowed his face. "Because you broke my heart," he yelled loud enough into the night air to scare an owl out of a nearby tree.

I ushered him inside so as not to air our dirty laundry to any other beings nearby. We went into the formal parlor and sat down on the stiff couch.

Southern manners dictated I should offer him something to drink, but I couldn't get over what he'd told me. "So all this time, you never knew my reasons?"

"To be honest, I couldn't bring myself to care. I'd never experienced rejection like that before. And I'll admit, I didn't know how to handle it."

Regret pounded in my chest. "I didn't leave you to teach you a lesson."

"But it did. I learned how to get over you."

His cold words stung. "Tuck, I'm so sorry."

He held up his hand. "That sounded harsher than I meant it. You did me a favor in the long run. I couldn't stay in Honeysuckle, so I went to Charleston and spent some time trying to be an adult. That's where I met Ashton, which has been the best thing to happen to me. It was his idea to start the development company."

My skin crawled at the mention of his friend, and more questions popped into my head. "How did you meet him?" I did my best to sound interested rather than suspicious.

"We met at a, um, club for men." Tucker coughed and avoided my gaze. "We got to talkin', and after a few drinks, I felt like I'd known him all my life."

"Sounds like a match made in heaven."

"The more we spent time together, the more Ashton liked the idea of coming back to Honeysuckle and improving a small town like ours."

How did Tucker not question why another young man would want to leave a city like Charleston and come live in a small, isolated Southern town like ours? Even when the town council considered change, it moved slower than molasses on a cold day. What kind of development would make a good business here in Honeysuckle?

As if reading my thoughts, Tucker explained. "You've been gone for a while, Charli. Things will move forward around here, and my family and I, plus Ashton, want to be at the forefront."

"What kind of changes?"

His face brightened. "You should see the plans we've come up with. There's a golf course. And a full-blown country club."

I smirked. "Just like your mother Clarice has always

wanted. A fancier place where she can restrict who can get in. Perfect for a town like ours."

Tucker pursed his lips. "It's not like that, Charli."

I didn't want to start an old fight that had nowhere to go. "And exactly what land would you be using for your plans?"

His expression confused me. "That's the thing I've been wanting to tell you. We were in the process of obtaining approval for most of the land for the golf course. But we needed to acquire some...specific property."

My gut already knew the answer at the immediate pang of my arm. "Whose property? No, don't tell me. Tipper's."

Tucker nodded.

"And you didn't think that was an important piece of information to share with his death and all?"

"I've been trying to talk to you."

I stood up. "I'm not a warden, Tuck. You knew that the knowledge of your development plans would have put you and your partner under suspicion, didn't you?"

Tucker sank into the back of the couch, scrubbing his hands down his face. "You know how it is here. You know how my parents are. I didn't want to bring shame on the family."

I placed my hands on my hips. "I'm going to ask you a simple yes or no question. Did you kill Tipper?"

He gaped at me in horror. "No."

"Who else knew about the property?" I counted my suspected list on my hand. "Ashton of course. Your father, I would guess. Anybody else?" I hoped he would spill the whole truth.

His face dropped with shame. "We weren't supposed to say anything," he delayed.

I threw my hands in the air. "Aunt Nora. You were supposed to say her name, so I would know that a small part of who I thought you were still existed."

Tucker stood up in defense. "I'm not the bad guy here."

"You hid your connection to a possible murder. How does that make you a hero?" I accused. "Just because you stood up to my aunt for me at Tipper's house doesn't absolve you."

He closed the distance between us. "How do you know I was there? I guess your brother could have told you. But then, how would you know I said anything about you?" He stood in front of me, blocking any escape route.

"Fine. I was there, too. I know about Aunt Nora wanting to find Tipper's will and invoking that ancient witch law loophole. If she inherits all of Tipper's possessions, then she'll be in charge of what happens with his land and house. I knew my aunt had a mean streak. I just didn't know how many shadows existed inside of her. This is the woman who's about to become your mother-in-law?" I poked Tucker's chest.

He crumbled like a biscuit that had been in the hot oven too long. "I swear to you, I never meant any harm to anybody. I think the idea came from Ashton, although maybe it had been mine first."

"To what? To poison him?"

"No," he protested. "To win the land off of him. To play

poker and get him so far in debt that he had to sign over his land. Ashton told me that it should be mine and my family's in the first place. And I thought that if I could get it back, then maybe my father would look at me with something other than contempt in his eyes."

I'd witnessed Hollis's treatment of his son. He turned a creative, dreamy boy into a hardened man in his like. I'd loved the boy but left the man.

Pushing for more information, I refused to let Tucker off the hook. "Did you win anything off Tipper?"

"It took us months," Tucker continued. "But we won here and there. Despite his imbibing habits, the old man was still sharp. I'd lost hope and wanted to come up with a new development plan and place for the golf course and country club. But Ashton insisted on following through."

My instincts screamed, alarm bells clanging in my head. I thought back on my first encounter with Ashton in the park when he shook my hand. When I'd seen him after that, he looked about as good as I'd felt.

"Where is Ashton now?"

"He wasn't at the dance," Tucker said.

Pulling on the chain around my neck, I touched the pink key hanging on the end of it. "I think I know where he is. I have to go find him."

Tucker grabbed my hand. "You're crazy. I was planning to go to the warden station in the morning, but I wanted to tell you first."

"Why?"

He released me and ran his fingers through his hair. "I don't know. Maybe to get you to see that I was worthy of you. That I could stand up for something good for once."

With sympathy, I squeezed his hand. "Tucker, you have to be worthy of yourself. If you had read my note, you would have known that I didn't leave you because of *you*. I left because of *me*. Because I knew I had to find my own path. And I just wasn't ready to be with anyone yet."

His voice lowered. "And what about now?"

He reached out to touch my cheek, but I flinched away, letting go of his hand. "I don't know. Maybe being with someone else is something I can explore if I get more time."

Tucker sighed. "But not with me."

"No. Not with you." I gave him the gift of honesty so he could move on. "Right now, I need you to go to the warden station."

"What are you going to do?" he asked with concern.

I squeezed the key and sent a small amount of intent into it until it tingled in my touch. Fingering it, I gathered up all my courage. "I'm going to solve things once and for all. And I'm going to be my own hero and save my life."

Chapter Twenty-Three

The fairy path shimmered closed in a cloud of pink sparkles once I pushed my way through to the other side. Gossamer had warned me to use it only in an emergency, and this definitely qualified. However, the effort sapped the last dregs of my energy. I doubled over, coughing and gasping for air.

"Yeah, I feel it, too." Ashton entered the room in Tipper's house where I stood. The glowing ball of light floating above his head revealed his disheveled appearance. "Who knew that old man had it in him."

A sick satisfaction settled in my stomach. "The curse got you, too?" The dark circles under his eyes and his shaky demeanor showed me that, like a virus, the curse had found its true home and taken root.

"Had I never met you," he spit out with venom, "maybe I would have gotten away with it."

"You poisoned Tipper," I accused.

He reached into his pocket and pulled out a glass vial. Holding it up, he let the light filter through its liquid contents. "Did you know that the same plant extracts that can heal us can also harm us? I learned a lot about plants and what they could do when they killed my mother." He furrowed his eyebrows.

"Who killed your mother?" I did my best to keep my distance from him, my eyes tracking the vile.

His lip lifted in a snarl. "My father and his family."

"Why would your father kill your mother?" *Keep him talking,* I told myself, taking slow steps towards the foyer.

Ashton followed me. "Are you in a hurry, Charlotte?"

"It's Charli."

"Charlotte. Charli. Birdy. What does it matter? We're both expiring. Breathing our last. Don't you want to know what you're dying for? If you leave, you may never know." He took a step to show me that even if I made it to the front door, he would do his best to cut me off anyway.

He had me. For the moment. "Fine. I'm listening."

Ashton coughed once, pulling his hand away and staring at the red splotch of blood dotting his skin. "You and I, we have a lot in common. Tucker told me that you never knew your real parents."

"I knew my real parents. They raised me." My brain worked overtime to process the scene.

The curse was working through him in a much more

insidious way than me. Maybe if I could outlast him, it would take him down first.

"Biological parents, then," he clarified with a dramatic roll of his eyes.

"But you just said your father killed your mother."

"For once, be a good little girl, and shut up and listen." His manicured demeanor cracked under his mania. "I had a wonderful mother. But I never knew my father. She did a remarkable job making sure that she took care of my every need so that I would forget to ask her who he was.

"She was the one who taught me all about plants and herbs, and how to use them. Mom used to run a table at the market in Charleston, and I would help her, selling essential oils to tourists. And on the side, she sold potions to those like us."

Charleston's council of witches enforced strict policies about the use of magic. Running a hybrid operation in that city cost a lot of money. I didn't have to ask whether his mother's business was legal or not.

His hand holding the vial shook, sloshing its contents, so he set the bottle down on a nearby table. "We did fine for a long time until the wardens in the city ran a sting on my mother. They set her up and then took her away. By this time, I wasn't a kid anymore. I did some digging and found my real father. Unlike us, he had real money since he was from one of the oldest families in town. Not once had he ever experienced what scraping by on almost nothing was like."

If I weren't trying to stay alive, I might be able to summon some sympathy for him. "Did you ask your father for help?"

Ashton sneered. "That was the last time I let my naïveté get the best of me. Yes, I went to their big house on the Battery. Tried to get him to come out and talk to me."

"And what happened?" I pressed, taking small steps toward the table with the vial.

"I found myself spending the night at the warden station. No formal charges were filed, but they put me through the ringer as a warning. And they thought that I would drop it. That's because they never had to work for anything in their lives. And *they* don't know what true hunger is." A look of determined contempt gleamed in Ashton's eyes.

"When did you tell him who he was?" I asked.

Ashton looked away for a second, recalling the memory. I took my chance and rushed toward the table with my arm outstretched. He snatched the glass container first, twisting and catching me around my neck with his arm.

"Oh no, no, no. That won't do, Charli." He dragged me into the formal parlor and tossed me away from him. "You do not want to play too much with what's in here. It could be dangerous. Tonight's the night of the dance. Let's see what steps the two of us have left to make."

I wanted to fight back, kicking and screaming. But the curse worked its way through my veins, too. The trip through the fairy path had drained too much out of me. Keeping my distance from him, I countered his moves as he maneuvered me around the room with his threatening presence.

"Good girl. Now, where was I?" He coughed again and wiped his mouth, smearing a red stripe onto his cheek. "Oh, right. My father. Rich men love to slum it, especially when looking for some fun outside of their marriage.

"I followed him for months, finding out his habits and where he liked to go at night. The good thing about being a nobody is that you can sometimes slip through the cracks. All I had to do was pay another nobody to let me in. When I finally told him who I was and where my mother was, I begged him to help her. And he laughed."

Ashton's pain reached me despite our current predicament. I often wondered what I would do if I ever found one of my parents. To know that one of them was rotten on the inside would break my heart.

"That must have been tough," I tried to empathize.

"Save your pity." He brandished the vial in the air. "Do you know that I could have killed him right there and then? I had brought some digitalis with me. Foxglove for the uneducated. It's an easy way to end someone's life. In small doses, you can help someone with a heart condition. But an overdose will end the life instead of save it. But I didn't use it."

Charli sucked in a breath. "Like the night of the engagement."

"You're thinking of your great-uncle, aren't you?" A proud smile spread on his red-stained lips. "Fine. I'll give you what you want. Yes, I used digitalis to kill him. But that wasn't the original plan. I wanted to make it look natural. Use it on him over time. Give him heart problems so that the town healer would notice, and then when he died of a heart attack, no one would think anything about murder."

"Why the big confession?" I pressed. "Aren't you afraid that I'll tell?"

"You're not getting out of here. At least, not alive. Neither of us is." He shook the glass container again. "Consider this my parting gift to you. The gift of knowledge. You're smarter than I took you for, Charli. I can't say the same about some of your family members."

His threat to my life shattered my fear. If these were my last moments, then I needed to make the most of them. My one final act could be finding Tipper's will if it was in the house.

Hiding my concentration, I mustered what magical energy I had left and focused it in my gut. Under my breath, I muttered the same rhyme I used before. *"Let me access all my skill and find the path to Tipper's will."*

Ashton regarded me with suspicion. "What was that?"

"I said, I thought you liked Aunt Nora." I clenched my fists, forcing my body to stay upright.

A sheen of sweat broke out on my brow, but I refused to show him the cost of my magic. A thin line shimmered across the room between an antique secretary, piled high with knick-knacks and overflowing with papers, and me.

Ashton paced in front of me, cutting off the direct route. "That dried up delusional witch? It took a few compliments and a little attention to turn her head and win her to my side. She brought it on herself, bragging to me about one day inheriting the Walker property, and I saw a quicker way to accomplish my goals."

I had been right all along. There had been a puppeteer behind Aunt Nora's actions. It didn't excuse her from her participation, but at least she hadn't been in on the murder.

"And what were those goals? To steal from my family member?" I took slow steps around the brocade chair, acting as if I wanted to keep my distance from him and trying to hide my real purpose.

Ashton watched me with curiosity. "No, to make myself a success in another town. To forget all about that young man, staring at his father and wishing he was better. See?" He pointed at himself. "The apple doesn't fall far from the tree."

"Whatever happened to your mother?" I distracted him with the one subject that softened him. "Surely, this hadn't been her plan for you."

"Well, she's not here to plan anything for me. She lost hope while they had her locked away. And when I told her about finding my father and what he'd said, she told me to wait. That she knew he'd do the right thing in the long run. Little did I know that day when she said that to me, it would be the last time I'd see her.

"Somehow, she got ahold of some oleander flowers. Beautiful but deadly when ingested. She committed suicide. And she was right. My father felt so guilty that he paid for my college education as long as it was far away from Charleston."

He stopped following me, and his shoulders hunched.

Sniffing, he straightened himself up. A small drop of blood trickled out of his nose.

"I thought you met Tucker in Charleston?" I asked, taking another step in the right direction.

"I had already returned to Charleston with the intent of setting myself up for life." He smiled at whatever memory replayed in his head.

"You mean blackmail your father for more money." I guessed. One more step and I might be able to reach the stack of papers that the thread pulled me to.

"Seemed as good a plan as any. Until I met Tucker and heard all the wonderful stories about this special town, full of idiots and dupes, your aunt becoming one of the biggest. And you becoming a close second." He darted past me to the stack of papers, grabbing them and throwing them in the air. White paper rained down and scattered on the floor. "What are you looking for, Charli? The will? Believe me, it's not here. I've checked."

I collapsed on a nearby chair, my hope withering. "How did you get in?"

He shook the vial in his hand again. "I'm good with plants. There are many mixes and combinations that can trick spells. Manipulate them. Even change them."

Pain throbbed through me, and I groaned in agony. Clutching my stomach, I doubled over and crumpled to the floor.

"The curse hurts, doesn't it? If your great-uncle hadn't been such a fool, it never would have affected you. But he screwed it up, and now you get to die with me." Ashton wheezed out a laugh that turned into a hacking cough. "You and I are coming to our end, aren't we?"

He dropped to his knees, careful not to break the vial in his hand. "I think the two of us should go down in flames, don't you?" He studied the liquid contents.

"How will poison set this place on fire?" I uttered.

"You think this is poison? When I went away to college, I set myself the task to learn all I could about the mixology of potions. I experimented with adding in a little magic here and there and came up with some wonderful results."

While he spoke, I risked one last attempt at finding the will. A sliver of a thread connected me to a few papers lying on the floor within reach. But the effort knocked the wind out of me, and I gave in to the racking wheezes and rattling coughs.

"Don't worry. I'll put you out of your misery," he promised, pushing himself off the floor for his triumphant last act. "This one here I call dragon's breath. It smells horrific because of the essence of sulfur contained in the beast's saliva. But a few drops of this can set a room on fire. I should know. I did the live testing."

"You," I managed between coughs, "are a monster."

The dark intent in his smile chilled me like the darkness that threatened to take me.

"I am my father's son."

I shook my head, following my last line of connection and crawling toward the papers. "You are what you chose to be."

He shook the vial again. "This amount should take out the entire house. What do you say, Charli? You ready to die?"

Shattering glass interrupted the verbose maniac. Loud cawing and a fluttering of black feathers filled the room. I screamed and lunged for the papers, grabbing them and shielding them against my body.

"Get away from me, you crazy bird." Ashton stumbled backward, and I feared the vial would break.

"Biddy, no," I cried out.

As he fell, the crow circled and caught the glass mid-air in her talons.

"No," screamed Ashton. Tipper's stalwart friend flew back out the window and into the night.

Closing my eyes, I chuckled. "So much for your plan."

"It may not be elegant, but I'll kill you myself," grunted Ashton. With a groan, he launched his body on top of me, his hands circling my neck.

I didn't know what hurt worse, the pain of his fingers squeezing off my last breaths or the agony of the curse working through my veins.

Either way, the truth had come to light. I could finally stop fighting and give in to peace. Life flickered out of me like the flame of a spent candle.

Another crash interrupted Ashton, and my dim brain wondered if Biddy had sprouted legs. Multiple limbs surrounded us.

"By warden command, you are under arrest. Hands up," Mason barked.

The pressure tightened on my throat until Ashton's body got yanked off of me.

"The man said to take your hands off the lady," a familiar voice growled.

Darkness swirled around the edges of my vision. I rolled onto my side to capture one last glimpse of the dragon I had slain.

"You think you've won," Ashton choked out. He produced a pill from his pocket and popped it in his mouth. "You think you had the last word. But like I told my father as I watched him take his last gasping breaths through his blue lips, I'm the one who gets to win."

Pink foam bubbled at the edge of Ashton's mouth as he collapsed onto the floor in a shaking mass.

Shouting erupted around me. Strong arms scooped me up from the floor, and two male voices tried to keep me going with reassurances.

"It's over, Charli."

"We've got you."

Chapter Twenty-Four

In a small Southern town, people rallied around each other to celebrate the good times and console one another in the bad. Support often showed up in the form of food. Based on the number of casseroles and dishes we received, and thanks to Nana's extra freezer and a couple of specialized freezing spells, we wouldn't have to cook for at least a month.

I placed a plate of gifted brownies on the coffee table in Tipper's parlor. It had taken me a few days to recover from the end of my great-uncle's death curse and the night of Ashton's confession. In the end, the right person had gotten punished, whether through the curse or his own choices. I didn't know why, but I still felt sorry for the man who got so lost that taking a life, even his own, was the only option in his eyes.

When Mason explained how he had arrived just in time at

the house that night, he told me that he had found Ashton's fingerprints on Tipper's flask using the phoenix feather. Because of how isolated Honeysuckle was, it had taken a little time to get confirmation from Charleston, but when he received it combined with Tucker's trip to the station after I sent him, he knew where to find me. And for a short time, he and Dash worked under a truce to get me.

I hadn't seen the wolf shifter in days. That didn't mean he didn't check in on me. But he always seemed to show up at the house when I was taking a nap or not there. I didn't know if he was still angry with me for my reaction the night he got taken in or whether he was afraid of the cursed girl.

Even though Doozy was gone, I still felt its mark on me. The sympathetic looks and polite congratulations barely covered the slight fear in some of the town's eyes. Only my close friends and family stood by me with unconditional love and support. And maybe that's why Dash's absence hurt a little more. I wasn't ready to forgive him yet for leaving, but maybe after some time, we could start from the beginning again.

Jed Farnsworth cleared his throat. "I know y'all been waiting for this moment. I'm gonna let my new partner in the firm take over from here." Ben sat down in the seat next to the older gentleman.

It turned out that when they pulled the crumpled papers out of my hand, they had almost tossed them away like trash. It took Matt's keen eye to notice that the script of the little community play on one side hid the will on the back of each page. While I had been recovering, my brother had taken the will to the advocate's office.

Matt sat next to me on the uncomfortable sofa, holding my hand. He squeezed it three times for good measure as we both drew in a breath to steady us. We'd been summoned to the house along with Clementine and Aunt Nora, who sat in separate chairs across from me. Our aunt did her best not to look in our direction. With Ashton's demise and clear guilt, she'd lost a valuable ally and someone she'd admired maybe a little too much.

Much to my chagrin and Nana's disappointment, there had been no way to prevent Aunt Nora from taking Tipper's place on the town council. Her bitter face puckered even more now that whatever plans she'd made with Ashton were ruined. No doubt she'd take her wrath out on the rest of the town, but for now, she remained civil with Southern politeness. We'd wait at least until after the will was executed, and then I would need to check my back for her knives from here on out.

"Let's get this over with," she demanded.

Ben regarded her with professional indifference and nodded. He held up the papers of Tipper's will and read off of the pages. A lot of the terms I didn't understand, but I perked up when it got to the section of bequeathing.

"To my great-niece, Clementine, I leave some jewelry and shiny trinkets for her. Pretty bobbles for a pretty thing."

My cousin straightened in the chair next to her mother.

Her satisfied smile and the lift of her nose gave her the air of something beautiful covering up something hollow.

Ben continued reading. "To my niece, Leonora. We've never seen eye to eye, and I think we can both admit that there was no love lost between us. Since I am not allowed to bar you from the town council, I shall leave you with a tool that has helped me to see the truth and aid me in making good decisions."

"What did that old fool leave me?" my aunt asked with too much greed in her voice.

Ben scanned the text. "His collection of flasks, which, if I'm reading correctly, is numbered over twenty."

"Minus one," clarified Matt, referring to the one that the phoenix feather had melted.

"Flasks? He left me flasks?" Aunt Nora screeched. "What else? There has to be more."

"Nothing else, Mrs. Irwin," Ben confirmed.

My aunt's top lip curled up in disgust. "Jed, is this true?"

The older advocate pulled his glasses down to the end of his nose and checked over Ben's shoulder. "Yes, I'm afraid that's it."

"I don't believe you," she huffed. "There must be *something* else."

Ben pointed at the paper. "There is, but I don't think you'll like it."

Aunt Nora clicked her tongue. "I knew it. What else does it say?"

Ben continued reading. "If the wretched, ungrateful

woman complains one iota, she gets nothing. Not even my good wishes for the rest of her endeavors. Good riddance to bad rubbish."

Aunt Nora bolted out of her chair, startling her daughter. "Come, Clementine. I refuse to sit here and listen to whatever these two receive from that old bat. We should have locked him up ages ago in a mental institution. Or hexed him seven ways to Sunday."

Matt held onto me to keep me from attacking her. I held my aunt in my hot gaze, trying to remember that she was my mother's sister. "Aunt Nora, may I remind you of the information Ashton shared with me and that I convinced Big Willie to consider but not to enact upon. Perhaps you should count your freedom to walk around this earth as your true inheritance."

"Lies," she spit at me. "Whatever he said, not a lick of it was true." She snapped her fingers. "Clementine. Come."

My cousin gathered her purse and followed her mother out of the house with a haughty huff. Both of their noses stuck so high in the air that I had a hard time believing they could see where they were going.

My brother leaned forward and took a brownie, biting into it with glee. "I love that Tipper's still got it, even when he's not here. You did good, too, Birdy." He ruffled my hair, and I batted his hand away.

Jed dabbed at the sweat beaded on his brow with a handkerchief. "I didn't think she'd like that. But Tipper's wishes are set in stone, and we're just carrying out them out. Go on, Ben. Read them the rest."

My friend beamed at my brother and I. "Hang onto your hats," he warned before continuing. "My niece, Raylene Walker Goodwin, was the light of my life. She was the sunshine to everyone in Honeysuckle Hollow. To her son and my grand-nephew Matthew Duane as well as her daughter and my grand-niece Charlotte Vivian, she was their sun, moon, and stars. All that I have left in this world, I give to them."

Matt dropped the brownie in his hand and stopped chewing mid-bite. "No way. All of what?"

Ben pointed at the paper and kept reading. "The deed to the land goes to my great-nephew. Matthew, take care of it and preserve it for future generations."

Jed pushed his glasses up his nose. "That'll give you some financial security, son. Its worth is far more then you could think of. He's also made some stipulations. You get the land and a tidy sum of money to help you care for it. But not the house."

"You get the land and his other property," clarified Ben.

"What other property?" Matt asked.

"Well," started Jed. "Your great-uncle owned almost half of Main Street."

"Which half?" I asked.

"The side with your mother's old store and the bakery. Not every storefront is full. There are a few vacancies because Tipper didn't really pay them that much attention. He was a decent landlord, fixing things as soon as they needed fixin'. And his rent was more than fair."

"That's right," I said. "That's the side of the street that your office is on, isn't it?"

"Our office," corrected Jed. He placed his hand on Ben's shoulder. "And someday not too far off, it'll be Ben's if he wants it. I'm getting a little older, and I'd much rather spend my time fishing than dealing with legal matters. I'll help him transition, and then I'll leave him to it."

"Congratulations, Ben. That was an unexpected surprise." I beamed at my friend.

"With everything you've been going through, it didn't seem that important." Ben shrugged. "But prepare yourselves because we're not quite finished."

"What else is there to discuss? Isn't that it?" I asked.

"Your brother owns Tipper's properties, yes," said Ben. "But your great-uncle made one important stipulation. That the house and a small portion of the land around it go to you, Charli."

The room spun, and I gripped Matt's knee for balance. "The house? All of it?" My eyes roamed over the room, the ceiling, the wooden floors, and all that the walls contained. "That crazy old, sweet man," I uttered, covering my gaping mouth with the back of my hand.

Jed chuckled at my reaction. "It comes with everything in it. And Tipper wanted this last part read out loud."

I leaned forward to listen to my beloved great-uncle's final words to me.

"My dear girl, I hope when you hear this that I've lived a long life roaming the world in the company of many women while you have found happiness in your life's pursuits. So, maybe you don't need what I am leaving you. But if you have not found your roots, perhaps this small gift will give you a place to call your own. An anchor and safe mooring while you live your life.

"And when you're ready, sell off any and all of my things to establish a little nest egg for yourself. May you search for and find many things in your life, and may you find your courage to overcome your fears and go after everything that you want. Take care of Biddy for me, and live your life like I've lived mine, for yourself and not for others."

We sat in silence as the quiet ticked by, marked by the grandfather clock that was now mine. I didn't know if I should cry in mourning, laugh in relief, or wonder in awe. Even from the beyond, Uncle Tipper would continue influencing my life. In the end, I couldn't blame him for the curse. And, as he always had in life, he left me with more questions than answers.

When we gathered our wits about us, Ben handed me the keys to the house. "I'm not sure I've ever seen his house locked except for when it was under warden protection," I said. "And even then, it was never completely empty."

"Well, it's yours now. Lock it. Don't lock it. It's your choice." Ben pulled me in for a quick hug.

I shivered under the enormous responsibility with such a big gift. Suddenly, the place seemed colder and more hollow than ever now that it no longer housed the spirit of a man who lived larger than life and gave more of himself than he took from others. The two advocates excused themselves and left.

Matt stayed behind, the two of us staring at each other in disbelief. "Does it bother you that this is where things almost ended with Ashton?"

"I don't know yet. We might need to sage the place a few times first. And maybe hire the Fairy Dust & Cleaning services."

"It definitely needs some help." Matt gawked around the place.

"And I fear that Tipper had become a bit of a hoarder in his later years. Cleaning this place up will be a mighty task," I admitted.

"But now it's *your* task, homeowner. Birdy, I'm glad the house went to you." He put his arm around my shoulder.

"Why?"

"Because I like Mom and Dad's old house. It's perfect for me and TJ."

"But what about when you have kids?" I asked.

"I don't know," he mused. "I think you and I grew up there just fine."

His observation eased a bit of my burgeoning guilt. "But if you ever want this place or need more space, you let me know, okay?"

As if sensing I needed a hint of normalcy, Matt grabbed me by the neck and gave me a noogie. I pushed him off and smacked him playfully. "Deal," he said. "I gotta go. You comin' with me?"

I shook my head. "I think I want to walk around Tipper's place for a bit."

"You mean, your place." Matt winked at me.

"It's gonna take a while for that to sink in. And I don't think I'll be moving in anytime soon." The thought of leaving Nana alone in her house worried me.

"Take your time. It'll be here when you're ready."

After Matt left, I walked slowly through every room of the house, my eyes lighting on every single possession. No doubt some of it was worthless, but more of it had great value either in monetary or sentimental reasons. Perhaps both.

When I'd circled the entire bottom floor, I paused at the staircase. I just didn't have it in me to mentally catalog the upstairs rooms as well. I needed time to let things process anyway.

Stepping outside, I debated on whether to lock the door.

"So did *she* get the house?" a voice startled me.

I turned around to find Beau waiting in the shadows on the porch.

"No," I admitted. "I did."

"Good. I'm glad it went to you." The old vampire's voice brightened, but he still carried sadness in his eyes. No doubt he still missed his greatest friend.

A thought took root inside me, and the bigger it grew, the more I agreed with it. "Beau, would you do me a huge favor?"

"Sure. Anything for you, Miss Charli."

"Well, it may take me a while to get used to this being my place. I'm not quite ready to move in. For now, would you mind living here and helping me organize Tipper's stuff?"

At the suggestion, pink tears rimmed the vampire's eyes. "Are you sure? I thought I was going to be homeless."

I didn't have to think hard about it. "It's a huge house for just one person. I don't see why you can't stay here for a while."

In his excitement, Beau poofed into a bat and back again at least two times. He wrapped his arms around me and hugged me tightly. "Now I know why you were his favorite."

I patted his back. "I think you mean my mother."

"No, Tipper was clear how much you meant to him. He told me once that he was the reason why you were in Honeysuckle in the first place, and that he had placed you with your mother and father."

That new and vital information bowled me over. "What are you talking about?"

Beau released me with a timid look on his face and covered his mouth. "Oh, I wasn't supposed to tell you that."

"That he had something to do with my adoption? I think you should tell me everything you know."

He wrinkled his nose at me. "But that's just it. That's all he ever said. I think I'll go inside and start organizing my room." He flashed a fanged grin and zipped around me, leaving me to my surprise on the porch.

I'd known very little about my adoption other than that I had been very wanted and that I was family from the second my parents had laid eyes on me. They'd known next to nothing about where I'd come from or who my biological parents were.

Most of the time, I didn't give a thought about my life before I was adopted. My family was *my* family, not by blood but by the choices of our hearts. But now, in very Tipper fashion, he'd left me with more truth to track down. Another mystery to solve.

Right on cue, Biddy called out to me from the sky. She landed on the porch rail, cawing and flapping her wings. My great-uncle's last words to me didn't mean that the crow was mine to keep. She was her own, and she could come and go as she pleased. But I would make sure to check on her and give her anything she needed whenever she wanted.

"You okay, old girl? You need anything?" I asked.

Biddy cocked her head from side to side, her yellow eyes regarding me. She chirped and squawked, hopping along the rail. As if satisfied with her inspection of me, the crow spread her wings and flitted to my shoulder. She balanced on her own, not needing to sink her talons into my skin this time.

I walked down the stairs of the house and onto the path toward the road. Biddy rode on me until we reached the edge of the property.

Turning around, I gazed at the house. Too many emotions mixed inside me. It would take time for me to feel normal again. Or maybe, my sense of normal might be shifted forever. And that might not be a bad thing.

Biddy squawked in my ear, and I scratched her head. "You ready to fly? Yeah, me too."

She nudged my head with the tip of hers, and without another sound, she flapped her wings and took off into the air. My heart soared with her, and I shaded my eyes to watch her free form until she disappeared into the horizon.

Epilogue

✿❧

I admired my reflection in the mirror, more satisfied with my appearance than the first time I'd worn my mother's altered dress.

Alison Kate continued to fuss with my hair. "I like it pinned up, but it's a bit formal. Maybe we should take it down for tonight?"

"Ali Kat, you've already put it up and taken it down five times. It looks good no matter what you do to it, and I appreciate your efforts. But everybody's going to think that the curse still has me if I don't get down to the party eventually." I winked at her in the mirror.

My friend backed away and inspected my hair. "We're leaving it up," she said with determination.

"Good choice."

"That dress looks fabulous on you, by the way. Patty Lou does some good work." Alison Kate made me twirl around.

I slipped on a pair of high heels. "She can create magic with a needle, that's for sure."

Loki did his best to trip me at the top of the stairs. Peaches took over that job halfway down, wrapping herself around my ankles. I picked her tiny body up and held her under my chin to feel her gentle purring.

"You keep your claws out of the silk. My sweet little Peach Cobbler Yum Yum Fuzzy Pants wouldn't hurt my mother's dress, would she? No, she wouldn't," I cooed at my orange kitten.

Nana met me at the bottom of the stairs. "That's a pretty big name for such a small little creature."

"Trust me, she'll grow into it." I rubbed Peach's orange fuzzy face against mine and set her down. Music wafted in from the backyard. "Is the rest of the gang here?"

"They're out back, eating food and waiting for you along with a few others," she said, leading the way.

I watched her take charge, directing people. At some point, I would have to muster the courage to ask her what she knew about Tipper and my adoption. But we were supposed to be celebrating, not digging up more information. My curiosity could take the night off.

Fairy lights twinkled over the entire lawn, most of them pink. Friendly faces cheered for me when I stepped into the backyard. Nana had gone all out with the celebration. Two tables spilled over with food, enough to feed most of Honeysuckle. Our invited guests quieted down and waited for someone to say something.

"I think they want you to make a speech, Nana," I whispered to my grandmother.

"No, sweet bird. They want to hear from you." She patted my back.

A shyness crept over me, and no spell would lessen my embarrassment. I panicked, unable to think of anything to say.

My grandmother whispered back, "When in doubt, keep it short and sweet."

Short and sweet. I could handle that. "Everybody," I began. My voice caught in my throat when all eyes gazed at me. I scanned the crowd to find those who gave me courage.

Goss floated beside Flint, her fluttering wings dusting her husband in pink. My gaggle of girls hugged each other close as they waited. Ben stood off to the side, but his eyes tracked Lily's movement. And Alison Kate held Lee's attention. At some point, I would have to help those boys find a clue so that my friends might have a chance to be happy together.

Matt hugged TJ around the waist, his chin resting on her head. With an admiring nod to me, Patty Lou joined her husband Steve behind the tables of food. And Mason stood at the back, wearing a nice suit and tie. He winked at me, his eyes shining in approval. His presence gave me a strange sense of strength. He'd done so much for me, and yet, I'd never had the chance to thank him. Since the night at Tipper's house, he'd never given me one.

With a cough, I started again. "I'd like to thank you for

your support. I couldn't have been here tonight without it." I looked directly at the detective. "I owe y'all my life."

Mason looked down at the ground, slipping his hands into his pockets. I scanned the crowd but couldn't find Dash. The wolf shifter still hadn't forgiven me.

"Charli," my grandmother prompted.

"I guess I should say, thanks a lot, and let's enjoy ourselves tonight." Everyone whooped and hollered while the music resumed.

After much food and drink filled our stomachs, we all got down to some serious dancing. It seemed like everyone wanted to make up for me missing the barn dance, and I got passed from partner to partner.

My brother teased me during a slow song, and my friends and I stirred up the dirt during a rousing one. Sweat trickled down my brow and the back of my neck, and I couldn't be happier or more carefree. Tonight was the perfect way to celebrate my life, say a proper goodbye to Tipper, and get on with things.

"May I have this dance?" Mason held out his hand to me. I placed mine in his and allowed him to lead me.

"I meant what I said." I leaned my head against his shoulder. "Thank you," I murmured into his warm body.

"My pleasure, ma'am," he chuckled.

"You seem to be picking up some of our customs, sir."

"What can I say? I'm starting to feel at home."

My heart picked up the pace. "Before long, you'll be

developing an accent," I teased. "And a serious addiction to sweet tea."

He pulled back so he could look at me. "As long as it's sweetened with honeysuckle syrup, right?"

With savvy moves, he twirled me out, showing off the movement of my mom's dress. With a slight yank on my hand, he led me back to him and pulled me in close to his chest, rocking us back and forth.

"May I cut in," a deep voice rumbled behind me.

Mason broke away from me, his jaw clenched. But he nodded once and handed me off to Dash.

The wolf shifter rocked me back and forth, his steps awkward and not as coordinated. He wore a nice shirt and clean jeans, and his beard smelled like cologne.

After the second time he stepped on my foot, he stopped. "I'm no good at this."

"You don't have to be," I reassured him. "It's just a dance. Two people figuring out a way to move together through a song.

"Yeah, well, I've never been good at moving with anybody," he complained. "Would you mind if I showed you something?"

I stopped dancing. "You're being very mysterious, Mr. Channing."

A mischievous glint flashed in his eyes. "I thought you liked mysteries, Charli Bird."

"Only my closest friends and family use that nickname."

Taking my hand, he pulled me out of the crowd of my friends. Once we were out of sight of the others, he wrapped his arm around my shoulders. "And what do I qualify as?"

I still hadn't come up with an answer to that question. "I'm not sure yet."

We made our way to the front of the house. Sitting beside the front porch steps was a shiny new bicycle.

"What's this?" I asked.

Dash placed his hands in his pockets and kicked at the dirt. "I wanted to surprise you with Old Joe. But it seems that my temper tantrum did more damage than I thought. It's going to take some time to fix your father's bike."

I touched the handles and rang the little bell on it. "You do know that this is a bicycle, not a motorcycle, don't you?"

He lifted an eyebrow at me. "You've seen what's in my garage. Of course, I know the difference. But I wanted you to have this to get around temporarily until I can fix Old Joe. And then, maybe you'd honor me by riding with me."

The thought of riding side-by-side on some road far away sounded tempting. Of course, if Dash asked me to, I'd ride behind him on his motorcycle any day.

"So am I forgiven?" the wolf shifter asked in a quieter voice. "I shouldn't have left."

"No. You shouldn't have. You should have stayed and been there for me. That's what friends do. They have each other's backs." A little bit of my frustration I'd bottled up came spilling out.

He winced. "I know. I just figured that you'd be better off if I wasn't around."

"You were wrong," I said. "Because I almost didn't make it."

His eyes flashed amber in the dark. "I would have killed that man if he hadn't taken that privilege away from me. Seeing you under his hands…"

"Trust me, it was no picnic for me," I joked with a weak smile.

Dash frowned. "I don't ever want to see you like that again."

"Oh, you won't. There are a bunch of people standing in my backyard that are determined to make sure I stay safe and out of trouble from here on out." I jutted my thumb to the back of the house.

"And yet, why do I get the feelin' that trouble will come find you anyway, Charli Goodwin?" He managed a smile but stopped himself. "Listen, I would completely understand if you never wanted to talk to me again. I wouldn't hold it against you."

"But I would hold it against me. I got a small glimpse of what life is like for those on the outside. And it can be a cold, lonely existence. Nobody deserves that, Dash. Especially you."

With a growl, he scooped me up and twirled me around.

"What are you doing?" I huffed through my hysterical giggles.

"I'm dancing."

"Put me down, you crazy man." I slapped his back and kicked my feet.

He dropped me with great care. When my feet hit the ground, my head stayed in the air, a little dizzy and confused.

Nana appeared out of nowhere on the front porch. "Young lady, you've got guests to attend to. Get your behind back there. You too, Dashiel Thaddeus Channing."

The wolf shifter's mouth dropped. "How did she find out?"

I couldn't hold back my mirth. "Small town. No secrets. And that woman has her ways."

"You Goodwin women," he muttered under his breath.

"Y'all movin' your feet yet?" Nana called out.

"Yes, ma'am," the two of us replied in unison.

My grandmother narrowed her eyes at us as we passed by, but her smile gave her amusement away.

When we returned to the backyard, Dash squeezed my arm and left my side. He joined Steve behind the tables of food, choosing a private conversation rather than mixing with the noisy crowd.

Mason stood on the other side of the yard, drinking sweet tea and watching me. He lifted his glass in the air and saluted me. I stood in the middle, not ready to make any big decisions tonight. Giving into the music and the call of my friends, I rejoined the party and left the next mystery for tomorrow.

DEAR READER -

Thanks so much for reading *Moonshine & Magic*. If you enjoyed the book (as much as I did writing it), I hope you'll consider leaving a review!

Southern Charms Cozy Mystery Series

Magic & Mystery are only part of the Southern Charms of Honeysuckle Hollow...

Suggested reading order:

Chess Pie & Choices: A Prequel

(*Available exclusively to Newsletter Subscribers*)

Charli Goodwin is engaged to Tucker Hawthorne, the admired "prince" of Honeysuckle Hollow. Underneath the perfect surface of their union boils an ocean of doubt. If he's such a catch, then why does she feel like she's on the hook?

When Charli's magical talents are put to the test to find something valuable to Tucker's family, she's set on a path that will test her love and show her where her true *happy ever after* may be.

Moonshine & Magic: Book 1

Charli Goodwin doesn't expect her homecoming to go without a hitch—after all, she skipped town, leaving her fiancé and family without a clue as to where she was going or why. Now that she's ready to return home, she plans to lay low and sip some of her Nana's sweet tea while the town gossips come out to play.

Unfortunately, on her first night back, Charli discovers the body of her crazy great uncle (hey, everyone has one). She suddenly finds herself at the center of a mystery that threatens the very foundations of Honeysuckle Hollow and the safety of every paranormal citizen in it—starting with Charlie herself.

With the clock ticking, will Charli's special magical talents be enough to save not only the town but her own life?

Lemonade & Love Potions (in the anthology *Hexes & Ohs*)

Charli Goodwin can't help herself when it comes to helping out her friends, especially a failed cupid trying to earn his way back into the matchmaking ranks. A singles mingle in her small Southern town should be the perfect event, but trouble with a capital *T* shows up when someone attempts to boost the odds of love in their favor.

Sweet honeysuckle iced tea, it's gonna take more than lemonade and a little magic to help Charli find out what's wrong, solve the mystery, and save Honeysuckle Hollow from disaster again.

Fried Chicken & Fangs: Book 2

An upcoming election and some new visitors to Honeysuckle shake up the magical small Southern town. When a beloved family member of one of the candidates disappears, it's up to Charli Goodwin and her special talents to get on the case.

What starts as a simple search uncovers a darker layer of manipulation and sabotage. Will she be able to figure out who is pulling the strings before the foundations of the town are destroyed?

Acknowledgments

There are many I need to thank for the creation of this book and the series.

For all the members in my Tiki Bar group, thank you for sharing your time, support, and knowledge with me.

I couldn't have entered the cozy mystery game without the help of some amazing authors! My many thanks go out to Amanda M. Lee, Annabel Chase, and ReGina Welling for allowing me to pick their brains on a regular basis. I also have to thank Sara Rosett, H.Y. Hanna, Leighann Dobbs, and Amy Boyles for their encouragement.

To my longtime writing pals, Lisa, Boyd, and Mel, you got me started on the cozy path. I hope some day you'll join me. In the meantime, thanks for the laughs, the kicks in the pants, and your unending belief in me.

April, thanks for being my test reader. Your additional

Southern expertise helped keep me grounded in my beloved setting.

For my family, y'all are as much a part of this book as the words. Thank you for the love.

Finally, I have to thank my very patient husband. You put up with repeated viewings of multiple cozy mystery series and movies, and helped me work out plot issues. You are part of why there is magic in the words.

About the Author

Bella Falls grew up on the magic of sweet tea, barbecue, and hot and humid Southern days. She met her husband at college over an argument of how to properly pronounce the word *pecan* (for the record, it should be *pea-cawn,* and they taste amazing in a pie). Although she's had the privilege of living all over the States and the world, her heart still beats to the rhythm of the cicadas on a hot summer's evening.

Now, she's taken her love of the South and woven it into a world where magic and mystery aren't the only Charms.

bellafallsbooks.com
contact@bellafallsbooks.com

 facebook.com/bellafallsbooks

 twitter.com/bellafallsbooks

 instagram.com/bellafallsbooks

 amazon.com/author/bellafalls

Made in the USA
Monee, IL
30 April 2021